Angels' Fall

Angels' Fall

Frank Herbert

WordFire Press
Colorado Springs, Colorado

WORDFIRE PRESS

Published by
WordFire Press, an imprint of
WordFire Inc
PO Box 1840
Monument CO 80132

ISBN: 978-1-61475-058-1

WordFire Press Trade Paperback Edition: April 2013
Printed in the USA

www.wordfire.com

INTRODUCTION

Frank Herbert will forever be known as the "author of *Dune*," the science fiction masterpiece that made his career and made his name. But he was an exceptionally diverse author who wrote in numerous genres, especially early in his career.

His first published novel was *The Dragon in the Sea* (Doubleday, 1955), a tense science fiction tale about the crew aboard a futuristic submarine in a pressure-cooker existence as they move behind enemy lines. *The Dragon in the Sea* proved to be a success, even resulting in film interest, and Frank Herbert wrote another novel, and another, and another—thrillers, mysteries, science fiction, mainstream (including the SF dystopia *High-Opp*, released by WordFire Press in 2012). His agent, Lurton Blassingame, couldn't find a publisher for any of them.

Herbert doggedly kept writing, never giving up, until finally seven years later he was able to sell *Dune*, which also garnered its share of rejections—and has now become the best-selling science fiction novel of all time.

Angels' Fall (originally titled *We Are the Hounds*) is one of those novels written after *Dragon in the Sea* and before *Dune*, a jungle survival adventure that features Frank Herbert's characteristic microcosm of people under intense stress. The following is how he described the book to his agent when he'd completed it:

December 18, 1957

Dear Lurton:

Here's the new novel. (Bev says it takes two people to write a novel: one to write it, and one to hit the writer over the head when it's finished. She borrowed my shillelagh for the occasion.)

From this distance (which somewhat garbles information) I get the impression of Doubleday that they're kind of the Ford Motor Co. in book publishing. You can't tell one novel from another without the license plates. Admittedly, this is over-simplification. But I'd hate to have this piece get lost on somebody's assembly line, and painted blue instead of red.

That's why I'm suggesting (a suggestion you may take only if you agree) that we try Hounds on a smaller publishing house, or one with a reputation for putting a heavy concentration of effort on a book they think will go (Scribners?). I can't be certain from here. But I do believe that this novel will run away if it's given any kind of push at the beginning.

(This is not to say that Doubleday didn't get all the mileage there was out of Dragon.)

The book selling business is booming out here. A friend's store is some 60% ahead of last year. (We helped him somewhat with his motivational research methods applied to his promotion.)

Season's greetings and all that.

Best regards

Frank

Five years later, with many rejections and no further novels published, Frank Herbert had parted ways with Lurton Blassingame, revised the manuscript substantially, and changed the title from We Are the Hounds to Angels' Fall. Then he went in search of another agent.

April 30, 1962

Dear Mr. Halsey:

Here is the opus we discussed over the telephone.

An earlier version of this went to my previous agent, Lurton Blassingame, in New York almost three years ago. [Note: it was actually five years.—ed] I asked for his comments and suggestions. Instead, he showed it to several readers, and returned it. Blassingame and I are no longer associated. The attached is a very different story from what he saw.

This one is written with a low-budget movie version in mind—minimal number of sets, four sustaining characters ... and you'll see what I mean.

Best regards

Frank Herbert

Unfortunately, *Angels' Fall* found neither a film studio nor a publisher. This lost work is now being published for the first time anywhere.

In that stealthy moment just before awakening, a nightmare invaded Jeb Logan's mind. It implanted an empty feeling that became—at the actual moment of awakening—a premonition.

And that set the pattern for the day.

It was a slow day starting. The first black clouds of the Ecuadorian wet season delayed the dawn. Daylight came somnolently out of darkness like a woman stirring beside her lover. Then the morning wind herded the clouds eastward toward the jungle.

But there was still no rain, and a dusty haze shrouded the dry highlands. It gave the sky the color of sifting ashes.

Sunlight flattened out in a few mica brilliants against the eastern edge of the Andean foothill town where Logan lived. The town was called Milagro after a local miracle, a legend recounted innumerable times: A young boy suffering from a jungle fever had awakened from a deep dream of his own and staggered into the dusty streets. Pointing to the sky, he shouted in Spanish, "See the angels! See the angels!"

The villagers had stared, and the little boy collapsed, sweating, burning. Some of the watchers thought they might have seen angels, too, up in the sky. The fever had already taken many of the people, and yet this boy miraculously recovered. He claimed that as he slept, shivered, sweated, all the while he had been with the angels. *Milagro*. Miracle.

In Jeb's own dream, a much darker dream, he had seen angels too. Great, soaring, heavenly creatures with pearlescent wings, surrounded by a halo-glow that was part humidity in the air and part the shine of a heavenly deity. In his dream they had been watching over him, soaring ahead as Jeb made his own way on a quest through the jungle, winding and curving on a course that made sense only with dream-logic. His path was twisted, unpredictable, and when he made the wrong choice and took an incorrect turn, the angels did not bless him for his independence. Rather, they reeled, struggled to attain heaven, and instead they tumbled, falling from the sky.

In the nightmare, Jeb had watched, felt the warning, the premonition. Yet he continued. This was his quest, not one determined by the angels of Milagro or anywhere else.

He had a journey to make.

He met a boat down at Puerto Bolivar. He had still been hypnotized by the mystery and the hothouse odor of the jungle above the coastal town. A luminous-eyed man all in white had squatted in the thick shade of the corrugated iron customs building, singing to the tune picked out on a pearl-inlaid guitar:

"Give me a while longer, death –
Stay your hand while my river flows on.
I do not yet want your dark sea.
For I have a love with grey smoke in her eyes,
And farewells are difficult for my tongue."

Jeb remembered his piecemeal translation of the song, stumbling through his rusty high school Spanish. Well, two years had changed that: now he could even dream the song in Spanish.

But the other details of his dream evaded him, driven away by the morning sounds. The futile questing of his mind left him troubled, unwilling to open his eyes: the first conscious touch of premonition.

Jeb stretched his leg muscles, felt the ripples of the single sheet that covered him. He was a long, knobby figure beneath the sheet: a moulding of angular shadows in soft focus under an olive drab canopy of mosquito netting. The weathered brown face protruding from one end of the sheet was angular, long: an Egyptian pharaoh's face with black hair peppered by grey at the temples.

"Well, what the hell," he muttered. "Time to get up."

He opened his eyes, blinked at a sudden memory: Hey! This the day that Bannon dame said she'd arrive! Well, by God! She's coming for nothing!

It had been a particularly frustrating telephone conversation. The long distance connection between Milagro and Puerto Bolivar had been dim and scratchy, and the woman at the other end full of Yankee determination.

"This is Mrs. Roger Bannon," she had said. "Are you the pilot?"

"Yes."

"What?"

"I said yes, I'm the pilot."

"We've never met, Mr. Logan. But you flew my husband and his partner to their rancho."

Then Jeb placed the name, recalled the husband: a scrawny little man with feverish eyes who'd hired Jeb to fly two men (Bannon and a partner named Gettler) to a jungle plantation on the Amazon watershed seven months before.

"What do you want, Mrs. Bannon?"

"I want to charter your plane for a flight to my husband's rancho."

"Sorry. No can do. My amphibian's dismantled for repairs."

"But the consul here says you have two planes!"

"Yes. But one's just a little single-engine float job."

"What kind of a boat?"

"Float! Mrs. Bannon. It won't do for that flight."

"But Roger's ranch is on a river!"

Here the connection had faded, and it had taken two full minutes to explain that he had too much liking for his skin to risk it by flying a single-engine floatplane over the Andes.

But she had persisted. "If it's a matter of money, Mr.

Logan, I'm perfectly willing to ..."

"No, dammit! It's not a matter of money! I'm just not ..."

"We'll catch tomorrow afternoon's train, Mr. Logan. I'm sure we can work out something when ..."

"Lady, you're wasting your time! Why don't you catch a mainline flight across to Belem and ...?"

"I'll see you the day after tomorrow, Mr. Logan."

And by God! She'd hung up!

Jeb had jiggled the hook, gotten the operator with her impersonal, "*Bueno?*"

Now, he squirmed on his bed, dreading the encounter with Mrs. Bannon. He suspected that it would be a class-one scene. Such scenes always left him with a desire to get drunk and stay drunk for a week.

Jeb frowned, stared up through the netting at the veined cracks of the yellow-brown ceiling. During the night a green spider had set out its web from a shard of the plaster. Gossamer filaments stretched down to the framework that supported the mosquito net. Now, the spider waited with one foot delicately touching a trigger strand of its web. Jeb's attention shifted to a scorpion resting on the wall beside his bed from its night's hunt.

The "Ark! Ark!" cry of toucanets came from the dead tree outside his south wall. American jazz blared from the radio in the *aberote* across the road. The quick *pat pat-pat-pat-pat-pat* of his cook-maid, Maria, making tortillas sounded from the kitchen below. And there drifted past his nose the thin vapor-trail bite of burning chiles, scorched to remove the skin.

It was all infinitely familiar, and somehow poignant.

For a moment, Jeb lay quietly savoring the morning. Then his thoughts scalpeled the edge of an old memory that easy living had allowed him to evade for a long time: stark, snow-blanched Korean hills, his hands fighting the controls of a crippled B-26 as it skimmed between cold peaks ... and the bloody dead figure of Swede Parker, his co-pilot, in the other seat—a gale pouring through the bullet-shattered windshield. Jeb re-experienced the chill of that wind: another touch of the premonition.

Now, what the hell's got me on this morbid kick? he wondered. *That crazy Bannon dame insisting that I fly her inside! Well, I'll ...*

The pig in the courtyard emitted a scream like a frightened woman. Immediately, Maria's voice lifted in a string of curses that she did not know Jeb understood.

"Dump your droppings in my kitchen!" she screamed. "You son of a fat whore! You spawn of uncounted illegitimate ancestors! I'll boil your testicles!"

There came the clatter of a thrown pan.

Jeb chuckled, folded back the mosquito net. His movement disturbed the green spider on the ceiling. She darted onto her web, stopped, retreated. The scorpion curved up its tail, scurried into a crack in the wall.

From the courtyard came another pig squeal, the quick scuffling of Maria's footsteps. A water tin banged against the tiled edge of the reservoir outside the kitchen.

Jeb lifted his wristwatch from the chair beside the bed, slipped it on his wrist, glanced at the dial. *Eight thirty! What's happened to the morning?*

He swung his feet to the floor, rocked forward, stood up and stretched to his full six feet two inches. His left hand hitched his red and white striped shorts higher about his waist. A yellow robe hung on the wall at the head of the bed. He caught the robe in his right hand, gave it a casual shake to dislodge insects, draped it over his shoulders like a cape, and walked out onto the balcony.

"Maria!" he called.

Her voice came from a recess beneath him: "*Si, señor?*" There was a slight quaver of age in the voice, but it sounded confident.

Jeb shifted his mental gears into Spanish: "Has there been a message from the airfield?"

Maria's replay was thick with the musical drawl of the altiplano Indians: "Manuelo sent to say that the airplane of two engines cannot yet be repaired. The little pieces have not arrived. And there was a wireless from the copper mine. They wish to receive their machinery."

"They'll have to wait until the amphibian's airworthy!" he snapped. "They know that!"

"Si, patron." Maria emerged from a door beneath him, stepped out onto the blue tiles of the courtyard. She was a fat, tubular woman encased in a brown dress the color of damp clay. The dress bound her into ribbed lumps as though she had been moulded by a corrugated culvert pipe. Her face was smooth, round, hook-nosed—topped by coarse black hair parted in the middle and braided in two long strands that hung like tassels across the grey shawl covering her shoulders.

Certain Chimu pottery bore likenesses that could have used Maria as a model. The genes that controlled her facial structure had swallowed Inca and Spaniard alike. The victorious Indian features now graced a woman who enjoyed a considerable reputation as a witch. It bothered Jeb not at all that his cook-maid was the local *bruja*, dispensing herbs and amulets along with her household duties.

Maria glanced up at Jeb, averted her eyes as she glimpsed the red and white shorts poorly covered by his robe.

"Is that all the news?" he asked.

She addressed the sidewall of the courtyard. "No, patron. The mayor wishes to enjoy your presence at a fiesta on the evening of Saturday. The boy brought an invitation. I opened it, of course, to see if it was something important that would require ..."

"*Ándalé*!"

Her gaze darted toward him, away. "Are you going to marry with the mayor's daughter, patron?"

Jeb grinned. "Maria, you're a nosey old hag!"

She smiled, displaying a glittering row of gold-capped teeth. "The Señorita Constancia is very beautiful, patron. She is a virgin of ..."

"A pure mango," agreed Jeb.

Maria pulled her shawl more tightly around her shoulders. "*Patron?*"

Jeb recognized the tone: it normally preceded a request for a day off, for a contribution to improve the church bell tower, for medicine for a sick nephew (because the *bruja* knew the limitations of her own magic).

"What is it?" he asked.

She shrugged. "Patron, last night I saw the spirit of my grandfather. Always, when I have this vision, there is violence, and someone dies." Again she shrugged. "Please be careful today, patron."

The dark eyes took another darting look in his direction and away.

There was suddenly no amusement in Jeb at this manifestation of witchcraft. He felt himself genuinely touched by her concern. There were in this town, he knew, people who paid Maria to have omens interpreted. For one brief moment he even considered telling her about his dream, and then he rejected the idea, half amused at himself.

In the distance, the train from Puerto Bolivar sent its whistle hooting against the hills. Momentarily, all other sounds hung submerged in the echoes. Jeb lifted his attention from the courtyard. Across the red-tiled rooftops he could see the outline of the first cordilleras lifting to the distant Andes and the *Anti-Suyo*: the great "Eastern Jungle" of the Incas. In the middle distance the green hills were split by the notch that spilled the Rio Mavari into the gorge below Milagro. From his balcony, Jeb could just see the edge of the river's upper pool where he kept the little floatplane.

A harpy eagle soared across the near hills, catching up Jeb's mind in the close awareness of flight. The eagle drifted into a thermal, rode away upward like a glider. He watched the bird until it became lost in the misty, heat-wrinkled air.

Maria scuffed her feet on the tiles. "Forgive me, patron, for bothering you with my vision. Do you desire your bath now?"

Jeb snapped his fingers at her. "Yes. And I want *you* to scrub my back!"

The old woman ducked her head to conceal a grin, spoke in a shocked tone: "*Señor!*" She shuffled out of sight below. There came the sound of water splashing into the ten-gallon tin that served Jeb as a shower.

And faintly behind that sound Jeb heard the exhalation of steam—like a tired sigh—from the morning train.

That crazy Bannon dame will probably be on that train, he thought. *Well, she can just go back on the train!*

From the railroad station, Milagro appeared imprisoned by dirty hills, their tops spiked with washed-out green bushes.

Mrs. Roger Bannon was not impressed. She stood in the dusty, packed-clay yard beside the station. Her gaze went first to the hills, then to the plaster peeling in scabrous patches from adobe walls, then to the dark-skinned people. The people bothered her. She felt that they were staring at her, but she could not catch an eye turned her way.

This is the absolute end of the world, she thought.

Mrs. Bannon was a petite woman, red-haired, with a rose petal translucence to her skin. A light blue suit, its simplicity and fit attesting a three-figure price tag, accented her smallness. The red hair was caught in a silver-grey scarf. Her eyes were green, quick moving, cynical.

She was thirty-six, and looked ten years younger.

At her left and slightly behind stood a red-haired boy, a twelve-year-old whose stance suggested an adult. He wore a casual tweed suit, white shirt, green tie. A leather camera bag hung from one shoulder. An expensive German miniature camera was suspended from his neck on a black cord. His eyes were green like his mother's but everyone who knew Roger Bannon felt something akin to shock that a child's face could be such a die-cast copy of the father.

The boy cleared his throat. "What a dump!" he said.

She had been thinking the same thing, and it startled her to hear the thought voiced.

"There probably isn't a decent hotel in a hundred miles," she said. She took a deep breath, and the ripe odor of

Milagro bit into her nostrils: burro dung, rotting fruit, carrion. The corner of the station at their left was used as a urinal by men returning in the night from the cantina-whorehouse across the tracks. The acrid urine odor dominated all the other smells.

"Will we get to the ranch today?" asked the boy.

She spoke sharply: "David, must you ask stupid questions?"

He shrugged, turned his attention to the pattern of sunlight and shadows on the station wall. Her mood was a familiar one. Silence was the best way to meet it.

One of her feet began to tap out a nervous rhythm on the dusty clay. The stationmaster had said it would be "*un momento*" while he obtained a horse cart for themselves and luggage. At least she thought he'd said "horse cart." The phrase book in her handbag wasn't much help.

I made three hundred and twenty-five thousand dollars before taxes last year, she thought. *My latest record will sell a quarter of a million copies at least. I open in Las Vegas on the twenty-first of October. I'll make two movies next year.*

What in Christ's name am I—Monti Lee Bannon—doing in this jerkwater village?

Her foot continued its nervous tapping.

"That guy's been gone ten minutes," said David.

"I can tell time!" she snapped.

"What'd he say he was going to get?"

"A horse cart or something I think."

"Don't you know? I thought you could talk Spanish."

"Oh, for Christ's sake, David! Just because I sing a few lyrics in ..."

"I was just asking."

She took a deep breath, opened her handbag, withdrew a pair of dark glasses, put them on. Her hands trembled.

"Here comes something," said David.

A black Victoria pulled by a sway-backed brown horse creaked around the corner. The stationmaster was one of the two figures on the raised seat. The driver was a wizened Indian in a black and white serape, blue shirt and blue trousers. He was barefooted. A straw sombrero shaded black marble eyes.

Mrs. Bannon glanced at him, took in the Victoria.

"Well, just in time for the coronation," she said.

Jeb was finishing his breakfast when he heard the horse coach draw up outside. There came the muted sound of voices, and he recognized a woman's Yankee accent.

Someone rattled the lock on the street door.

Well, I'd best get this over with, he thought. He wiped his mouth on a coarse napkin, stood up, went out into the courtyard.

Maria was just starting down the steps from the balcony.

Jeb waved her back. "I'll take care of this one, Maria."

"Si, patron." She returned to the balcony.

Again the street door rattled.

Jeb entered the atrium, unlatched the door, drew it open.

A red-haired woman stood before him, her eyes hidden behind sunglasses.

His first impression was: *My God! She's little!*

"Yes?" he said.

"Are you Jeb Logan?"

"I am."

And he thought: *Oh, Jesus! She's one of those cute little tomboy tricks!*

Monti swallowed. She had worked out a plan of action, but now, confronted by the tall, rough masculinity of Jeb Logan, she wondered if she'd have to change her tactics.

"I'm Mrs. Bannon," she said. "Mrs. Roger Bannon. I talked to you on the telephone from Puerto Bolivar."

He thought: *Dammit! I'm going to stick to my guns!*

"You've had this trip for nothing, Mrs. Bannon," he said.

She forced a smile. "Let's talk it over, anyway."

He glanced toward the Victoria. David stood beside the

luggage that the driver had stacked on the cobblestones. The significance of the boy's red hair was immediately obvious, and Jeb was struck by the resemblance to Roger Bannon. *Hell! She's got a kid as big as she is!*

"There's nothing to talk over," said Jeb.

"You flew my husband and his partner in there, didn't you?"

"And a half ton of their gear besides, but I'm not about to ..."

"All right then." She turned, addressed David: "Son, have the luggage brought inside."

"Look, Mrs. Bannon, I'm too ..."

"Are you going to leave me standing out here in the street?" she demanded.

Jeb took a deep breath, closed his eyes, opened them. He stepped aside. "Be my guest."

A group of Milagro urchins came up and stopped beside Jeb's door, staring at David. The boy lifted his miniature camera, took a picture of the children. The scene struck Jeb as intensely decadent. He spoke sharply: "Kid! Get that stuff in here like your mother said!"

David looked startled, lowered the camera. "Yes, sir!"

Monti stepped past Jeb, walked through the atrium into the courtyard. She wrinkled her nose at the barnyard smells.

Jeb followed, noticed her sniffing.

"I guess the pig smell is pretty high," he said. "It has a regular sty down at the other end of the courtyard, but the damn thing outgrew it. The gate won't hold him."

"I'm sure one can get used to anything," she said.

Jeb frowned, raised his voice: "Maria!"

She appeared at the balcony rail above them. "Si, patron?"

He gestured toward the entrance where the coach driver was stacking the luggage. "Have him put that stuff in the guest room."

"We've been up half the night on that beastly thing they

call a train," said Monti. "There was a drunk ..." She shuddered.

Maria nodded to Jeb, disappeared in the direction of the stairs.

"Have you eaten?" asked Jeb.

Mont took off her dark glasses, fingered them nervously. "We brought food from the Hotel at Puerto Bolivar."

Jeb stared at her, suddenly overwhelmed by a sense of recognition. Then his mind slipped a cog, substituted a movie screen for his courtyard background.

"Hey!" he said.

Her head jerked up.

"You're the singer," said Jeb. He snapped his fingers. "Monti Lee!"

She smiled. It was a static response, emptied of all friendliness by years of overuse. "I suppose Roger's told you all about me," she said.

And she thought: *Now we'll go through routine "A" about what it's like to be an entertainer ... and gosh! it's sure interesting to meet you.*

"Your husband never said a word," said Jeb. "I had no idea.... I mean, him married to you. I never thought ..." He broke off in confusion.

"Roger has hidden charms," she said.

David came in from the street, crossed to the tiled edge of the reservoir. He saw the pig under the bougainvillea, lifted his camera, took a picture of it.

Jeb scowled.

"Now, about flying us to the rancho," said Monti. "I thought ..."

"It can't be done," said Jeb. "I'm sorry."

She found a cigarette in her purse, fished out a pearl-inlaid lighter, touched flame to cigarette, spoke through the smoke: "You took Roger and the Gettler person in there. What's so difficult about ...?"

"This is a shirt tail outfit with only two planes, Mrs.

Bannon. The twin-engine amphibian I use for the long hauls is grounded for repairs. My other's a single-engine float job I use only for short hops—mostly passengers to the ranchos up the Rio Mavari."

"How long before you'll have your amphibian ready to fly?"

He shrugged. "God knows. Maybe a month. Maybe two."

Anger painted two bright spots in her cheeks. She stamped a foot. "The train was bad enough! Then that horse cart! Now I have to deal with a white man gone native!"

Jeb said, "I'm sorry these things bother you."

She thought: *I'm going at this all wrong.*

"I apologize," she said. "The consul told me you were pretty stubborn. But I'm prepared to bid high." Again the practiced smile. "And I like stubborn men."

"Have you flown much, Mrs. Bannon?"

"With airlines ... certainly."

"Your husband's clear over on the Amazon watershed, Mrs. Bannon. Now, there are regular airline flights from Puerto Bolivar across to Belem. From there you could ..."

"Nuts!"

"Well, what's wrong with ...?"

"Lots of things, Mr. Logan." She took three furious puffs on her cigarette, ground it underfoot. "My papers were all cleared for Ecuador, but it still took me two days to wade through the red tape. I didn't have a letter from my hometown chief of police!"

He chuckled.

"Verrry funny! If I go over to Belem it'll just be more of the same—only this time in Portuguese!"

"What's your all-fired hurry?"

"I open in Las Vegas on October twenty-first, and I've only ..."

"That only gives you a couple of weeks here! You'll have to ..."

"I know what I have to do, Mr. Logan. Now what I want

to know from you is just how much it's going to cost me?"

"You're wasting your breath, Mrs. Bannon."

"The consul said that if the price was right, you'd do it."

Jeb made a slow, pointed examination of her figure. "He's right. And there are even some things I'll do just for the fun of it." His gaze hardened, and his voice lowered almost to a growl: "But that doesn't include committing suicide!"

"Oh, it can't be as bad as all that. Single-engine planes make much longer flights all the ..."

"How the hell do you know what my plane can do? You come here fresh from sitting on your fanny through an airline milk run, and you think all I have to do is ..."

"What's your price, Mr. Logan?"

"You don't have that much!" He raised his hands. "Look, if that one engine failed up there over ..."

"Can't you coast down to a lake or a river and ..."

"Judas Priest!" Jeb smacked his forehead with the palm of his left hand. "*Coast* down to ... What do you think this is, a toboggan?"

Monti blushed. "I realize you might run into some problems that ..."

"Come here!" He grabbed her arm, hustled her into the room beyond the kitchen that he used as an office. It was a cool room, dim after the glare of the courtyard. An ancient roll-top desk occupied one corner. A crude trestle table stood against the opposite wall, its top covered with a jumble of maps. Jeb found one map in the pile, spread it on top.

"That's the map the consul showed me," she said.

Jeb put his hands on the map, leaned forward, closed his eyes. "Lady, why the hell are you picking on me? There must be a thousand other guys who ..."

"But you flew Roger to his ranch. You know where it is."

"I see." Jeb opened his eyes, looked at the map.

David came in from the courtyard, stood beside his mother. "Is that the map that shows Dad's ranch?"

"Hush," said Monti.

"There are some things the consul didn't tell you," said Jeb.

"He mentioned the gas problem," said Monti.

"Oh, he mentioned the gas problem."

"And he told me the range of your plane."

"He told you the range of my plane."

"He said it'll go maybe seven hundred miles on ..."

"Fine! Then we come down at some little native village, and we tell them to dig an oil well right away because we ..."

"We sent a telegram to the village of Ramona," she said.

"That was very enterprising of you, Mrs. Bannon."

She nodded. "They wired back that they have gasoline."

"Brazilian army gas for their patrol planes," said Jeb. "Besides, that's in Brazil ... where you'll meet some more red tape—in Portuguese."

"It's just a village," she said. "The only papers we'll need are green ones with George Washington's picture on them."

"Ah, the power of the Yankee dollar," he said.

She smiled. "And Ramona is only about three hundred and fifty miles from here. I measured on the map."

"Wonderful." He nodded. "Now, shall we step out of your dream world, Mrs. Bannon?"

"What?"

Jeb put a finger on Milagro. "Here we are with a single-engine float plane." He moved his finger across to a dot on the Amazon basin side. "And this is the gay native metropolis of Ramona: five hundred souls, assorted insets, lizards, amoebic dysentery, two cantinas and warm beer."

"Not to mention gasoline," she said.

"Of course. And the straight-line distance between Milagro and Ramona is a *mere* three hundred and fifty miles."

"About half your range," she said.

"True. Except that my little plane doesn't have oxygen. Your straight-line route runs over peaks that'd push us up to twenty-two thousand feet. We'd have to fly down here through the pass. That's only seventeen thousand feet. Still without oxygen—and closer to six hundred and fifty miles."

"Well, your plane'll fly that far!"

"You're right. And what's more, there are even places along that route where we could stop for gas. If we had *wheels* and if they happened to have some gas!"

"But you could fly it in ..."

"Sure! Through some of the worst air in the world! And if we have to come down in that area with nothing but those jim-dandy puddle sticks under us—we have bought it! For good!"

"I think you're vastly overplaying the ..."

"Lady, I haven't even told you the half of it! Just for the ducks, let's say our engine conks out, and we *do* find a stretch of wet grass or a piece of water that'll take us. There we are. This little bird of mine doesn't have a radio, either."

"I don't get you, Mr. Logan. You're a pilot. You're supposed to keep a plane in the air. Yet, you talk as though the most important thing is staying on the ground!"

"Mrs. Bannon ..." He stopped, swallowed, spoke slowly and carefully: "Mrs. Bannon, an airplane is a machine for going up into the air *temporarily*. When you forget that qualification, you're on the way out: in pieces. Now, I grant you that there are some barnstormers and crackpots who'll ..."

"The consul told me you were a combat pilot in Korea. Wasn't *that* kind of dangerous?"

His eyes narrowed. He nodded. "Yes. There were even some life insurance companies that wouldn't write policies on us. But we were out to kill somebody, or get killed. That's how war is, you know. But that's over for the moment. I no longer want to kill anybody: not you, not your boy here ... not myself. Nobody! I want to age gently in the flesh, become an *old* pilot. I'm in a business that ..."

"That's *temporarily* not making any money from the look of things!"

"True."

"You can't even afford a radio for your ..."

"Wrong. My plane's just *temporarily* without a radio. It *had* a radio. And I even had another pilot working for me until recently. By some odd coincidence, the pilot and my radio vanished at the same time. So ... you see?"

"Mr. Logan ..." She shook her head. "I just don't have the time to fight with you ... or to bargain with you ... or anything. I'll pay you twenty-five hundred dollars to fly us to my husband's ranch.

Holy Mother! he thought. And he scowled. "Why, this all-fired ..."

"If we can get gas at Ramona, could you carry enough extra to return?" she asked.

He nodded.

"Is there any other complication?" she asked. "I mean ... well, I see your point about distances. What's the flying distance from Ramona to the ranch?"

Jeb glanced down at the map. "About four hundred and fifty miles." Sudden anger overcame him. "But by God! You don't fly a single-engine plane to the limit of its range over these mountains and that jungle!"

Monti put her left hand over her eyes.

Jeb took a deep breath, exhaled: almost a sigh. "Couldn't you come down later, Mrs. Bannon? I mean after this engagement or whatever it is on the twenty-first of October?"

She shook her head without removing her hand from her eyes. *What can I tell him?* she asked herself. *That I have to do this to save my marriage? But maybe that's not true. I'm not being honest with him or myself. I don't really know why I'm doing this. Except that I'm not getting any younger, and ...*

Monti lowered her hand from her eyes. "Let's just say that I *have* to go in there, and that I'm willing to pay whatever it costs to get my way."

"Even to getting yourself and your boy killed?"

She swallowed. "I don't think it's that dangerous."

"You mean you won't let yourself believe it's that dangerous. Would you consider leaving the boy, and just going by yourself ...?"

"David has to go with us. That's part of it. I'm bringing him down to stay with his father."

Jeb stared at her. "Does Bannon know you're coming?"

"No. It's a surprise."

"I thought he'd written for you to come down ... that everything was okay ... that ..." He broke off. "Do you have even the faintest idea what that rancho is?"

She shrugged. "Some kind of a plantation. They're growing stuff for drugs."

David cleared his throat, spoke in a squeaky voice: "And they're trading with the Indians." He blushed.

Jeb glanced at the boy, back to the mother. "That's a jungle plantation, Mrs. Bannon. It's new, raw. And there are Indians: Jivaro. The Jivaro are not tame Indians."

"My dad never said it was dangerous," said David.

"David's very healthy," said Monti. "He's had all of his shots: yellow fever, typhoid—everything. I'm sure he won't catch anything."

"Except maybe a poison dart—or a spear in the guts!"

She paled. "You'll go to any extreme to get out of taking us!"

"A visit might be all right," said Jeb. "A *short* visit, but ..."

"Poison dart!" said Monti.

"There's always the possibility that a Jivaro will take a sudden dislike to you," said Jeb. "And he may decide to add your *tzantza* to his collection for no reason you'd ever understand."

"What's that?" asked David. "A *tzantza*?"

Jeb kept his attention on Monti, spoke coldly: "A shrunken head."

She drew a sharp breath. "You're just trying to frighten me!"

He shrugged. "Some people go in there and never have a bit of trouble with the Jivaro. Some say the Jivaro are damn fine Indians, but ..."

"Roger would've said something if it was dangerous!"

"I guess so."

"I'll pay you thirty-five hundred dollars," she said.

The haunted mood of his morning dream returned to Jeb. It enfolded him like a thrown net. He felt swept up in a current he couldn't escape, and this feeling aroused a core of determination within him. He shook his head. "No!"

"Forty-five hundred, Mr. Logan." She managed a bitter smile. "You see, I'm a determined woman."

He remained silent, shocked.

"How long would it take us?" she asked.

He shrugged.

"About nine hours?" she asked.

"More or less."

"That's about five hundred dollars an hour," she said.

"It's a lot of money for one ride," he said.

Her mouth shaped into the reflex smile. "And what's money if it won't buy what you want?"

David took Monti's arm. The boy looked pale, angry. "Mother, let's go back and find somebody else. This guy's afraid!"

Jeb took the sting of the words, drew in a deep breath, fought for control. Then: "You're right, kid. I'm yellow. Scared as hell. That comes from having brains enough to know what can happen in those mountains and that jungle."

"I'll make it an even five thousand dollars," she said. "Take it or leave it."

He felt the net draw closer, thought about five thousand dollars: the money to buy a new port engine for the amphibian, to buy new radio equipment, to bring in another relief pilot ... money to grease a few official palms and smooth out the red tape.

Mother and son stared at him.

Jeb took his flying cap from its hook above the map table, jammed it on his head. It was a symbolic gesture. Monti knew his decision before he spoke.

"All right!" His words were sharp, bitten off. "We'll go to Ramona. If they'll sell us gas at Ramona, we'll go the rest of the way."

She exhaled a long, sighing breath.

And Jeb knew from the feeling of the net around him that they'd be able to buy gas at Ramona.

Monti spoke the thought: "They'll sell us the gas."

Jeb stepped to the door, recalled the small mountain of luggage they'd unloaded from the Victoria. He considered the flying distance, worked the almost automatic calculation of weight-over-fuel that was like an instinct with him. It gave him a perverse feeling of pleasure to say: "Start cutting down your luggage. You can take sixty pounds between you."

"What should we wear?" she asked.

"Cottons ... Khaki. It gets damn hot over there." He glanced at his wristwatch. "Let's get moving. We've just about enough time to make it before dark."

Already, his mind was moving ahead into the flying problem: *We'll be heavily loaded. I'll have Manuelo stir up the river ahead of us with a motor boat—give us a little chop to help get off. Dr. Iriarte has Jeep cans for carrying the extra gas. I'll have to send some boys after them. Now, where the hell did I put my jungle kit?*

"Maria!" he called.

"Si, patron?" She came out of the kitchen, tears running down her cheeks.

Jeb looked at the tears, surprised.

"Patron, you are going in the airplane!" she said. "My vision ..."

His trapped feeling became anger. "Maria! Stop that damned foolishness! Send some of those children off the street to bring Dr. Iriarte's gas cans. All of them! Get my jungle kit, then start making us a lunch."

She bowed her head. "*Si, señor.*"

The courtyard became a scene of bustling motion.

Jeb found himself caught up by the excitement, but he still felt that he had been outmaneuvered. And there was the dark instinct from his nightmare.

He would not have called himself a deeply superstitious man, but in the minutes just before the takeoff he almost cancelled the flight.

It was the fretful stiffing of Premonition ... the dream.

Something about a river ... and death.

But the mood passed. The pilot within him took over. There came the moaning of the motor at full throttle. The pontoons stuttered through the light chop of Manuelo's motor boat. Then they were off the water, lifting up into the clean air where sawtooth peaks stretched across the horizon: a stark barrier in black rock and cold white snow.

The plane's cabin was an isolated piece of civilization: clean fabrics, glistening Plexiglas, chrome, the round eyes of gauges—and the droning motor in the background.

Monti sat on Jeb's right. She had changed into a man's tan shirt, dark green riding breeches, Jodhpur boots. The silver scarf still tied her red hair. An indrawn look pinched her features. Already, her mind was projecting ahead to the meeting with Roger.

Will he be happy to see us? Of course he will! What a godforsaken place for him to choose. Why couldn't he just sit back and let me support him? What's he trying to prove? Jesus! It's been more than seven months! Has he changed?

David sat directly behind her, crowded by the stack of empty Jeep cans tied down beside him. The boy wore a light blue shirt and jeans: colors that accented his sunburned look. Like his mother, he was silent, but unlike his mother, his eyes moved to catch each change in the landscape.

For the first time since they'd left the States, David was allowing himself to recognize his own feelings and thoughts. Excitement tensed his throat and chest. The veneer of adult cynicism that had rubbed onto him from the Bohemian atmosphere surrounding his mother began to slough away. More and more, there appeared a twelve-year-old boy filled with the vibrancy of adventure.

I'll bet there's lots of hunting at the ranch, he thought. *And Indians. After mother leaves, and we're alone: Dad and me ...*

He chewed nervously at his lower lip.

The plane entered the pass. Peaks climbed the sky above

them on both sides. Turbulent winds shook the little ship. The passengers bounced and jerked. Wings creaked. The Jeep cans banged.

David lifted the camera from his neck, took a picture through the side window. The thin air added to his feeling of exhilaration. He took another picture straight ahead through the propeller blur.

Then they were through the pass. The ground receded. The air became even rougher from the thermal winds pouring up from the hot country ahead.

"There's the jungle," said Jeb.

David lifted against his safety belt, peered ahead.

It was a cauldron of liquid green boiling over the edge of the world. The immensity of it filled him with a momentary sense of fear. The green stretched out forever, and it was not life—it was something alien, an enemy.

Jeb tipped the plane's nose down slightly, eased back on the throttle, adjusted the carburetor heat, the trim tabs, reset the gyrocompass.

That David's a funny kid, he thought. *Not like a kid. He acts too grown-up to be happy*. And then he wondered at himself: *Does being grown-up mean being unhappy?*

The mountains slipped behind. Now, the jungle poured beneath them.

An hour and twenty minutes later the dark adobe walls and tin roofs of Ramona came under their left wing. The town sat on a point to the north side at the juncture of the Rio Tapiche and Rio Itecoasa. A wide stretch of dirty concrete steps reached down to the water on the Itecoasa side. Launches and dugouts nosed against the foot of the steps like a jumble of thin insects.

Behind the town a thick wall of jungle held civilization at bay along an indefinite balancing line: here a finger of cultivation invading the green, there a creeping-in of wild growth attacking the houses.

Figures moved along the concrete steps, looked up.

A rippling shadow of the plane passed over the town and out across the Itecoasa. The river was a sheet of dark glass roiled by an imperfection where the narrower Tapiche joined it.

Jeb banked for an upriver landing.

Monti glanced at her wristwatch. "Two thirty-five," she said. "I thought you said it'd take more than six hours."

He tugged at the visor of his cap. "We were lucky and found a tail wind."

"Where's all the danger that frightened you so?"

Jeb smiled. "So it's been milk run—this far."

She sniffed.

He dropped the flaps, aimed the plane up the Itecoasa. Now, they were low enough that the river became a wide, flat lake between low walls of green. Heat poured in the vents: a burning wash of air that inflated the cabin with moisture and a kind of molten tension.

"My god, it's hot!" said Monti.

The plane feathered out on a cushion of air, splashed down opposite the town. Jeb gave it right rudder, taxied up to the con–crete steps to dark people with volatile features. Voices called out in Portuguese and Spanish. Hands clutched at the wings. Jeb shut off the motor, fearful that one of the dark figures would stumble into the propeller. He opened his door, slipped down to the float.

Now, he became conscious of the town's odor: an exhalation of bad breath—fetid earth, rotting fruit and flesh. Black flies arose from the bottoms of the launches and dugouts, invaded the plane.

Monti slapped at her arms.

Jeb singled out one of the smiling, jabbering faces around the plane, pressed a bill into the man's hands, told him in Spanish that he was in charge of keeping the *aeroplano* secure. The man replied in Portuguese, but apparently he understood. He immediately started ordering his companions to stand clear.

David released his safety belt, leaned forward. "May I get out, Mother?"

She stared at the scene outside, her mouth drawn into a curve of distaste. "I guess so, but stay in sight where we can call you."

Two soldiers in green uniforms, peaked caps, carbines over their shoulders, appeared at the top of the steps.

Jeb worked his way along the float, leaped to the steps and climbed up to the soldiers. They stared at him suspiciously until he passed over his pilot's license and Brazilian flight permit folded around two fifty-milreis notes. The documents came back to him without the money.

"Gasoline?" They looked at each other with a kind of resigned wonder at the stupidity of all foreigners. One shrugged. The other shrugged.

"*Un momento, señor*," said one.

They went back into the town, strolling unhurriedly down a palm-shaded street through green shadows and hot patches of sunlight.

Jeb fidgeted, stared at the town, at the river.

I was a damn fool to take her word about the gas here, he thought. *If we can't get any ... we're stuck.* He looked down at a scattering of outboard motors on launches and dugouts. *Oh, hell! We'll get gas here all right. We just won't like the price.*

Presently, there appeared at the head of the steps a small, chocolate-dark fat man with thick-lidded bloodshot eyes. He wore a wrinkled blue suit, a damp white shirt, a red tie spotted by perspiration.

"A message about gasoline?" he asked. "By wireless? What message? What gasoline?"

Jeb sighed. Another fifty-milreis note changed hands.

The man looked speculatively at the airplane, as though weighing its probable salvage value. He glanced at Jeb, smiled, turned back into town. He strolled at the same casual rate as the departed soldiers.

Jeb made his way back down the steps to the plane.

Monti leaned out the door on her side. "What luck?"

He held out his hands, palms up. "*Quien sabe?*"

Twenty minutes later a crude hand truck bearing two fifty-gallon drums rumbled and sloshed up to the top of the steps. It was pushed by what could only be described as a *swarm* of children.

The drums bore a Brazilian government seal with a legend in Portuguese warning that they contained gasoline "for official use only!"

Again the chocolate-dark man joined Jeb on the steps. "The gasoline is very expensive here, *senhor*." He shrugged apologetically.

"How much?"

"In dollars, *senhor*?"

Here we go, thought Jeb. He nodded.

The man held up two fingers. "Two liters—one dollar."

Jeb winced. He knew that the dark little man would almost double the money on the black-market exchange, thought: *Maybe I can shave that some.*

Without warning, Monti spoke from just behind Jeb: "How much does he want?"

Jeb turned, surprised that he had not heard her come up. "He wants fifty cents American per liter."

"Pay it."

"But ..."

"I said pay it."

Jeb nodded, turned back to the vendor of gasoline, who was smiling broadly at Monti. "Agreed. Start pouring gas."

The man bowed, waved to his *swarm*.

Presently, the official gasoline began gurgling into the wing tanks and the Jeep cans that were brought out and lined up along the steps. The laboring children scrambled about their work, pushing and shouting. The air became thick with the cloying smell of gasoline.

Jeb looked around for David, saw him at the top of the

steps taking photographs of the scene.

"I think I'll look at the view," said Monti. She started toward David.

Latin eyes followed her movements. Comments were called back and forth by the men on the steps. The children grinned and laughed.

Monti turned to Jeb. "What are they saying?"

Jeb smiled. "They say you have a boy figure—that your breasts are smaller than the average hereabouts ... that you don't have a proper female bottom. Things like that."

The anger spots colored her cheeks. "Well! That's too damn bad!"

"Take it easy," said Jeb. "Women have to get used to that sort of thing in a Latin country."

"We'll see about that!" She turned, resumed her climb to the top of the landing, and looked out at the river. A familiar feeling swelled in her.

"Your damned show-off compulsion!" her father had called it.

She called it "my show-*them* feeling."

The built-up personality of Monti Lee—the ballad singer, the torch singer—came over her. She visualized a microphone before her, called up the Spanish lyrics that had been coached into her for a movie about Mexico.

One deep breath: the husky voice rolled out over the dirty landing, into the humid, odorous, insect-filled air.

"Quiéreme mucho, dulce amor mio ..."

All work on refueling the plane stopped.

She had them under control when she hit the second line.

Someone raced up the steps. Presently a guitar sounded behind her, filling out the melody. Then another guitar ... maracas. An older boy from the *swarm* picked up the counterpoint by tapping two hardwood sticks.

Her voice sank to the closing verse: *"... tan separados vivir ..."* She left it hanging there.

The landing erupted to shouts: *"Olé! Olé!"* They wanted

more.

She gave them "Siboney" ... "Babalu" ... "Sin Ti" ... "Luna, Luna, Luna."

Finally, her voice grew tired.

But they wanted still more.

She looked down at Jeb on the landing below her. His face was drawn into a craggy frown. "Tell them I can't sing anymore," she said.

"Tell them yourself!"

"Wha ... Oh!" She began to laugh. "I don't speak their language. I just know the words to some songs. They're just ... noise."

"Some noise!"

He waved the guitarists away, turned to the crowd on the steps. "The voice is tired," he said. "No more voice."

"Ahhhhhhhhh ..." It was a long multiple sigh of regret.

One of the guitarists wanted to know, "She is a star of the *cíne*, no?"

"Kind of," said Jeb.

"Oh."

Another stepped forward. "You are staying the night? There is a fiesta that ..."

Jeb shook his head, glanced at his wristwatch.

The guitarist turned to Monti. "*Señorita, quiere usted un* ..."

"She doesn't speak Spanish or Portuguese," said Jeb.

"But ..."

He explained about "noise."

This amused everyone.

"We are flying on over the jungle to the rancho of her husband," said Jeb. "We must hurry to arrive before dark."

Slowly they retreated. Work resumed.

David crossed to Monti's side, frowned. "Mother! Why must you make such a show of yourself?"

"That's what buys your beans, sonny boy!"

It was ten minutes to four before they got off the river.

Jeb aimed the plane across the roiled juncture of rivers, using the wavelets to help break the grip of the water. They lifted sluggishly, heavy with extra gasoline. He pulled up the flaps, played the controls delicately to avoid extra strain on the already overstressed wings. They circled back over the town.

People ran along the steps. Hats were waved.

"How long to the rancho?" asked Monti.

"Maybe two and a half hours," said Jeb. "I'll push it. Your exhibition back there wasted time. I'll have to waste gas now to make it before dark."

"That'll teach them who has a boy figure," she said.

Jeb smiled, shook his head. He checked his instruments, glanced back at David. The boy sat in the corner behind his mother, crowded by the Jeep cans of gasoline. The cans rattled faintly in their lashings.

"How're those cans riding?" asked Jeb.

"All right, I guess."

"Let me know right away if they shift around."

"Yes, sir."

Jeb turned his attention back to their course.

David peered down out the side window. Far below them, the loops and whorls of the Tapiche were a snail track curving through the omnipresent green. Excitement keyed up the boy's senses, made him feel desperately alive.

Will dad ever be surprised!

A chuckling happiness bubbled within him. Reflected sunlight exploded in a glare-flash from the river. David squinted. He saw Jeb reach out, adjust the gyro compass, noted the empty socket in the panel where the radio had been.

"What's that thing you keep fixing?" asked David.

Jeb looked over his shoulder. "Huh?"

David pointed at the compass. "That."

"Oh." Jeb turned back. "That's the gyrocompass. It's steadier than the magnetic compass. We have to fly a pretty straight course overland to conserve gas."

"Couldn't we follow the river?"

Jeb smiled. "It's eight or nine hundred miles to the rancho by river. That land down there is pretty flat in lots of places. The river wanders all over the map."

"How fast are we going?"

"About one seventy ... maybe a little more."

"Will we get there before dark?"

"Sure. And some to spare."

Monti stabbed a glance at David. The boy fell silent, sat back. Jeb looked at her.

"That was some performance you put on back there in Ramona," he said.

She frowned. "Not one of my best." Anger showed in the way she clipped off her words.

"What were you trying to prove?"

"I don't *have* to prove anything, Mister Logan. Leave the brilliant questions to my psychoanalyst!" She waved a hand toward the instruments. "You just fly the plane. That's what you're being paid to do."

Jeb shrugged, thought: *Man! What an acid tongue! No wonder Bannon chose the jungle!*

They passed over a clearing, stark galvanized metal roofs standing out against the green.

Monti said, "If *we* had to cut way down on *our* luggage, why'd *you* bring that big heavy valise I saw you cram into the back?"

So that's what's eating her!

"That's our survival kit," said Jeb.

"Survival kit?" She turned squarely toward him.

"In case we get forced down." He reached around behind her, tapped the seat back. "There's a loaded .44 magnum revolver and twenty-five rounds of extra ammo in the seat pocket behind you. There's a machete under the seat."

"Are you trying to frighten me again?"

"Nope. You can starve to death down there just as quick

as you could out in an open boat on the ocean. So you carry a few necessities ... just in case."

"Such as what?"

"Oh ... fishing gear, snares, food concentrates ... a twenty-two pistol and a few boxes of ammo for it ... atabrine, terriamiacin, a pellet stove, tea, a flashlight and extra batteries. Things like that."

"Stupid!" she muttered.

"You wouldn't think so if we ever needed that kit."

She turned away, sniffed.

David said: "What's this thing on the floor under my feet?"

"That's the grapnel for anchoring us to the beach when we land," said Jeb. "Sorry we had to put it under your feet. No other place for it with this load."

"Oh, that's okay." David sat back. "We flew over some buildings beside the river back a ways. What were they?"

"Agricultural experiment stations," said Jeb. "Abandoned now. The help had a falling out with the Indians."

He turned, looked across the Jeep cans out the windows. "That's sure a big mountain over on our left."

"That's Tusachilla," said Jeb. "Active volcano. See that ring of black near the summit? She put on a show a couple of months ago. I flew some scientists in near there. Vulcanologists."

"There's not much around here, is there?" asked David. He sounded frightened.

"Not much civilization," said Jeb. "Your dad's rancho is at the head of navigation on the Tapiche. There's an army post—one sergeant and a radio—about a hundred miles downstream from the rancho. Then—nothing but the river and a few Indian villages for almost a thousand miles."

"Beastly country!" snapped Monti.

"One of the last frontiers," said Jeb. "That's one of its attractions, Mrs. Bannon."

"Oh, call me Monti," she said. "Roger's mother is Mrs.

Bannon."

Jeb glanced around at the height of the sun, adjusted the throttle for a few more revolutions. "Is that your real name: Monti? Or is that one of those names they pick for an actress?"

She sighed. "It's really Montana."

"After the state?"

"My father was a gold camp lawyer there. Later, he was a judge. I was born at a place called Meadow Creek after we became respectable."

"Montana's a good name," said Jeb. "It means *mountain* in Spanish."

"What's in a name?" she asked. "As the Bard so appropriately put it." She squirmed into a more comfortable position, took a deep breath. "May I call you Jeb?"

"As you said, 'What's in a name?'"

"How well do you know my husband, Jeb?"

"So-so. About as well as you get to know anybody after flying with 'em a couple of times."

"What makes him come to a Godforsaken place like this?"

"*Quien sabe?* Maybe he's looking for something."

"But there's *nothing* here!"

"Nothing except what you make for yourself. Maybe that's what he wants."

Anger flooded her. "You can't talk simple sense with a man! All of you go wandering off into ... into philosophy!"

Jeb smiled. "So what's unusual about a man wanting to make something for himself?"

"He's running *away* from himself!"

"*Quien sabe?*"

She was silent for almost five minutes, then: "Do you know Roger's partner, this Gettler?"

"Franz Gettler? Yeah. He's been around these parts a bit longer than your husband. I've ferried him a few places."

"Where's he from?"

"I think he was prospecting in the Serra do Craval before he hooked up with your husband."

"No, I mean where's he from originally?"

"Some place in Westphalia, I think. He spent some time in the States, too. I heard he was a professor of some kind at one time."

"Hardly likely!"

"You never can tell."

"What's he like?"

"Big guy. Blond. Accent."

"Do you like him?"

"Oh, now look here ..."

"I mean it: Do you like him?"

"What's that have to do with ..."

"I want to know what he's like."

"Your childlike faith in my judgment is very touching," said Jeb.

"Well, you must know if you like him or not."

"I don't know. Never thought about it. He's a kind of a cold fish. Always feeling things, making funny cracks about texture."

"What do you mean?"

"Oh ... my amphibian's got plastic upholstery. He ran his hand along it, said it felt dead. Things like that."

"He sounds crazy!"

"Well, maybe he doesn't have all his marbles. Some people get eccentric from being alone too much in the jungle."

"Why'd Roger choose him for a partner?"

"How the hell do I know?"

"Would you choose someone like that for a partner?"

"Gettler knows the jungle."

"Huh! I don't see why anyone would *want* to know it."

Jeb shrugged, scanned the sky.

A passage of turbulent air shook the plane. The cans of gasoline banged and scraped. Time passed in the droning somnolence of motor sounds, the flowing of the green sea beneath them. The air became more turbulent. Jeb became conscious of a stronger smell of gasoline in the cabin. He spoke over his shoulder to David.

"How're those cans riding?"

"There's a little bit of gasoline spilled down the side of one of them," said David.

Jeb frowned, studied the winding river track ahead.

Monti began humming faintly to herself.

The tune filled Jeb with disquiet. He tried to place the reason, and recognized the melody: The lament of his morning nightmare.

Immediately, the sodden sense of premonition came back, started the perspiration in his palms. *This is stupid!* he told himself. *I've got to stop this!*

"Is that another one of the *noises* you sing?" he asked.

She seemed to return from far away. "Huh?"

"That tune you were humming."

She hummed another stanza. "Oh, that. I heard it in Puerto Bolivar. It was on a jukebox. Sad kind of song."

He translated the words for her.

She shuddered. "What a morbid thing!"

David leaned forward between them. "How much farther?"

"About an hour," said Jeb. "The rancho's in those foothills straight ahead." He glanced up at the wing tank gas gauges. "We'll be letting down pretty soon to top off our tanks."

"Couldn't we make it without that?" asked Monti.

"Yes. But I want to get rid of those cans. They make me uneasy."

"Where're you going to land?" asked Monti.

"A wide stretch of river up ahead. There's a beach."

"Will there be Indians?" asked David.

"Probably not," said Jeb. "No villages along this stretch."

"I saw a village back a ways," said David. "Are they good

Indians or bad Indians?"

"I guess they're pretty tame," said Jeb. "Except when they get all hopped up on *cachasa*."

"What's *cachasa*?"

"Mostly fermented saliva. The women chew some stuff, spit it into a gourd."

"Do they really dr ...?"

"David!" Monti whirled on her son. "Stop asking so damn many questions!"

He sat back. "Yes, Mother."

She drew a nervous breath, extracted a package of cigarettes from her blouse pocket.

Jeb glanced at her. "No smoking."

She jerked her head toward him, glaring.

Jeb nodded toward the rear. "The gas."

She frowned, returned the cigarettes to her pocket. "Sorry. I forgot."

He tipped the left wing down, began a slow, banking turn. "There's where we'll refuel."

The river ahead widened, stretched out in almost a straight line—a thick finger pointing at the hills.

Jeb pulled back the throttle. The jungle moved up toward them at a deceptively rapid rate. There came a moment of gliding suspense. Then the floats touched the river with a cushioned bounce. They slowed, turned toward a low sandy beach on the right.

Damp heat poured in the vents. It was sticky, and with a feeling of actual weight.

Sand gritted under the floats. The plane's nose lifted, stopped.

Beyond the beach the jungle arose in steady waves of color: harsh lines standing out in the bold flat light of the low sun. There was a deep blue-green at the bottom, a sun-bleached sage at the top. Above the green towered a candelo tree with bat-falcon nests cluttering the forks of its branches. The front line of the forest was a wall of *mata-polo* trees hung with a twisted screen of lianas.

Jeb shut down the motor. Silence flooded in upon them.

A flock of violet swallows dipped across the sand, lifted and turned over the trees. Behind them came a squall of black flies that enveloped the plane, faded away in a diminishing drone.

Heat devils shimmered above the beach, twisting the lower level of the jungle into dancing lines.

"It's beautiful," murmured Monti. "I never realized it could be so beautiful."

"And it's deadly," said Jeb. "You're not allowed even one mistake out there. Never forget that."

"But it looks so peaceful."

"Are there wild animals in there right now?" asked David.

"Lots of them," said Jeb. He opened his door, released his safety belt. "You can stretch your legs on the sand, but stay away from the jungle's edge." He lifted the revolver from the seat pocket, tucked it into his waistband.

Monti noted the motion, grimaced.

A swarm of gnats hummed in the open door, settled on every stretch of bare skin. Jeb slapped at his neck. "The bugs can be fierce. We'll make this quick."

He stepped onto the float, took the grapnel and line from the rear, anchored the plane, and began refueling.

Monti got out her side. David followed. They wandered up the beach, voices lowered in a murmured conversation.

An odd pair, thought Jeb.

The memory picture of Bannon came back to him: the skinny frame, the sandy hair, the deep-set eyes with their mystical light. There was a kind of overpowering calm about Monti's husband. It reminded Jeb of the relentless Latin-American courtesy.

How'n hell did two like that ever get together? he wondered. *The boy sure looks like his father. Especially the eyes.*

The thick smell of gasoline began to make Jeb dizzy. He

wiped perspiration from his forehead with the back of his sleeve. Flies and gnats crawled over his skin, buzzed and hopped, their bites like fire. He hoisted the last can from the rear seat, topped off the wing tanks. The can remained half full. Jeb re-tied it in the rear, carried the empties across the beach, and hid them inside the screening lianas.

Monti watched Jeb working. David kicked at the sand behind her. She ignored the splash of sand, puffed thoughtfully on her cigarette.

This Jeb is like Roger, she thought. *What makes people like them come to the end of nowhere?* The cigarette burned her finger. She dropped it, stubbed it out with her toe. *Why'm I here? What do I want from Roger? Dammit! I should never have married him! We should've had an affair ... and that's all!*

She stared at her toe marks in the sand.

God! But I need him!

"Won't Dad be surprised?" said David.

A feeling of love for her son passed over Monti. "He most certainly will, dear."

David came around to stand half-facing her. He looked away at the plane. "Do you really love Dad, Mother?"

Her mouth twitched. She glared at the boy. "Don't ask stupid questions!"

Jeb leaned out of the plane, called to them: "Come along. We don't have much more daylight. Have to hurry." He stepped down to the float, helped them aboard, brought in the grapnel and cast off. The current caught the plane as he climbed into his seat.

Abruptly, David pointed upstream. "Hey! Look!"

Around the upper reach of the river nosed a *caoba* dugout with five Indians: a sinewy rippling of bodies, painted paddles flashing in the late sunlight. A stolid figure sat in the bow holding a *pindu* cane pole across his lap. His hair was cut squarely across his forehead in low bangs, his face marked by red streaks of *achiote*.

Jeb started the motor, swung out into the river, faced downstream away from the canoe.

The Indians backpaddled, waited.

Jeb pushed the throttle ahead: the motor roared. They gathered speed—faster, faster. He rocked one float off. Then they were airborne, reaching out over the jungle in a wide turn, and back above the upturned Indian faces.

"Those are Zaparos," said Jeb. "Fairly tame."

The plane climbed faster now, freed from part of its load. Again the jungle took on its appearance of a soft green carpet.

"It looks so calm down there," said Monti.

"Just on the surface," said Jeb.

"Will I be able to swim in the river?" asked David.

Jeb shook his head. "That river's one of the deadliest parts of the jungle, full of piranha."

Monti whirled toward him. "Those terrible fish that eat you alive?"

"That's right."

"My God! I almost went wading back there!"

"It probably would've been safe enough if you'd stayed close to shore," said Jeb. "The river's clear. You could've seen them coming."

"Can you fish for them?" asked David. "Are they good to eat?"

"Yes, to both," said Jeb. "Just don't fall in."

"You just stay away from the river, David!" snapped Monti. She shuddered.

"The jungle's not really peaceful," said Jeb. "It's just a matter of difference in time sense."

"Time sense?" asked Monti.

"I saw a movie once," said Jeb. "Taken by some naturalist. He exposed one frame every hour—pictures of a jungle vine. That vine just boiled up—writhing and slithering like a snake to choke off the tree it was attacking. All that plant life just *looks* slow and silent ... and tame. He took pictures of some pods: they jerked open, hurled out their seeds. The seeds leaped upward toward the sunlight. That's the jungle as it really is."

"You make it sound horrible."

"Depends on your point of view. When you come right down to it, that's what all life's really like."

"Men! You spread your damned philosophy around like a dirty smell. It spoils everything it touches!"

Jeb chuckled.

The plane droned onward. More and more orange crept into the light as the sun sank lower. Jeb glanced at his wristwatch. "Almost there. Timed just about perfect for the light."

"It wasn't so dangerous after all, was it?" asked Monti.

"We've been lucky," said Jeb. "If we ..." He broke off, stared ahead. A thick blue column of smoke arose from the jungle-carpeted hills.

"Looks like a fire," said Monti.

Jeb nodded, throttled back.

The plane crossed the snake-track winding of the river. He banked, began a slow glide toward the water, keeping as much attention as he could on the smoke.

"What would they be burning?" asked Monti.

"Probably clearing land," said Jeb.

The plane swept out over a wide reach of water.

Jeb tensed.

A line of dugouts swarming with coppery backs stretched across the river. All faced downstream. Paddles foamed in the water.

Downriver from the Indians stood a single canoe with one figure in it, a white man in an Aussie hat, tan clothes. Desperation showed in the way he flailed the river with his paddle.

"Something's wrong," said Jeb.

The lone figure suddenly stopped paddling, took up a rifle. He turned, fired at the pursuing dugouts. One canoe overturned. The others scattered for shore. Water geysered in front of the retreating canoes as the rifleman fired once more. He put down the rifle, looked up at the plane sweeping overhead. Now, he lifted his paddle, waved downstream with frantic, chopping gestures.

"Is it Daddy?" asked David. His voice came out high-pitched, squeaking.

"I couldn't see," said Monti. She turned toward Jeb.

"It looked like Gettler," said Jeb. He dropped the flaps, banked to circle back. In that moment, the nightmare premonition came back like a tight band around his chest.

Death and a river! And Maria's vision!

"What're you going to do?" asked Monti.

"Land and pick him up."

"Why was he shooting at those Indians?" asked David.

"David! Please be quiet!" barked Monti.

The plane passed over the dugout a bare ten feet off the water, splashed down ahead of it. Jeb reached back, pulled the magnum revolver from the seat pocket, circled back toward the canoe.

Now, there was no mistaking the occupant of the canoe: It was Bannon's partner, Franz Gettler. He was a heavyset blond man with sharp Teutonic features, overhanging eyebrows. There was a bull-like quality to the man, a brutal and instinctive violence to his movements. He paddled with swift dipping motions that rocked his canoe, sent it surging toward the plane.

Jeb scanned the matted greenery of both banks for a sign of the pursuers. There was nothing. Only the overturned dugout floated sideways downstream like the back of a floating alligator—the sole reminder of violence.

Monti put a hand over her mouth. "Something's happened to Roger! I can feel it!"

Gettler's canoe came under the left wing, swung in beside the float. Jeb opened his door.

"You're a blooming miracle!" shouted Gettler. "Let's get

the hell out of here! Fast!"

"Jivaro?" asked Jeb.

"You're damned right: Jivaro!"

"Where's Bannon?"

Gettler grabbed the strut. "Dead!" He handed his rifle up to Jeb. The plane rocked to the man's weight as he lifted himself up onto the float. Jeb passed the rifle back to David, leaned forward as Gettler clambered into the rear.

"They attacked about an hour ago," panted Gettler. "No warning. No damn warning at all!"

Jeb slammed his door, swung the plane downriver.

"They must've spitted Bannon at least ten times," said Gettler.

Monti gasped, bit her lower lip.

Jeb heard a sob from David. "This is Mrs. Bannon and their boy," he said. He scanned the water for obstructions, pushed the throttle ahead. The plane's nose lifted.

Something splashed into the river directly in front of them. There came a booming roar from the bank to heir right. A crashing sound of torn metal filled the air. The plane shook violently, and the motor set up an immediate clattering, banging. Jeb throttled back, passed the revolver to Gettler. "Use this! They're on the right bank!"

"What's happened?" asked Monti.

"Muzzle-loader," said Jeb. "They hit the engine."

The thick smell of burning oil filled the cabin. Dark smoke clouded the air, streamed in the vents. Jeb closed them. The plane held a speed of about twenty miles an hour, but the motor coughed and bucked as though it would quit any moment.

Monti's voice climbed almost to a scream. "They're going to catch us!"

"Not unless the engine conks out," gritted Jeb. He scanned his instrument panel, fussed with the mixture. The motor smoothed slightly, but its racket was still deafening.

The plane's right hand door swung open. The magnum

revolver roared in their ears. A stench of cordite was added to the oil smoke.

They rounded a bend in the river. Jeb opened the throttle another notch, reduced it as the motor increased its erratic banging.

"I think we've got a badly cracked head ... and probably worse," said Jeb. "It'll never get us off the water."

Monti stared at him. "What'll we do?"

"If we can't fly, we'll float," said Jeb. "We'll try to reach the army post downstream."

"Army post!" said Gettler. "One sergeant and a radio!"

"We'll make it if we can stay afloat," said Jeb.

Again the magnum roared.

They rounded another bend. The river stretched ahead, shimmering with a glassy haze. In that moment, the sun sank behind the mountains, and the sky became a luminous silver.

For the first time, Jeb had a moment to take stock of the situation. And a thought smashed through his mind, stunning him: *A river and death!*

He shook his head. *Nuts! It's just a coincidence! But there was Maria's vision ... Christ! Next thing I'll be wearing an amulet of monkey balls!*

A roar from Gettler shattered Jeb's musing, "Hey, kid! Leave that rifle alone!"

"I'll kill 'em!" screamed David. "They killed my Dad! I'll kill 'em! I'll kill 'em!"

The plane rocked to a struggle in the rear.

"I said leave that rifle *be*, kid!"

Jeb looked back as Gettler forced David into a corner, wrenched away the rifle, and jammed it behind the rear seat.

David's face was contorted. Tears streamed down his cheeks. He had lost all of his pseudo-adult reserve.

Gettler said, "I'm sorry, kid, but you might kill one of us."

Monti spoke in a tone of washed-out calm: "David, try to be brave ... and quiet." She took a quavering breath. "You won't help by making a commotion in here."

And she thought: *That was a dirty trick ... a dirty, stinking, filthy trick you played on me, God! Letting me arrive just when it was too late!* She buried her face in her hands. *I mustn't think this way! I mustn't think at all!*

A feeling swept over her that she was up for try-out in a new play—without script or rehearsal, without knowing the words or music, or what part she had to take.

"I think we've outdistanced them," said Gettler. He closed the right hand door, sank back into the seat behind Jeb.

David chewed his lower lip, stared out the window. *It's all her fault,* he thought. *If it hadn't been for her, Dad never would've come here. Always jawing at him! Never giving him a moment's peace!*

Jeb raised his voice above the banging engine sound, spoke over his shoulder: "Are you sure ... about Bannon?"

Gettler spoke carefully, as though balancing his words one against another: "I'm sure. They hit our cultivation crew about six-thirty, when the men were all tired and ready to quit for the day. I was out on the river knocking over some 'gators, or they'd have got me, too."

"You were damned lucky," said Jeb.

"Yes. I heard the shouting, then I saw Rog come out of the house with a rifle. But there were a couple of them at the back of the house by then. They came through the house and got him before he could turn."

"They've been chasing you ever since?" asked Jeb.

"Yes. I knocked off several from the river, then got the hell out of there. Thought I was done until you showed up. What brought you?"

"Mrs. Bannon and the boy were coming for a visit."

Gettler cleared his throat. "You picked a bad time to visit. I'm certainly glad you did, though."

Jeb mulled over Gettler's story. Something about it bothered him. *He was out shooting alligators. Would the*

Indians attack across cultivated land—out in the open—if they heard rifle fire? I always thought they were more cautious than that. Unless it's a religious war of some kind.

"What set them off?" asked Jeb.

"God knows." Gettler leaned forward. "Is that motor going to hold out?"

"God knows that, too," said Jeb. "Did you kill any 'gators before the attack?"

Gettler's voice was suddenly wary: "Why?"

"I'm looking for a reason for the attack."

"I got two of them," said Gettler. "But the Indians don't object to killing 'gators."

So he was shooting—according to him, thought Jeb. *And the Indians would've heard rifle fire.*

"We're far enough ahead now," said Gettler. "Better try your radio. Maybe you can contact that army post."

"We don't have a radio," said Jeb.

Gettler said, "Ugh!" as though someone had hit him. Then: "Well, it's less than eighty miles to the post."

"We'll make it tonight some time, given any luck at all," said Jeb. He glanced at his instrument panel through eyes watering from the oil smoke. "I hope she doesn't start to overheat."

Monti began to sob: dry and wracking. Her shoulders jerked as though she were fighting away from someone.

"I'm sorry," said Gettler. "There was nothing I could do. Nothing."

Out of the corner of his eye Jeb saw one of Gettler's long-fingered hands come forward, stroke Monti's hair. It was a sensuous gesture—disquieting.

Monti shook her head. Gettler withdrew his hand.

The river channel narrowed to no more than twice their wingspan. They were hemmed in by a shadowy wall of overhanging trees. Jeb snapped on the landing lights. They picked out two caverns of brilliance that soon became filled with fluttering, darting insects. The light touched the riverbank, outlined twisting medusa roots that clutched the dark red clay.

A melon curve of new moon lifted into the eastern sky. It was the color of molten copper: the color of a native's back glistening in the sun.

Gettler tipped his head back, stared up at the moon. He felt the false coolness of the plastic cushion against his neck. It carried a reminder of civilization—refinement. For the first time since he'd started running, he allowed himself to think.

I get another chance! A tight smile played along his lips. *You were wrong, Rog: I did get away with killing you!* He thought of the surprised look in Bannon's eyes when the bullet smashed into him. Just that once they'd lost their irritating calmness. *If only those bastard Indians hadn't been watching! Always sneaking around! Spying! And who would've thought they'd give a damn whether one white man killed another!*

He put his left hand into the game pocket of his hunting jacket, felt the four leaf-wrapped packets: four raw emeralds of the clearest transparency, their color a rich, vibrant green with the luminosity of crème de menthe. The smallest would cut down to ten carats; the largest would go three times that size. And there was no real way to tell how many more there were in the clay mountain behind the rancho.

You were stupid, Rog, thought Gettler. *Just plain stupid to think I'd forget such a find just to save your noble savages!* The dark shadow of Monti stirred in front of Gettler, sent him off on a new tangent in his soundless conversation with the dead man: *And, Rog—if I want—maybe I can have your woman, too. How's that for a joke?*

Reflections from the landing lights revealed the interior of the plane, distracted Gettler from his musing. The soft curve of fabric overhead filled him with a sense of luxury. Every glint of light on chrome—the foxfire green of phosphorescent dials, the purposeful controls added to this feeling. He thought of what the gems in his pocket meant in wealth and luxury. His mind rejected the uneven banging of the damaged motor, and he imagined himself flying smoothly over the jungle: over everything unclean and contaminated.

Jeb Logan had gambled his life too many times on his ability to detect motor trouble by ear alone, and now he could not blank out that irritant clamor as Gettler had. He tolerated the sound for an hour and ten minutes, then turned off the ignition, nosed the plane into deep sedge at the upriver end of a narrow island.

In the sudden stillness, the whining hum of insects came to them like a memory of the engine sound. Then the metallic chime-call of river frogs intruded. The wing lights picked out the cold green reflection of their eyes. Jeb turned off the lights. The coughing bark of a red monkey sounded from the left bank. Patrolling bats flickered overhead, and skimmed the water to drink.

David spoke in a low, frightened voice: "Why've we stopped?"

"I want a look at that motor," said Jeb.

Monti stirred from a lethargic crouch, looked around. *I don't know what's happened to me,* she thought. *It's too soon to think. I won't think yet.*

"Is the motor any worse?" asked Gettler.

"Probably," said Jeb. He stared out at the darkness, sensed the watching animal life around them, thought: *When you're in the jungle there's nothing else. It flows over you, through you. And it says: "You're nothing! I could chop you down anytime!"*

"What do you mean *probably*?" asked Gettler.

"I mean it sure as hell can't be getting any better from the sound of it," said Jeb. "There's a flashlight wedged on the ledge behind you. Hand it here, please."

Gettler passed the flashlight forward.

Jeb took it, said: "You can start unlashing that Jeep can beneath your feet. I want to dump it into the wing tanks and get rid of the can. Too much fire hazard this way."

"Can't we put up with it this way until we get to the army post?" asked Gettler.

"Just give me the can," said Jeb.

Gettler grunted, bent to feel the lashings. "How much gas do we have?" he asked.

"There's about three gallons in that can, and one more full one in the luggage compartment behind you, plus about forty gallons remaining in the wing tanks."

He opened his door, swung down onto the float. Immediately, the insects descended upon him. He felt them swarming over his face, touching his lips, his nose, his eyes. When he turned on the flashlight some left for the new attraction. Jeb worked his way forward, dropped into the sedge, waded across to the other float, climbed up. The light revealed a jagged hole in the cowl. He lifted the flap, shone the light inside.

The bullet has smashed into the head of the first cylinder, ricocheted back and down. Smoke curled out of a crack along the cooling baffles and through a hole torn in the valve cover. A splinter of metal had smashed the top plugs on the first two cylinders. The bullet had taken out the bottom plug on the second cylinder. That left four cylinders, and the motor completely unbalanced.

Jeb shrugged. *What a mess!*

"How bad is it?" called Gettler.

"We've got four cylinders," said Jeb. "I started out with six." He closed the cowl flap, turned to emptying the gas cans.

Presently, the smell of gasoline filled the air. It drove away some of the insects. Jeb straddled the cowl, listened to the gas gurgle into the tank. The moon set while he worked. He looked up: a wilderness of stars flooded the sky. And when he lowered his gaze, he could see the tremulous shimmering of the stars on the river surface. Quite suddenly, the river became for him an immense loneliness locked between jungle walls. He sniffed the odorous night: thick with the baited and the repelling perfumes that marked one line in the jungle's endless battleground.

What if the Indians beat us to that army post and the radio? he wondered. *We have to follow the river. They could go straight over the hills—or signal ahead with drums.*

In that moment, Jeb realized that there was no way to beat the Indians to the army post if this was actually a race. He tossed the last empty can into the sedge, slid down to the float, found a length of driftwood that he used to push the plane off into the current.

Monti came out of her lethargy. "Have we gotten away from them?" she asked.

"I think so ... at least for now," said Jeb. He wedged the pole against the strut, clambered back inside, slammed the door.

"You're sure this thing won't fly?" asked Gettler.

"I'm sure." Jeb handed back the flashlight, said: "If anybody's hungry, there's K-ration in that big valise in the luggage compartment. You can pull your seat-back forward to get at it."

Gettler took the light, said: "Here, kid. Hold the flash for me." The light flared, threw raw shadows ahead. A blackish brown *helicon* butterfly hurled itself against the windshield, clung there.

"I'm not hungry," said Monti. She slapped at insects on her arms and neck.

"I don't feel like eating, either," said David.

"That makes three of us," said Jeb.

"I'm going to keep up my strength," said Gettler.

There came the sound of scrambling from the rear. The light wavered. The plane rocked. Presently, the light went off.

"Aren't you going to start the motor and get going?" asked Gettler.

"The river's going our way," said Jeb. "As long as there's

no wind to foul us up we can use the free ride."

And he thought: *There's a real chance that we may need our gasoline. If that army post's been hit, we face eight hundred miles of river!*

"It's only thirty-five or forty miles ahead," said Gettler. "Two hours with the motor."

There came the sound of cardboard tearing as he opened the ration box.

Jeb cupped his hands over the altimeter, studied the luminous dial. "We were at twenty-eight hundred feet elevation when we picked you up. We've come down fifty feet. My map shows the army post at twenty-six hundred feet. That means a current of around eight knots between here and there."

"Five or six hours," said Gettler. "Maybe seven. I say use the motor."

Jeb shook his head. "I say save the gas."

Gettler absorbed this. "You think we're going to need it?"

"Yes. I think that's a possibility."

Silence settled over the cabin, broken only by the sound of Gettler eating, the occasional slap of a hand killing insects.

The plane floated on a black carpet with the deeper blackness of the jungle slipping past on both sides. They turned in an eddy, floated sideways.

"Why do you think we may need the gasoline?" asked Monti.

Jeb shrugged. "If the Jivaro want to beat us to that army post, they can—motor or no motor."

"Do you think they'll try to beat us?" she whispered.

"They know where we're going," said Jeb. "And they know that the sergeant at the post can talk through the sky to summon airplanes with bombs. That's one of the things they fear. They don't like airplanes."

"Have they been bombed?" asked Monti.

"Several villages have been flattened after Indian raids," said Jeb. They know about bombs."

"They should kill them all with an atom bomb!" said David.

"I still say use the motor," said Gettler. "We could beat them."

"Don't be foolish," said Jeb. "Our only hope is that they may fear the dark more than they do the planes we can call by radio!"

Gettler leaned forward. "Start the motor."

"No."

Violence hung in the air—in the controlled breathing.

Jeb thought of his revolver tucked in Gettler's belt. The nerves of his back twitched. Then he heard Gettler take a deep breath, exhale, settled back.

"Are they really afraid of the dark?" asked Monti.

"They're supposed to be," said Jeb. He opened his door, slid down to the float, groped on the rear floor for the grapnel and line.

"What're you doing now?" asked Gettler.

"I'm going to make a sea anchor," said Jeb. "There'll be a breeze up the river before long. The anchor will keep our nose pointed downstream, give us a little control."

"What's a sea anchor?" asked David.

Jeb smiled involuntarily, thought: *The boy will be all right in spite of his loss. You can't suppress youthful curiosity.*

"It's a kind of a drag that floats just below the water surface," said Jeb. "Only the current affects it. The wind will blow against the plane, and the current will pull the anchor downstream. That'll keep our nose pointed the way we're going—keep us from getting tangled up in the trees. And our motion downstream against the wind will give the plane's control surfaces something to work on: I'll be able to guide us a little."

"How're you making it?" asked David.

"With a piece of wood I found along the shore back there."

"Oh."

There came a low splash as he dropped the anchor into the river. He paid out the line, fastened it to the struts.

"Let me have the flashlight," said Jeb. He reached inside, felt the smooth cylinder pushed into his hand. The switch clicked under his thumb, and a shaft of light leaped out to the jungle wall. It illuminated a cluster of sago palms in front of the reed-like screen of a line of *cana brava*. The light began to siphon in a flow of fluttering, darting insects. Jeb turned it off.

"Maybe six hours at this rate," said Jeb. He glanced at the luminous dial of his wristwatch. "About three a.m. we can start watching for the radio tower."

"We could make it in two hours with the motor," muttered Gettler.

"And chance piling into a log or 'gator, and holing a float," said Jeb.

"Your landing lights seemed to show everything," said Gettler.

"Yes, and the lights and motor sure advertised our presence, too!"

"They know we're here," said Gettler. "They know exactly where we are."

"We couldn't hear rapids with that motor banging away," said Jeb.

"No rapids between here and the army post," said Gettler.

Jeb clambered back inside, shut his door. He glanced at Monti. "Why don't you lean back and try to get some sleep?"

"No, thanks." She shook her head, a shadowy half movement in the dark.

"They know exactly where we are!" snapped Gettler.

"What can we do when we reach this army post?" asked Monti.

"The sergeant'll radio for help," said Jeb. "An army plane'll come to fly us out. Then I'll have to worry about flying in a new engine to get this ship out."

"I'll get you a new engine," she murmured.

"We're wasting time!" snarled Gettler.

Jeb whirled. "If they want to go over the mountain straight to the post—how long? How fast could they get there?

Gettler was silent for a long minute, then: "Three hours at the outside."

"We couldn't possibly beat them," said Jeb.

Gettler sighed. "I guess you're right."

Jeb faced forward.

Monti began breathing in ragged gasps as though she were choking. Jeb gripped her arm. "Are you all right, Monti?"

She nodded, then: "Mr. Gettler ... are you sure, are you absolutely sure ... about Roger?"

"I saw it," said Gettler. "They kept stabbing him with those damned barbed spears, twisting them. There was blood all ..."

"Why don't you shut up!" barked Jeb.

"Easy now," said Gettler. "She asked the question. She knows these are *head* hunters."

"I hope the soldiers kill every one of those Indians!" snarled David.

"They'll kill enough of them, son," said Gettler.

Again, the feeling of uncertainty swept over Jeb. Something about the scene upriver: Gettler pursued by the Jivaro ... something about it didn't fit Gettler's story. The dugouts had been stretched across the river, boiling with coppery bodies that ...

Jeb tensed.

There had been no ceremonial spears and blowguns: none of the flashy painting and decoration that meant war. The Indians had been dressed and geared for hunting or fishing.

Jeb turned, held out his hand. "Let's have my revolver."

Gettler did not move. "Let's leave it where it is."

Something warned Jeb not to press the issue. His mind went to the little twenty-two revolver in the survival kit. He turned back.

Monti leaned against her door. "It's so hot," she said. "Doesn't it ever cool off?"

"Toward morning we should get a little relief," said Jeb. "Why don't you try to get some sleep?"

"Would it help to open the doors?" she asked.

Jeb slapped a gnat on the back of his hand. "Take your choice: heat or bugs."

She sighed.

"We'll be at the army post before morning, won't we?" asked David.

"Shortly before dawn," said Jeb.

The first hesitant puff of the night breeze rocked the plane. The wind steadied, blowing softly up the river. The plane swung on its submerged sea anchor until it pointed downstream.

"Why don't you all try to nap?" asked Jeb. "I'll take the first watch." He tried the rudder controls. Slowly, the plane drifted sideways toward the center of the stream. The anchor-plus-wind did give some control.

"I'll watch with you," said Gettler.

"What Jivaro tribe was it?" asked Jeb. "Which headman?"

"I didn't ask them," said Gettler. He stirred restlessly. "What'n hell do you think I ..."

"I thought you might have recognized their paint," said Jeb.

Gettler coughed, rubbed the handle of the revolver in his belt. *Logan suspects!* He said: "I was too busy getting away."

Something very phony here! thought Jeb.

"Maybe you'd like to go back and have another look!" said Gettler.

"I saw enough the first time," said Jeb.

Gettler pushed himself against the back of his seat. *Will I have to kill them, too? Will I?*

"As long as you're going to watch anyway, I'll take forty winks," said Jeb. He turned sideways toward the door, listened tensely to Gettler's movements, thought: *If he naps later, I'll jump him, get the gun. I'll stay awake.*

Slowly, Gettler relaxed. *I don't have to decide now.*

Jeb could just make out the darker shadow of the shoreline in the starlight. The hypnotic flow made him drowsy. He concentrated on trying to see through the blackness, senses strained to their limits. There was the movement of the river dragging them against the breeze, and it awakened in Jeb a sense of mystery. Tonight the river was haunted, peopled by the ghosts of every passenger it had ever carried.

And the night was hushed out of fear—not out of peace. The serenity of their movement was false.

It was like the false serenity of landing a plane: slowly gliding down the imaginary wire of the landing path with the motor ticking away. Yet that was one of the moments of greatest danger.

His head nodded. He shook himself awake, glanced at his wristwatch. The luminous dial revealed that an hour had passed.

Where'd the time go? he asked himself.

Gettler moved restlessly in the back.

The plane had floated closer and closer to the left bank. Now, a wing caught a trailing vine. They turned, dragging heavily.

Jeb sat up, started to open his door.

But the current against the sea anchor pulled them free, swung them back toward center stream.

Jeb relaxed, tipped his head against the seat back. He could hear Gettler's uneven breathing.

Doesn't the bastard ever sleep?

Another hour passed: another and another and another ...

The river widened, slowed.

Jeb fought the monotony, trying to keep his eyes open. *Could we float the plane clear down to Ramona?* he asked himself. *Christ! It'd be almost impossible!*

He became conscious of a reddish fire glow downstream on the right bank, snapped upright. "Trouble!"

The others stirred around him.

"I've been watching it," whispered Gettler.

"What is it?" whispered Monti.

"Fire," said Jeb. He looked at his wristwatch, leaned forward to peer at the altimeter. "We should be just about at the army post."

"That's it," said Gettler. "The fire means they've been here ahead of us! I told you to use the engine!"

"So we could get here in time to be slaughtered," said Jeb. "You know we couldn't have beaten them!" He stared into the surrounding darkness. "Are they still here? That's what I want to know."

The plane drifted closer to the fire glow.

Gettler shifted his weight, passed the rifle to Jeb. "You may need this," he whispered. He leaned across David, opened the right-hand door.

"It's coals," said Jeb. "Nothing but coals. The night breeze has stirred them up."

An eddy swung them toward the right bank, then pulled them away. The current tugged at their anchor, as though impatient to get them away from here.

Jeb became acutely conscious of the tense breathing around him, realized that he was holding his own breath.

"Are you sure it's the army post?" whispered Monti.

Jeb nodded. "I've landed here before."

"This is it all right," whispered Gettler.

Something barked and gibbered in the jungle beyond the coals.

David leaned forward close to Jeb's ear, whispered: "Can they see us out here?"

"They couldn't miss," said Jeb. "Their eyes are trained to see unusual movements."

"They see us all right!" snarled Gettler.

"Then why don't they attack?" asked Monti.

"You tell me," said Jeb. He reached down, found the flash on the floor under his feet, pointed it toward the coals, and pressed the switch. The shaft of light silhouetted the girder structure of a radio tower toppled crazily into the jungle. Something ran on four feet from a mound near the river edge into the jungle blackness. They could see a warped and blackened tin roof flat on the ground. Smoke curled around its edges.

Jeb turned off the light. The welcome darkness enfolded them. "There was one body near the river bank," said Jeb. "It was burned. Might've been Jivaro."

"How long ago do you figure?" asked Gettler.

"Four or five hours," said Jeb. "They must've started for here the minute they began chasing you. Some of them came over the mountains on foot. We never could've made it."

"Where are they?" demanded Gettler. "Why don't they attack?"

Jeb sensed the note of hysteria in Gettler's voice, thought: *I had a premonition against coming on this flight. I should've believed it. I had a premonition against wasting gas tonight. I was right. From now on I believe.*

The plane drifted past the coals, around a bend. Again they were isolated in the darkness: a floating metal oasis at the bottom of the abyssal depth that was the night.

Jeb responded with a feeling of weary loneliness. He thought ahead to the winding, twisting river course: the rapids, the sunken limbs, the shoals of deadly piranha ready to tear flesh from bones, the hunger and the disease.

And the probability of Indian ambush.

The plane around him felt fragile and inadequate: a corrupt and impermanent thing. He wondered that he had trusted his life to this machine high above the jungle when it was so vulnerable.

Getter's low rumble broke the shocked silence that filled the plane: "How far to Ramona?"

"More than eight hundred miles by river," said Jeb.

"Aren't there any settlements along the way?" asked Monti.

"Indian villages," said Jeb. "We're in Jivaro country now. No telling how far their control extends. They raided clear down to Ramona twelve years ago."

"But you said those Indians in the dugout where we refueled were some other tribe," she said.

"Zaparo," said Jeb. "Probably a trading party that came up to get curare."

"Curare?"

"Dart poison. The Jivaro witchmen are the only ones in these parts who make it."

"Will this thing float us down to Ramona?" asked Gettler.

"Your guess is as good as mine," said Jeb. He turned. "Have you ever been up the Tapiche by launch?"

"No. but I've talked to some who have."

"How many rapids?"

Gettler counted on his fingers, musing: "Eight or nine. Maybe more. I'm not sure. Depends on the season and the height of the water. But how could we run even one in this thing?"

"Under power," said Jeb. "Provided the gas holds out and the engine doesn't quit on us."

"Are you sure you can't get this thing into the air?"

"No. But I'm reasonably sure I couldn't keep it there."

"How long would it take us to float down to that town?" asked Monti.

"I don't know," said Jeb. "What's your guess, Gettler?"

"Six weeks or more—with luck. How're we fixed for drinking water? Got anything to boil it in?"

"I've enough pills to purify about sixty gallons. There're two canvas water bags in that survival kit. Water's no problem. I'm worried about food. We'll have to stop and hunt ... and if the Jivaro follow us ..."

"They'll follow," muttered Gettler.

Jeb stared downriver. The sense of worry about Gettler still nagged him. He felt the smooth metal of the man's rifle against his palms.

"If we could steal a canoe we could make better time," said Gettler.

A sudden negative feeling gripped Jeb. He held tightly to the safety belt beside him until the feeling passed, the rifle still in his right hand. Presently, he propped the weapon into the corner at his left, reached across Monti, closed her door. A faint, musky perfume filled his nostrils when he leaned close to her. It left him with a keen awareness that she was female ... and desirable.

"We need a canoe," repeated Gettler.

Jeb shook his head. "The plane gives us some safety. It's some protection from darts, arrows. They don't have many of those muzzle-loaders. The few they have don't shoot very straight."

"One of them shot straight enough to stop us," said Gettler.

"A chance hit," said Jeb.

"A chance ..." said Monti. "Do *we* have a chance?"

"Certainly," said Jeb. "If we don't panic."

A shocking laugh—almost a giggle—came from Gettler. "Like the man said: If we can only keep our heads!"

Far off, a night bird called: "Tuta! Tuta!" with a fluting voice like a woman.

Jeb shuddered. The near hopelessness of their position pressed in upon him. They were at the beginning edge of the rainy season with eight hundred miles of jungle river stretching ahead: rapids, chasms, whirlpools, clutching snags. Weariness was a weight upon his shoulders and upon his eyelids.

The flux of night sounds pulsed in his temples. He stared

out into the darkness, saw the witch light of fireflies along the shore, smelled the wind from the jungle like an exhalation of evil breath.

In that moment he felt that the jungle rejected all civilization with a conscious and purposeful effort: an active hostility. He saw the jungle as a reservoir of unrestrained savagery that alerted every civilized hackle.

And the waiting Indians were like the embodiment of all he feared: a focus of cruel intelligence that did the jungle's bidding.

I will not submit! he thought.

"They're out there in the jungle ... looking at us right now," said Gettler.

"I don't like floating in the dark," said Jeb. "We could come on a snag, get caught in rapids—anything!"

"There're no rapids right away," said Gettler. "Forty miles or more. Not until we start down off this plateau."

"We'll watch for an island," said Jeb. "It's not very likely that they'll be waiting for us on an island."

"Good idea," said Gettler. He settled back into his seat, thought: *So my second chance won't be easy! All right, I'm used to fighting. I'll make it even if it kills these soft fools!*

The river tugged gently at their anchor, and all of them sensed their alliance with this current dragging itself endlessly down to the sea like a black chord of emptiness.

But now ... no longer empty.

The hoots and cries of howler monkeys greeted the dawn. Their intrusion aroused the birds to mysterious morning talk in the sheltered blackness of the forest: staccato peepings, churrings up and down the scale, intermittent screeches.

A pearl luster crept across the sky, became a milky silver light that gave definition to the river. To the west climbed foothills—one foothill after another—piled waves of hills pounding against the Andean escarpment.

The plane sat nose-in to the trees on the right side of a narrow island. It floated quietly like a great water bug. Dancing flames of forest flowers wavered in the tree overhead. A sluggish current twisted into random whorls against the floats. Vagrant curls of morning mist hung on the water like puffs of torn gauze.

Inside the cabin Jeb Logan stirred to wakefulness, stared downstream. The river was like a cathedral aisle between tall trees. His gaze dropped to Monti beside him. She was still asleep, curled into a fetal crouch against her door. She had the look of a small child about her: the red hair disarrayed, an unlined expression of innocence on her face.

Thoughts and feelings of protectiveness passed through Jeb. He resisted an urge to reach out and pat her shoulder, turned his head to look at Gettler.

The Aussie hat was off, revealing a graying wheat stubble of hair. Gettler's head was thrown back. He breathed with a low, burred rasp. There was an appearance of fallen greatness about the man. Heavy pores indented his skin to a harsh, leathery brown. A day's growth of beard roughened his chin and cheeks. Frown creases laced the corners of his eyes and mouth.

Jeb's attention shifted to David. The boy's pale blue eyes stared straight ahead into the dense, somber green of jungle growth on the island. David flicked a glance at Jeb, resumed his watchful staring. There was a washed-out look to the boy's face that made his freckles stand out. A section of sunburned skin on his forehead was beginning to peel away in flakes of grey-white.

Gettler turned the watch over to the kid, thought Jeb. *Well, why not? Young senses are alert.*

He turned back to Gettler, noted the handle of the revolver curving up from the man's belt. Jeb considered reaching out and taking the gun, then he became aware of a change in Gettler's breathing, looked up to two eyes like drops of hot tar staring at him through slitted lids.

"What time is it?" rumbled Gettler.

Monti stirred restlessly.

"Just dawn," said Jeb.

Gettler turned to David. "All quiet, son?"

"Yes, sir."

Jeb straightened, looked downstream. The mist had risen slightly. It veiled the near reaches of the river. "Time to shove off," he said.

"Let's keep our eyes open for another dugout," said Gettler. "Then we could make time."

Jeb's jaw muscles hardened. "I'm sticking with the plane!"

"You're a fool," said Gettler.

"Okay! But I'm riding it out in the ..."

"Listen to me!" snapped Gettler. "I know the jungle. You move fast here or you don't survive."

"You can go by yourself anytime," said Jeb.

"I'll keep that in mind," murmured Gettler.

Jeb looked around at the interior of his plane, at the smooth tan fabric of the ceiling, the chrome efficiency of the instrument panel. He put his hands on the wheel, moved it.

Angrily, he jerked his hands away, shifted his weight, felt a tingling cramp in his legs.

A feeling that something or someone had betrayed him filled his senses.

"Are you going to shove us off, or shall I?" asked Gettler.

"I'll do it," said Jeb. He opened his door, slipped down to the float, untied the vine he had used to fasten the plane in the night. A broken cane pole bobbed in the driftwood caught against the upstream float. Jeb recovered it, pushed the plane into the current, glanced downstream.

There was not a breath of wind. The makeshift sea anchor rested on the float, grapnel hooks trailing wisps of reedy grass. He decided to leave it there, clambered back into the cabin.

Without anchor and wind to hold the plane steady, it twisted at the push of every random current. There was a certain majesty about the movement: slow, sweeping turns to the river's rhythm.

Jeb sniffed. The smell of gasoline was almost gone, and he detected the odor of mildew mingled with the musk of human sweat. Mildew. Already the jungle had a beachhead within the plane.

Monti stirred, rubbed her eyes. She turned toward Jeb, smiled. Then, slowly there came an unfolding as she awoke: a look of confusion replaced the smile. She shook her head, turned, stared hopelessly out her window.

"We'd better think about shooting some game today," said Jeb. "Those K-rations won't last forever."

"The first thing is to take stock of what we have," said Gettler. "What's in that kit behind this seat?"

Jeb turned. "There should be seven K-rations left. Water purifying tablets. I told you about them. Some antibiotics. Fishing gear. A pellet stove. Tea. Snares. Another flashlight and spare batteries. We've a machete. And there're twenty-five rounds of extra ammo for that revolver in the seat pocket here."

"Is that all?" asked Gettler.

"A light poncho," said Jeb. And he thought: *Okay, so I'm not telling about the .22 revolver!*

It was as though David had read his mind. "Didn't you say there was a .22 revolver?" the boy asked.

Jeb swallowed. "Didn't I mention that?"

"No, you didn't," said Gettler. "What else do we have?"

"I've got a scout knife," said David. "And matches in a little waterproof box my Dad ..." he grimaced. "... my Dad sent me last Christmas."

"There are more paraffin matches in the kit," said Jeb.

"I have my camera and the attachments here in this bag," said David. "And ten more rolls of film." His voice lowered. "That's not much good to us, though."

Monti held up her pearl-inlaid cigarette lighter. "Here's a cigarette lighter." She fished a cigarette from her shirt pocket. "Anybody for a smoke?"

Gettler shook his head.

"I kicked the habit," said Jeb.

Monti lighted her cigarette, spoke around the first exhalation of smoke. "How noble of you."

"I couldn't afford the U.S. imports when I first came down," said Jeb. "And I couldn't stand the native product."

"What's in your luggage back here?" asked Gettler.

"Mostly clothes," she said. "A shaving kit I was going to give ..." she shrugged "... to Roger. Some toilet things, perfume, make-up. A carton of cigarettes. A can of lighter fluid. Nothing that'll do us much good."

"We may need the lighter fluid," said Gettler. "This is going to be no joy ride."

Monti sniffed. "Why don't we stop the melodrama. There'll be search planes out right away."

"Why?" asked Gettler.

"They won't be able to make radio contact with that army post. They'll come to investigate."

"And they may decide it's a simple mechanical failure,"

said Gettler.

"They'll be out within a week, anyway," she said. "When they find out *I'm* missing. The papers will have a field day. My agent'll roll on the floor in purest ecstasy, and we'll pack them in at Las Vegas."

"We're on the edge of the rainy season," said Gettler.

"When the rains start there'll be no aerial search," said Jeb. "They may send a boat up the river, but even then we'll have to cover maybe six hundred miles on our own."

"Why look at the worst side?" demanded Monti.

"Because that's what we have to be prepared for," said Gettler.

"You haven't told us what you have," said Jeb. He looked at the bulges of Gettler's jacket pockets. "What's in your pockets?"

"Extra clips for the rifle," said Gettler. "A hunting knife and some matches."

Jeb turned around, looked downstream. They had drifted around a bend. Ahead, the emerald green of the hills turned to a misted blue in the distance. Already, the sun was becoming an instrument of torture. And the humidity! Sweat rolled off his skin without evaporating. He saw in his mind's eye the long curving and re-curving slant of river, a vaguely wandering trench through the wilderness.

A striated claw of hills loomed closer ahead. Jeb wondered which claw carried the river channel.

"We'd better eat," said Gettler. He turned around. "Scrunch forward, son."

David leaned over his mother. She reached up, patted his cheek.

Gettler groped behind the rear seat, came up with K-rations, sat back. "Is there any water?"

"There should be a one-quart canteen full in the bottom of the kit," said Jeb. "And there're two canvas bags."

"That's something else you didn't mention," said Gettler. Again he squirmed around, felt in the luggage compartment.

Hunger suddenly awoke in Jeb's stomach. His hands trembled. His mouth burned with thirst. "Let's have the canteen up here."

Gettler passed it forward. Jeb took it, offered it to Monti. She shook her head. He drank greedily, put down a sudden nausea.

David said: "What's that?"

"A water bag," said Gettler. "You take it now, and get down on that float out there, dip it full of water and drop in one of these pills."

"Careful you don't fall in," said Monti. She opened her door, leaned forward.

"This river's full of piranha," said Gettler. "I've never seen them so thick."

David scrambled down to the float, dipped the bag full of water, returned to his seat. Monti slammed the door.

They ate in silence, hunting out the last morsels.

Presently, Jeb leaned back, took a deep breath. The sun was high enough now to burn the mist off the river. The heat was mounting. *The tropic warmth seemed to have a definite moment of beginning,* he thought. One instant it wasn't there, then it overwhelmed the sense threshold to wash the body in perspiration.

"I have to go to the toilet," said David.

Monti looked out, studied the patchwork shadows along the shore.

"I've been looking for a place to land," said Jeb.

"Another island," said Gettler. "One we can see clear across."

"What I had in mind," said Jeb.

Monti shook her head, took a shivering breath, turned to stare straight ahead at the quicksilver track of the river. The plane seemed suspended in a vaulted cavern of motionless air that was slowly inflating with heat until she was sure it must explode.

Jeb looked at her. "Are you all right, Monti?"

She nodded, unable to speak, thought: *There's a laugh for you! Am I all right? Hell, I've never been all right! Except a few times with the guy who's back there dead.*

"I have to go to the toilet bad," said David. "I can't wait."

Monti whirled. "You *have* to wait!"

"You better get out and hang onto a strut, son," said Gettler. "We'll look the other way if it bothers you."

"All right." David opened the door, clambered out.

Monti said: "Could one of those blowguns—the ones with the poison darts—reach out here from the bank?"

"Just about," said Gettler. "Adds a certain spice to the elimination problem." He smiled. "We could hang our jackets over the windows if *you* want to use the float."

She turned a look of pure venom on him, whirled back to stare straight ahead.

"Let's face the fact that we're real people," said Gettler. "We're not like characters in the women's magazines, people who never sit on a toilet."

She ignored him.

David returned to his seat.

"Feel better, son?" asked Gettler.

David blushed, shrugged.

"Gettler, give us the poncho from the kit," said Jeb.

"Why?"

"Just hand it here."

Gettler turned around, grunted as he pulled the poncho from the luggage compartment. Jeb took it, fixed it over the windows beside Monti.

She glanced at him, smiled faintly, took a deep breath. "I never did read those magazines," she said. She slipped under the poncho, opened her door, stepped down to the float. The door closed.

A minute passed in silence.

"Wasn't there any way you could've saved my Dad?" asked David. He looked up at Gettler. "Any way at all ..."

Gettler's hands turned white as he gripped them into

fists.

David said: "I mean ... you got away and ..."

"Shut up! Will you?" Gettler was shivering, face contorted.

Monti's door opened. She climbed into the seat, took down the poncho as she entered, wadded it under her feet.

"I'm sorry," said David. "I just wish ..." He swallowed, fell silent. A confusion of angry, fearful thoughts warred within him.

"What's wrong?" asked Monti.

"David just wishes it'd been me who got killed instead of Roger," said Gettler. His voice lowered: "Can't blame him."

"Oh, no ..." said David. "I ..."

"Be quiet, David," said Monti.

And she thought: *Yes. Why wasn't it that big oaf?*

Silence settled over the cabin.

They drifted along a widening stretch of river where the current slowed. The root-laced banks crept past in a time-clogged, dragging suspense.

Jeb stared hypnotically at the shore, and the thought came to him that the moment of immediate past was never quite discarded—and the future never quite had a starting point. All fused in one gliding, stretched-out smoothness: a positive momentum down an endless incline.

He turned his head, studied the feathered softness of hills on the right, and suddenly beyond the hills glimpsed the snow cone of Tusachilla with its black tonsure of volcanic ash.

Now, the river was lined with mango trees in dense foliage broken by the lighter sage of tropical mistletoe and an occasional fur-coated *chonta* palm.

Above the near reaches of the river hovered two black and white *urubu* vultures. They hung seemingly fixed in the burned-out steel blue sky as though they had been painted there on a false backdrop. A flock of tanagers—deep glistening turquoise—swept overhead, dived into the jungle wall, were swallowed by it as though they had never been.

Monti had watched the birds. *It's the same with us,* she thought. *Nothing marks our passage here: no broken branches, not a leaf disturbed. We might never have been for all the sign we leave.*

Then she thought about Roger.

"Those birds," she said. "I don't know why ... but they remind me of something Roger said once. I think he read it out of a book."

"Oh?" said Jeb.

"Something about all life being holy," she said.

A deep rumble that could have been a chuckle came from Gettler. "That's from Blake. Christ! I can hear Roger saying it. He was *full* of philosophy!"

"That he was," said Monti.

"Arrrrrgh," said Gettler. "I've studied philosophy in six languages. Did any of it tell me the world is just like that jungle out there?"

"You couldn't argue with him," said Monti. "He'd smile and quote somebody on peace and understanding."

"The jungle's the finest school of philosophy in the world," said Gettler. "Completely pragmatic. Ask about good and evil! The jungle has one answer: *'That which succeeds is good!'* And it kills to maintain its status quo!"

Monti turned, looked at him. "Were you really a professor once?"

Gettler drew back, lowered his head. A look of confusion, of retreating, passed over his face. A tic moved his left cheek. Every feature revealed a deep inner struggle as though something were rising to the surface.

Why should that question bother me? he asked himself. *Certainly I was a professor!* His mind swept through a violent pulsing of memory, like a deck of cards riffling before his eyes. There was the university at Bonn. And the class in comparative logic. And there was one of his students he hadn't thought of in ten years: *Karl ... Karl ...* The last name evaded him as new memories attacked his reeling mind.

What's happening to me?

His hands came up, claw-like, pressed against his forehead as though to dig out the offending memories.

Abruptly, they were gone, leaving him feeling wrung out, weak. Now, he was angry with this woman because she had exposed him to something he had believed dead and buried—with the burial place carefully hidden. He opened his eyes, saw her staring at him.

"Is something wrong?" asked Monti.

"Yes!" He hurled the word at her. "This world's full of stumbling fools!"

Monti drew back.

"Was I a professor? Arrrrrgh! You've a head full of cotton! What difference does it ..."

"You *were* a professor," she said. "Why don't you like to ..."

He spoke quickly to stave off the memories: "Because I was stupid! I never taught anyone anything! We were all innocent lambs in the jungle!"

"Something happened," said Monti. "What happened?"

"I happened!"

Jeb said, "Look, it's almost ..."

"I grew claws," snarled Gettler. "I learned to eat meat. And I came out here to the only honest teacher in the universe: the jungle. Now, shut up! Or I'll show you some of the things the jungle taught me!"

She recoiled, eyes widening, looked to Jeb.

David glanced at his mother, turned on Gettler. "Stop talking to my mother like that!"

Jeb froze. *Gettler's crazier than a loco ape,* he thought. *He may explode!*

But Gettler took a deep breath, startled them by laughing. He patted David's knee. "No harm intended, son. Just joking. Rest easy, young Galahad. You don't have any maidens to protect today."

Monti faced forward. *How could Roger associate with a beast like that?* She thought of the river track ahead. *I couldn't stand six weeks with him! But that's silly. We'll be rescued soon. The minute I'm missed. There'll be a big hue and cry.*

Jeb leaned against his door, studied the current ahead. He scratched at the stubble of beard on his chin. *Something's very wrong with Gettler. His story about the Indian attack doesn't ring true. What's he hiding?*

The sun climbed higher, blasted down upon the river. They floated in a great bowl of burning sunlight with the plane at its center, the tiny cabin a moist hell. A pall of silence settled over their world. Not an animal stirred or cried. Only the insects remained as a token of life: tiny black flies with a bite like fire, random clouds of blue and white butterflies—a fluttering pastel mob that danced across the path.

Monti suffered in her own private hell: fear of *bugs*. All the wraith forms tortured her ... every whirr, hum, stridulating and chafing buzz touched the nerves of her spine. She saw in each jigging, dancing horde only image of grotesque, sticky tentacles reaching for her.

Toward noon the current speeded, swept them around a bend. They whirled toward a low scrub-covered island. The water coursed around the island to join below it.

"It looks clear," said Jeb.

"Are we going to stop?" asked Monti. She felt that she had to get out of the plane, to run and escape the insects—anything to avoid insanity.

"What do you think, Gettler?" asked Jeb.

"No sign of Indians," said Gettler. "It's out of dart range from either shore. Pull into the upper end."

Jeb slipped down to the pontoon, grabbed up the cane pole he had wedged against the strut, pushed toward a shallow beach of water-rounded pebbles. The float beneath him grated on bottom. He studied the river for signs of piranha, jumped off into muggy water above his knees.

Gettler dropped down to the other side.

They swung the nose of the plane into the beach, put out the grapnel.

Jeb waded ashore, studied the island's scrub, swung his gaze along both banks of the mainland. The jungle on either side was a green wall with giant creepers weaving random draperies on every tree.

Cicadas whined in the island scrub, and there was the sudden musical whirr of a hummingbird's wings. The bird—a glorious bronze green—darted across the island, hovered over an invisible flower lower in the scrub.

"That hummingbird says it's safe on this island," said Jeb.

Monti and David joined them on the beach.

"Is there any insect repellant in that kit of yours?" asked Monti. "These bugs ..." She shuddered.

"Have a look," said Jeb. "I'm not sure. Try the box with the red cross on it. That's our first aid kit."

A black and white vulture lifted from the lower end of the island. Its pinions clattered loudly in the still air. The vulture flapped across the treetops. Another followed ... and another ... and another, until a stream of them sailed away over the jungle.

The four figures on the beach stared after the vultures.

"Did we frighten them?" asked Monti.

"More likely they were just ready to go," said Gettler.

"What were they eating?" asked David.

"Fish or a pig, something like that," said Gettler.

Monti returned to the plane, rummaged in the compartment behind the rear seat. A trail of the tiny black flies followed her like thin shreds of smoke. She straightened, examined a bottle, uncapped it, began putting its contents on her face, neck and arms.

Jeb turned his attention back to the island, took a deep breath, sniffed the air. It was thick with the heavy, drenched hopelessness of a tropical mid-day—and just the faintest touch of ancient carrion.

Monti rejoined them. "I found something labeled *'Bug-Go',*" she said. "It repels me, so it should work on bugs."

Gettler moved away from them along the beach.

Jeb looked down at Monti. "Don't leave the open beach. Lots of fer-de-lance in this country. That scrub looks like a good place for them."

"That's a poisonous snake, isn't it?" she asked.

"One of the worst."

"This country's so beautiful, and you make it sound so deadly."

"It is deadly." He looked after Gettler, then to the far shore. The jungle felt ominous, peopled with evil. "It's the dangers you can't see, that you don't suspect—those are the worst."

"What should I do?" asked David.

"Guard the plane," said Jeb. "Watch that the anchor holds."

Gettler was moving toward the far tip of the island. He carried the rifle carelessly in his right hand. The game pocket of his jacket bulged strangely.

Jeb stared at the bulges. *What's he got in that jacket? Rifle bullets like he says? Or what?*

"What's he looking for?" asked Monti.

"Something to eat," said Jeb. "A turtle, a 'gator."

"Are the Indians over there right now watching us?" asked David.

"In the jungle? Probably. Anyway, we'll assume that they are."

"Why don't they attack, then?" asked Monti.

"Their way is to wait in ambush," said Jeb. "They'll choose their own place and time."

He looked at David. The boy's face was beginning to turn brick red in the sun.

"You'd better get in the shade of the wing," said Jeb.

"We'll have to rig you a hat of some kind. The sun'll boil you like a lobster."

"Do what he says," said Monti.

"I'll look for a leaf to make you a sunshade," said Jeb. He glanced after Gettler. "But first, I want that little revolver out of the survival kit."

"Mr. Gettler took it," said David. "I saw him."

Jeb stopped. "When?"

"Just a few minutes ago when you were pushing us into the island. Before he got out."

"The son of a bitch!" snapped Jeb. "He's got his hands on every weapon we own!" He pushed David toward the plane. "Get into the shade."

Monti followed. She pulled the silver scarf across her forehead almost down to her eyes. It gave her a curious, Arabian look. "Why would he take all the guns?" she asked.

"You tell me," said Jeb. "Is he planning to desert us?"

"I don't like him," whispered Monti. "He makes me feel afraid." She hesitated. "Back there when ... when you hung up the poncho and ... I got out, I kept expecting him to peek." She shuddered. "Dammit! I've posed in the nude, but ... It's those little eyes. They make me feel dirty!"

David moved into the shadow of the wing.

Jeb looked down at Monti. Welts of insect bites marked her cheeks. A streak of dirt slashed across her chin. The man's shirt she wore looked wrinkled, damp, soiled. But none of these things subtracted from the elements of her beauty.

She averted her eyes under his stare.

The strong lines of her face—lines that made cameramen gloat—defied the harsh noonday shadows. Pieces of history had washed over uncounted beautiful women to produce this face. It refused to bow now to the worst possible light.

Jeb spoke brusquely, "Excuse me. I want to look at the motor. And I'm going to rig a fish line."

Monti stared after Gettler. "What is it about that man?"

she murmured. "He's an animal ... yet ... Why would he take all the guns? Doesn't he trust us?"

"He can't stay awake forever," said Jeb. "Had you thought of that?"

Monti's lips thinned. She put a hand to her cheek.

Gettler had stopped at the lower end of the island. He bent over something on the beach.

"I've the strangest feeling," she said.

"What?"

"That it's his fault. About Roger."

"How do you mean?"

"Call it a woman's intuition. I can feel it. Roger would be alive now if it weren't for him." She nodded toward Gettler.

"Nothing except intuition?"

She shrugged.

Jeb told her about his own suspicions, about the pieces of Gettler's story that did not ring true.

Monti stared into Jeb's eyes. "Could he have murdered Roger?" she whispered.

Jeb frowned. "I suppose so."

"But what about the Indians?" she asked. "They were chasing him."

"Would Roger have made friends with the Indians?" asked Jeb. "I mean—would he have gotten really close to them?"

Her eyes widened. "It's the very thing he would've done! *Noble savages* he called them in a letter."

Jeb looked down the island at Gettler, who now was stalking through the scrub.

"Why?" she asked.

"I'm just guessing," said Jeb. "I've got nothing to go on except suspicions. But why would he take all the guns?"

"What do you mean?"

"If your husband went through any kind of an adoption ceremony with the Jivaro, and then Gettler murdered him, it'd be a point of tribal honor with them to avenge the killing."

Monti put a hand over her mouth. "Could he ..."

"Sure he could! But we don't know that he did. For all we know, he's told us the literal truth!"

"But why would he take all the guns?" she asked.

"There's one thing," said Jeb. "If he did murder Roger, we can't let him know that we suspect. He'd slaughter us in a minute."

Across the island, the heliograph of a golden moth wing splashed in the sunlight. Jeb glanced at it. A big green *cacique* oriole flew out of the jungle, floated behind the moth on an air current, twisted down.

And there was no moth.

The scene left Jeb with a deep feeling of disquiet. For a moment he had identified with the beauty of the moth. And the jungle had taken it—quickly, silently.

"What'll we do?" asked Monti.

"We'll watch and wait," said Jeb. "First chance, we'll get the guns back."

At the foot of the island Gettler suddenly sprang into action. He ran across the scrub, raised a twisted limb in one hand. The limb crashed to the ground once, twice. He tossed it aside, bent, lifted something that wriggled and squirmed in his hand. He swung the thing, smashed it against the ground.

"What's he got?" asked Monti.

"Looks like a lizard."

David joined them. "Are we going to eat that thing?"

Jeb looked down at the boy, wondered: *Did he hear us talking about Gettler? And if he did hear us, will he give us away?*

There was no time to explore the problem with David.

Gettler came tramping up to them. He carried a gold-spotted green lizard by one of its hand-like feet. The lizard was about two feet long. Bright spots of blood dripped from its grinning jaws.

"Do you expect us to eat that?" asked Monti.

"Hell! These are good eating!" boomed Gettler. "Taste like chicken."

"He's right," said Jeb. "They're a delicacy."

Monti shuddered. "I couldn't *possibly*!"

"You'd better forget your squeamishness," said Gettler.

"I'll start a fire," said Jeb. "We can cook it here and eat it on the way."

"Vultures cleaned a tapir on the lower end of the island," said Gettler. "There's real food: a jungle pig."

Monti grimaced at the lizard. "I'd as soon eat snake!"

"And we may eat that, too," said Gettler. "You eat what the jungle gives you or you die."

"It can't be any worse than frog's legs," said David.

"Better," said Gettler. "Come along, son."

He led the way down to the river's edge below the plane, pulled a thin bladed clasp knife from his pocket.

"What're you going to do?" asked David.

"Give you a lesson in anatomy," said Gettler.

David crouched beside him.

Gettler flipped the lizard onto its back, half in the water, slit it open lengthwise, spread the cavity.

David gulped.

"Up here's the thoracic cavity," said Gettler. "These are the lungs." He pulled them out. "The stomach." This, too, came out and onto the rocks beside the lizard. "Let's see what it's been eating." Gettler slit the stomach sack. "Insects ... some kind of a worm ... a fruit pod. Catholic taste."

David bent closer, fascinated. He had heard the conversation between his mother and Jeb Logan, and their words had filled him with fearful suspicions about Gettler. But Gettler's hands moved so deftly. His voice was so gentle.

"Why'd you take all the guns?" asked David.

Gettler swished his knife through the water. "Did your mother tell you to ask me?"

"No, sir. I saw you take them. Why didn't you leave one at the plane ... in case the Indians attacked?"

"Do you know how to shoot a gun?" asked Gettler.

"Yes, sir. My ... Dad taught me."

"Maybe next time I'll leave one of the guns with you," said Gettler. He poked at the lizard entrails with his knife. "This is the liver."

"Doesn't Mr. Logan know how to use a gun?" asked David.

"Can you keep a secret?" asked Gettler.

David frowned. "I ... guess so."

Gettler glanced up the beach where Jeb had a fire going next to a large rock. "Mr. Logan hasn't been in the jungle as much as I have. There're ferocious animals here that if you shoot at them, they'll attack. I'm afraid he might shoot at the wrong thing."

"Like what?" asked David.

"Jaguar. Boa constrictors."

"Golly!"

"I know you'd be careful," said Gettler.

"Did my ... Dad know lots of things about the jungle?" asked David.

"More than I know about it," said Gettler. "He was a real expert."

David nodded.

Again Gettler prodded the liver. "The liver's what stores the food stuffs that the body needs. And it helps purify the blood." He moved the knife blade. "This is the pancreas. It secretes insulin and digestive juices."

"You know all kinds of things," said David.

Gettler frowned, wiped the knife against his pants, put it away. "Here. Save these." He handed David the lizard's heart and a section of lung. "Fish bait."

David swallowed, took the bloody pieces. "What kind of fish will it catch?"

Gettler swished the lizard through the water. It left a red stain that drifted away on the current. He threw the rest of the entrails into the stain.

Abruptly, the water flashed with a shoal of piranha. The dark surface boiled in a writhing commotion as they fought for the bloody entrails.

"*That* kind of fish," said Gettler. "And there's a lesson for you in *natural* science. Don't fall in the river or you'll feed those fish."

"Would they really eat a human being?" David stared wide-eyed at the turbulent water.

"Right down to the bones," said Gettler. "Come on. Let's cook our dinner."

"Yes, sir."

"And remember our secret. We wouldn't want to hurt Mr. Logan's feelings."

"Gosh, no."

Monti was persuaded to take a tentative bite. She savored the meat, then ate ravenously, throwing the picked bones out the open door of the plane beside her. She watched the passing shore as she ate. Food dispelled some of her gloom.

They'll start searching for us soon, she thought. Her mind turned to Gettler. *When we're rescued. Then we can find out the truth of what happened at the rancho. The government will send soldiers. They'll get at the truth.*

Jeb, too, watched the passing jungle, saw the heat devils spiraling from the treetops. Now, the river bank was more open: lined by cabbage palms and with tree ferns weaving delicate patterns below.

Shadows were longer as the sun began its descent toward the peaks in the west.

Infrequently, in the spotted sunlight beyond the river's edge, Jeb's eyes caught flitting movements. It occurred to him that live things in the jungle were mostly sudden—darting so quickly that you seemed to see them only after they'd gone: like frozen afterimages.

A loose rumbling sound from the rear of the plane caught Jeb's attention. Snoring. Gettler? Jeb turned, and his muscles locked.

David was bent toward Gettler, a look of total concentration on his young face. His right hand crept toward the butt of the big revolver in Gettler's belt.

Gettler was sleeping with his mouth open, the rifle cradled against one knee.

David heard us! thought Jeb. *The crazy kid's going to start a battle royal! I've got to stop him!* He watched the slowly moving hand. *But maybe he can get it!*

Jeb glanced quickly at Monti. She stared out her window, oblivious of the tableau in the rear. Jeb returned his attention to David. The boy's hand hovered over the gun butt, moved down, touched it.

Gettler's eyes jerked open. His hand smashed out, caught David on the nose, hurled him into the corner.

"I thought so!" bellowed Gettler.

David cowered in the corner, blood flowing from his nose, running down his chin, down his neck, staining his shirt.

Jeb had started to dive for the gun himself. He froze as Gettler jerked up the revolver, waved it menacingly.

Monti had whirled at the sound of the slap. She reached for David, drew back as Gettler thrust the gun toward her.

"Did you put him up to that?" he demanded.

"Up to what?"

The gun muzzle moved toward Jeb.

"I just wanted to look at the gun," said David. "You said you were going to let me." He wiped the blood away from his chin. "Why'd you hit me? You gave me a bloody nose!"

Gettler's face underwent an abrupt transformation: the cheek muscles sagged, his eyes lost some of their glaring fire. He lowered the gun, turned to David, spoke as though he had just that moment awakened:

"Sorry son. But you shouldn't have done that."

"I didn't mean any harm," said David.

"Don't ever do that again," said Gettler. He produced a red bandana from one of his jacket pockets. "Here. Press this against your nose."

He lied to me, thought David. *He doesn't really want me to have a gun.*

Jeb wet his lips with his tongue.

Gettler's attention shifted. He stared at Jeb through slitted eyes. "What're you trying to prove, Logan?"

And David thought: *He's trying to prove that you killed*

my dad! Did you? The question formed on his lips.

"David, are you all right?" asked Monti.

"Yes, Mother."

"You shouldn't try to play with guns, David."

"I'm sorry, Mother."

We're at the mercy of a madman! thought Monti. *He could have killed Roger!*

Jeb had followed the same line of thought, but now, something else occupied his mind. *David has some power over Gettler. How can we use that?*

"In the jungle you have to sleep on a hair trigger," said Gettler. "Never trust anything that touches you to be safe. Do you understand, David?"

David wiped his cheek with the bandana, nodded.

Gettler looked at Monti. "There's the one thing your husband never learned about the jungle, Mrs. Bannon. He was too trusting, always hobnobbing with the savages. Precious lot of good it did him!" He lowered the revolver to his lap.

"What do you mean he *hobnobbed* with them?" asked Monti. "Did he visit with them in their villages?"

"Stayed for weeks at a time," said Gettler.

Jeb said: "Do you want me to look at David's nose, Monti? See if it's okay?"

"You heard him say he's all right!" snapped Gettler.

David shook his head. "It's already stopped bleeding. I'm okay."

Roger visited with the Indians, thought Monti. *They would've accepted him. He was that kind.* There was no longer any doubt in her mind. *Gettler murdered him!*

Gettler glared at Jeb. "What're you staring at?"

Monti put a hand on Jeb's sleeve. He turned around, faced forward.

The back of Jeb's head fascinated Gettler. *I could kill him right now! He suspects. That's as bad as knowing. It's his fault the woman and boy haven't warmed to me. He dies if I want him to die!*

Gettler suddenly felt that he occupied a pool outside of time—remote and godlike. *If Logan dies I'll have the woman and boy all to myself.* His face took on a dreaming look, filled with a drunken expression of power. His hand on the butt of the revolver tingled and trembled.

"Hadn't you better put that gun away?" asked David. "It might go off and hurt somebody."

The mood was shattered. It dissolved completely, and he swung on a hurtling pendulum into a ragged chaos of memories. One face dominated the memories: a boy. His name was ... was ... *Peter*! And Gettler asked himself: *Why is Peter talking about guns? We never let him play with guns.* His mind dodged the question, relaxed into a lecture hall memory, the familiar podium beneath his fingers. Ahhh. Comparative logic: the mind slashing through a wilderness of dark things to the one bright kernel sprouting in a glade.

And Jeb thought, *I've got to get those guns away from him!*

Silence invaded the plane: an impressive solitude magnified by the heat and hypnotic flow of shoreline.

Jeb stared at his hands. He had never before been forced into a position where both fear and idleness forced him to look inward. The experience was both terrifying and fascinating. *Fear is the penalty of consciousness,* he thought. He felt that somewhere in his past had reached a glowing summit where there were no complications of before and after. It was a plaintive half-thought: a looking for a place of no doubts.

The images within my mind are part of me, he told himself. *I don't need to fear them. They're the past.*

But he sensed that there might be a tip-over point with introspection, that somewhere within him lurked a memory, which could engulf him.

Monti lighted a cigarette, her second of the day. She studied the glowing tip. The same pressures of introspection were at work on her, and she found them equally disturbing. Her reaction was to run away to the present, a place just as repugnant.

The future, then.

They'll start looking for us soon. She looked up at the sky. *A plane could come over any minute now.* Her attention went to the mountains in the western horizon. The mountains grew and diminished as the river twisted through its blue furrow.

The plane drifted on an enchanted river that meandered between curtains of drooping lianas. They rounded a bend, and the current carried them toward the towering brilliance of three *Fernán Sanchez* trees: a startling red against the overpowering green. Water was slowly undercutting the witch finger roots that clutched at a muddy bank.

Rising waves of heat encased the plane in dead air. The sun was a throbbing inferno that drifted over them, crushed them.

The river edge became quilted with evening shadows. Night swept upward from the trench of slow current to the blazing peaks. The sun dipped behind the mountains. Amethyst vapors in the sunset produced a space of polished ruby water ahead of them—like flowing blood.

There came a moment at dark when the river seemed to cease all movement. Then they were into the damply cushioned night: the time of the timid and the terrible.

The melon slice of moon was slightly larger, a thin curve of bright metal. Its light spilled over the jungle edge like a pale waterfall, flooded the river with a cold glow of silver.

In the plane, the absence of the sun was a weight lifted from their heads. They nerved themselves to eat the last of the K-rations.

Something splashed in the river behind them.

Slowly, the hush of first-dark was replaced by the noises of the early night: low rippling calls that could have been a bird or animal, the distant scream of a prowling jaguar, a flutter of wings overhead, the chiming of frogs.

Monti's voice came low and devoid of energy: "Do you think the Indians have given up?"

"Not likely," said Jeb.

Are they really after Gettler to avenge my husband? wondered Monti. And again she began to doubt her suspicions.

"They'll choose a narrow place in the river," said Gettler. "Probably at rapids."

"I wish I knew what set them off," said Jeb.

"Plain filthy nastiness!" snarled Gettler. "That's the way they are!"

"One atom bomb would kill all of them!" said David. "When I grow up I'm going to drop an atom bomb on them!"

"Then you'd never know why they did it," said Jeb. He stared ahead along the moon trail.

Gettler said: "Logan, you'd better keep ..."

"Oh, stop it!" snapped Monti. "It's so close in here! We have to be together, so why can't we make the best of it?"

"Arrrrrgh!" said Gettler.

"Maybe if we talked about ourselves," said Monti. "If we got to know each other better."

"The practical female," said Gettler.

"We did a movie on the Mississippi—oh, six or seven years ago," said Monti. She counted on her fingers. "Seven years."

"I saw it," said Jeb.

"I thought then how wonderful it'd be to just drift down a river," she said. "So peaceful."

"You played the part of a captain's daughter," said Jeb. "A river boat captain."

She laughed. "It was a terrible story, as trite as something from a third grade reader. But I liked the songs. And it was light-hearted. We had fun."

"There was a song about moonlight on a river," said Jeb.

She hummed two bars. "That one?"

"Yes! God, it seems like yesterday! I was in Washington, D.C. I took a Pentagon secretary who lived way out in Maryland. And I got a ticket for speeding on the way back. Big fat patrolman who said, 'The war's over, Mister!' So it was."

"This isn't like the Mississippi, is it?" asked Gettler. "No Jivaro on the Mississippi to separate you from your head."

"There are *several* differences, Mr. Gettler," she said.

"I would prefer you to call me Franzel," he said.

"What's in a name?" asked Jeb.

Monti chuckled. Then: "Franzel?"

"Yes. As you say: we are thrown together, and should make the best of it."

"Franzel," she said.

And Gettler thought: *That's what Gerda called me: Franzel.* And his mind sheared away from the memory. He found himself thinking of a graduation ceremony in 1934. There had been a sprinkling of jack-booted National Socialists in the audience, but no one had paid much attention—then. There had been no disturbance. Dr. Auber had been the speaker, his theme: "Freedom for the Academic Mind." Dr. Auber had disappeared the following week.

"Where were you seven years ago, Franzel?" asked Monti.

"I thought it was a very good speech," said Gettler. "If you chain down the academic mind, it discovers nothing new."

"What?" asked Monti.

Gettler shook his head. "Eh? Oh, yes. I was just thinking about someone who's been dead many years. I wonder how he encountered death. As an illusion? Or as a cataclysm?"

"I asked where you were seven years ago?" said Monti.

"Seven? Lovely number. Full of religious significance. Let me see. Seven. I was in New York. Yes. There was a position at Columbia, but someone else got it. His wife was a friend of someone important in the school administration."

"That's too bad," said Monti.

"Oh, no! It was a narrow escape! I could've been trapped in civilization!"

"Trapped?" asked Monti.

"Civilization is bossed by women," said Gettler. "The jungle is where men are supreme. This is *man's* last frontier. We don't like you here."

David crouched in his corner, listening. The words were strange and fascinating to him. He found Gettler's voice compelling, and the man's thoughts were contagious to the young mind.

"What's it like—the movie life?" asked Jeb. "Is it as hectic as the magazines make out?"

"It's a living," she said. "A job."

"Women make a hell out of the world!" said Gettler. "They're dictators in a marriage! So literal. So practical. So down to earth!"

David listened in enchantment. *She did try to boss my dad,* he thought.

"Is it *hard* work?" asked Jeb.

"God, yes. You're lucky if you get six hours of sleep a night when you're shooting."

"They're supposed to hold the secret of duration," said Gettler. "But they lose the secret because they always try to take over the ways of men!"

"We did a story about bullfighters," said Monti. "In Mexico."

"I saw that one, too," said Jeb. "In Korea. A Quonset hut bijou. No heat. Damn near froze to death."

"Another company was doing a similar kind of story in Spain at the same time," said Monti. "It was a race. Jesus! Twelve and fourteen hours a day!"

"And women keep superstition alive," said Gettler. "Intuition? What's that but superstition? Men are the creative beings. Women destroy creation."

And David thought: *Dad never would've run away if it hadn't been for her! He'd be alive right now!*

Monti turned, looked into the shadowy rear of the plane. "What're you going to do when we reach civilization, Franzel?"

Gettler broke off a ranting thought. *Her voice! How like Gerda's voice!*

"What am I going to do?"

He thought about the emeralds in his jacket. "I like the American Southwest," he said. "The houses are air-conditioned. Lovely clean air. You can put perfume in the air. I will have a swimming pool. The beds will have silk sheets. Silk is so clean to the touch. There will be a shower with glass walls. So antiseptic, glass. No filth. No perspiration. I'll ..."

He stopped, cleared his throat.

"Go on," murmured Monti.

"This is stupid!" said Gettler.

David filled the pause. "I'm going to kill Indians! All I ..." Abruptly, he was crying.

Gettler's voice came strangely soft and pleading: "Please don't cry, son. Please. Look: you lean back here and go to sleep. Let Franzel worry about killing Indians."

"I'm sor-ry," sobbed David. "It's ... just ... that ... I ... never ... ever ... got to know him. Now ... I'll never have the chance!"

Monti turned, pressed her face against Jeb's shoulder. Silent sobs shook her.

Jeb took her shoulders, pulled her head down onto his lap. "You try to get some sleep, too," he whispered.

Slowly, she quieted. She felt herself giving up to fatigue. *Jeb's like that part of Roger I loved best,* she thought. *Gettler's like the part I hated.*

It was a curious thought. Her mind turned it over and over until sleep broke into the circle.

David's crying subsided.

Gettler made murmurous sounds over the boy. *Like Peter, he is. How like Peter.* But again his mind refused this trail. *It will be a small house with one servant. And I will discourage visitors.*

The moon path crawled beneath the plane, rippling with spider lines in the eddies, flowing like painted silk in the broad reaches.

Jeb stared downstream.

The Jivaro can't hold off much longer, he thought. *They know all the best places for an ambush. The experts say they won't attack at night, but ...*

This thought turned every shadow into a source of peril. Jeb strained his senses against the night.

Gettler tipped his head back, looked up at the moon through the side window. Bronze earthlight filled out the hidden circle. There was a look in this darker area like a human face. Then he recognized the face: Roger Bannon. Good old Rog. The face looked deeply introspective as it had whenever they'd talked philosophy. There was even a dark spot on the moon that could only be Roger's pipe.

And for the first time, something like remorse touched Gettler.

So I killed him. He should've realized how important the emeralds were to me. He should've known how much I hate filth! How I need clean things around me! Everything was fine until the emeralds. Maybe the emeralds killed him. Or the part of me that had to have the emeralds.

David had seen Jeb pull his mother down. He looked at the single silhouette in front where there had been two. His mother's Bohemian life had given David a knowledgeable cynicism beyond his years.

Will she marry this pilot or just have another affair?

He was beyond feeling hurt or surprised about his mother: only curiosity.

Before the moon went down they beached the plane on a narrow islet no more than fifty feet long, the center criss-crossed with logs deposited in the last flood.

Jeb took the first watch. He listened for a deepening of Gettler's breathing. *Let him fall into a deep sleep and I'll get the gun from his belt!*

But every slight shift of motion in the plane, the bump of flotsam against the floats, animal sounds from the jungle all brought a momentary holding of breath, a waiting silence from Gettler.

And at midnight he straightened, said: "Now I will take the watch."

"All quiet," said Jeb.

"Good."

Jeb turned his head against the seat. Monti's head was still cradled in his lap. She breathed quietly, evenly. He noted that the mildew smell was stronger in the plane. And there was an acrid tang of rust. The smells filled him with a feeling of melancholy, as though deterioration in this symbol of civilization represented all human decay and mortality.

A flock of parakeets announced the dawn. They chattered and gossiped in the jungle beyond the island. A misty, bluish-white morning light covered the sky. Smokey mist hid the river upstream and downstream. Smaller birds added their sounds to the day: flutterings, chirps, twitters.

Jeb heard the birds as though their calls pulled him a long distance up to wakefulness. He awoke sweating, and feeling strangely weak, sat up.

Monti had moved away from him in the night. She slept curled against her door.

There was a feeling of moist, unhealthy warmth in the air of the closed cabin.

Jeb leaned forward to look through the overhead curve of windshield. His back ached from sleeping in a cramped position. The sky was an empty grey slate prepared only as a setting for one vulture that sailed into view across the treetops, wings motionless. The vulture tipped majestically, beat its wings, flew upstream. Jeb lowered his gaze, noted the plush growth of parasite moss covering the underside of the tangled logs on the island. He turned around.

David sat silently awake in his corner. His eyes were red-rimmed, sleepy. Gettler beside him stared downstream, trying to see through the mists.

"We'll meet rapids today," murmured Gettler.

"This is our second day," said David. "Will they be looking for us yet?"

Jeb shrugged.

David lifted his camera. "I got my camera ready to take pictures of the plane when it comes for us."

"Don't get your hopes up," said Gettler.

Jeb opened his door, slipped down to the float, froze motionless with one hand on the door. Something moved in the log jam. Then he recognized it: a river pig, the kind the Indians called *carpi*. Jeb looked up to Gettler, saw that he had seen the pig.

"Give me the rifle," whispered Jeb.

Gettler hesitated, then passed the gun out the door.

Jeb kneeled on the pontoon, waited.

The pig came around the end of the logs, stopped with its tusked snout pointed at the plane. It looked like a curious old man surprised by an intruder.

Jeb sighted, squeezed the trigger. The rifle bucked against his shoulder, and its sound filled his ears.

The pig flipped onto its back, jerked once, was still.

A scream erupted from the plane: Monti! "Where? Where are they?"

"It's just a pig!" shouted Gettler. "Food!"

Jeb stood up, looked into the cabin. Monti sat stiffly upright, shivering. Her left hand was pressed against her cheek.

"I ... I thought it was the Indians," she quavered.

"Jeb shot a pig, Mother," said David.

Gettler opened the right hand door, clambered out, went to the pig. He brought out his knife, began cutting off the hams.

David leaned down to Jeb. "Mr. Logan?"

"Yes?"

"Is it dangerous to shoot at jaguars and boa constrictors?"

"What?"

"Will they attack you if you shoot at them?"

"Not usually. Why?"

David lowered his voice, related Gettler's story.

Jeb looked across at Gettler working over the pig, felt the weight of the rifle. He swallowed, glanced up at Monti.

She seemed completely hypnotized, all attention focused on the weapon in Jeb's hands.

He wet his lips with his tongue, slowly worked the bolt. The empty casing clicked out, dropped into the river. Jeb glanced down at the gun, felt a wave of frustration. There were no more cartridges in the magazine. He shook his head, passed the useless weapon to Monti.

She looked into the empty magazine.

"Why's he afraid to let us have a gun?" whispered David.

"I don't know," said Monti. "Now hush."

"David, I have a job for you," said Jeb.

"Yes, sir?"

"See these caps on the floats?" Jeb pointed down at a round lid near the front of the pontoon. "They unscrew. There's a little pump in the luggage compartment. I want you to check the floats, and pump out any water in them."

"Aren't you going to do anything about the guns?" whispered Monti.

"What can I do?" asked Jeb. "Let's be patient. Our chance will come."

"But he may kill us all!"

"Not unless we excite him."

"He's crazy!"

Jeb nodded. "Yes. But I think we can keep him calm."

"Do you hear that, David?" asked Monti.

"Yes, Mother."

Jeb worked his way along the pontoon to the beach, collected driftwood, started a fire. He could hear David pumping out the floats. Presently, Monti and David joined him at the fire.

"There wasn't very much water," said David.

"How much?"

"About an inch."

"In each one."

"Yes."

"Did you put the caps back on tightly?"

"Yes."

Gettler came up with the bloody meat. "Not very well hung, this meat." He grinned through his beard.

"Too bad we can't smoke what we don't eat," said Jeb. "It won't always be that easy to come by."

"Aren't there fruits and things we could pick?" asked Monti.

Jeb nodded toward the far shore about two hundred feet away. "That tree leaning over the water is papaya. There may be no Jivaro back in there watching us. Then again ..." He left the thought hanging.

"How far d'you figure we've come?" asked Gettler.

Jeb looked upstream where the mist was beginning to lift. "Maybe a hundred and sixty miles from the rancho."

"No farther?" asked Monti.

He shook his head. "The current averages three or four knots in the dry season. Figure it yourself."

"Even counting the first night when you used the motor?" she asked.

Jeb nodded.

"When the rains start we'll go faster," said Gettler.

"We'll be rescued before then," she said.

Gettler looked at the sky: darker now in the west. The snow cone of Tusachilla appeared abnormally close in the clear air. A tuft of black smoke curled eastward from the volcano.

"Easterly wind," said Jeb.

Gettler nodded, bent to cooking the meat.

"What's that mean?" asked Monti.

"Rain before long," said Jeb.

Gettler left the meat on a spit over the flames, straightened. "We'll hit white water today." He turned, studied the plane. Both pontoons trailed green reeds. Mud caked their tops. A length of vine hung from the left wing.

Jeb followed the direction of Gettler's eyes.

The plane looked deceptively ready to fly, aluminum and

paint still glistening along the sides. But the mud and vines were like symptoms of dissolution. And there were other signs: the dark bullet hole in the engine cowl, a smudge behind the cowl from oil smoke.

"Shall I fill the water bag?" asked David.

"And don't forget the purification tablet," said Gettler.

David went to the plane.

Gettler pulled a box of rifle cartridges from his jacket, jounced them in his hand, stared directly into Jeb's eyes.

Jeb's face darkened.

Gettler returned the cartridges to his pocket without smiling, turned away.

And Jeb felt that he had looked death directly in the face. He had never felt it so strongly: not even during the war.

Monti leaned against a log. The rifle shot that killed the pig had shocked her from a dream. Now, she remembered the dream: There had been an amorphous grey place full of frightening shadows. She had raced away from every hint of terror. And at every turn, Roger had appeared—eyes full of that maddening calm, voice pitched to that enraging reasonableness: *"It's time to forget me, Monti. You must forget me, Monti."*

Over and over and over and over and over ...

"Meat's ready," said Getter.

Monti shook her head.

The sun lifted over the jungle, and they felt its first impact.

They ate quickly, cast off.

Almost immediately, the river took on a new character. The hills drew closer, bent down over them. A faster current tugged at the pontoons and the sea anchor that Jeb tossed into the flow. More lines of eddies trailed from the shores, curved on the dark surface of the water.

For a time, a band of long-tailed monkeys paced them, roaring and chittering through the trees along the left bank. The monkeys abandoned the game at a river bend.

"The rainy season's overdue," said Gettler.

"It'll be hell in the rapids when they start," said Jeb.

"What's that?" asked David. He pointed downstream.

A column of smoke stood vertically out of the jungle: a grey exclamation point.

"Jivaro!" snapped Gettler.

"That smoke's at least ten miles away," said Jeb.

"Signal smoke," said Gettler.

The column of smoke broke off, dissipated.

"Does that mean they're going to attack?" asked Monti.

"It told those downstream where we are," said Gettler. "They're waiting for us."

"The first rapids you talked about?" asked Jeb.

"Maybe."

The river straightened, and the hills beside them dipped even lower. A thick twisting of hardwood trees along the shore gave way to lines of sago palms backed by rising waves of the overpowering jungle green. Only infrequently was the green broken by the smooth red-skinned trunks of *guayavilla* leaning over the water.

Around another bend, they surprised a long-legged red bird feeding in the shallows. It lifted on silent pinions, flew downstream.

Another bend—swifter current.

They heard the roar of rapids, felt another quickening of river flow even before they saw the white foam.

Quite suddenly, no more than half a mile downstream at the end of a straight sweep of current, they saw the snarling boil of foam, misting spume hurled into the air. The sound grew louder: a crashing, violent drumming without rhythm.

Jeb brought in the sea anchor, wedged it tightly against the strut, lashed it there, leaped back into the cabin, primed the motor.

Start! Please start! he prayed.

The current picked up more speed. They felt that they were hurtling toward the maelstrom.

He pulled the starter. The engine coughed, backfired. Again he pulled the starter. The motor caught, began to die. He nursed the throttle. A great banging, spitting roar came from the engine, drowning out the sound of the rapids.

"No sign of Indians!" shouted Gettler.

Smoke from burning oil fanned out behind the plane, began to fill the cabin. Jeb closed the vents. A line of foaming rocks broke the current.

To hell with everything! thought Jeb.

He pushed the throttle in to the limit, wondered if the crazily rocking motor would jerk from its mountings. But the little plane began to skim, and for a brief heart-skip they were airborne above the first rocks. Then the straining engine coughed twice. Water caught the floats. The river dipped down, roared and leaped, down, down through ever steepening banks. Jeb fought the controls. The plane lurched and twisted. Spray filled the air. Roaring of river and motor competed for domination.

Something wrenched at the right hand float. A tearing sound of tortured metal battered the air. The nose dipped, came up. They skimmed out of the gorge into a wide bend. The river flattened out in a slowly frothing boil as though in exhaustion from the rapids.

Jeb aimed for a white line of sand beach on the left, cut off the motor at the last possible moment. The right wing dropped—lower, lower and lower as the torn float drank up water. The left hand float grated on sand, spun the deeper float in a short arc.

The damaged pontoon gurgled, sighed out a burst of bubbles. Six inches of air remained between the tip of the right wing and the surface of the river.

Jeb took two deep, gulping breaths.

"Now, we find a dugout," said Gettler.

"Maybe," said Jeb.

Monti lifted her face from her hands. "I thought it was the end."

"Were there Indians?" asked David.

Jeb looked back up the foaming steps of the rapids. "I don't think so."

"This was not the place," said Gettler. "That means there is a better place downstream for an ambush."

"Let's have a look at the pontoon," said Jeb.

"It's done," said Gettler. "Kaput."

Jeb opened his door. Immediately, the sound of the brawling water grew louder. Insects began to invade the cabin. Jeb slipped down to the slanted top of the left float, studied the jungle beyond the beach: a confusion of interlaced branches, vines, creepers and tree ferns. A damp track at their left crossed the sand, disappeared at a dark hole in the undergrowth: game trail.

"There could be an army of Jivaro ten feet inside that jungle, and we couldn't see them," whispered Gettler.

"Game trail over there to the left," said Jeb.

"I saw it," said Gettler.

"What kind of game?" asked David.

"All kinds," said Jeb. He sniffed the air.

A line of ripples moved upstream toward them, pushed by a wind out of a furnace. The ripples fanned out before the wind, grew as the wind grew. Then the wind died, and the air around them trembled in the heat.

Jeb took a deep breath. "We don't solve anything just sitting here." He scanned the river for piranha. The water ran as clear as a sheet of glass. Mica sparkled in the sand of the bottom. Reflections danced and shimmered on the metal underside of the wing. A pressure of heat radiated from the sand beach.

No sign of piranha. Jeb slid off into the water. It was warm. He splashed around beneath the tail, waded out to the damaged float. Another examination of the water. No flashing of deadly fish. He bent down, ran a hand along the outside of the float.

Just back of the leading edge his fingers encountered a

jagged rip in the metal. He explored the break, straightened.

Gettler still sat in the plane, attention fixed on the wall of jungle beyond the sand.

He's frightened silly! thought Jeb.

Monti opened her door, leaned out. "That water looks cool."

"It's warm."

"Can we fix the float?"

"It's only about a foot long, and maybe an inch wide in the worst spot."

"What could we use to fix it?"

"I can see a gum tree in the forest there," said Jeb. "Bark, gum and vines. We can pound the metal back into some kind of shape with a rock."

"We must find a canoe," said Gettler.

"You hunt for one while we're fixing this!" snarled Jeb.

Gettler paled.

"How'll we get that float out of the water?" asked Monti.

"Vines," said Jeb. "Run them from the float around a good solid tree beyond the beach and back to the float. Put a strong limb between the vines, turn it. You twist the doubled vines."

"Back in Montana we called that a Spanish Windlass," she said.

"Some big leaves under the float will make it slide easier," he said. "Just goes to show there's a complete supply house and repair shop here if you only know how to use it."

"Too bad we can't fix the motor the same way," said David.

Jeb sighed. "Yeah."

"I say get out of here while we still have our heads," said Gettler.

"Go ahead," said Jeb.

"Is there danger from Indians?" asked David.

Gettler looked downstream to where the beach sand trailed off into a red clay bank. He seemed to be having trouble with his breathing.

"If they were going to attack, they'd have been on us before now," said Jeb. "We're sitting ducks." He took a deep breath. "Hell! They may've quit a hundred miles back."

"Not the Jivaro," muttered Gettler.

"We're wasting time," said Monti. "Cut the vines and let's get started."

"Machete's under your seat," said Jeb. "Let's have it."

The sun climbed higher as they worked. Insects clung to every patch of exposed skin. The air took on the consistency of molten tar full of inflated tensions.

Slowly, with creakings and poppings, the damaged float came out of the water onto the sand. A rivulet ran out of the hole.

Gettler flopped down in the shade of the wing, cradled the rifle in his arms, studied the jungle. Earth and sky around them had sunken into a deep and sultry oppression.

He reflected the same mood.

"I feel a little dizzy," said David.

"Get into the shade of the wing there," said Jeb. "You've been working out here without your sunshade."

"That leaf!"

"You should use it," said Monti

"It won't stay on!"

Jeb pulled one of the small canvas buckets from the survival kit, picked up the machete, crossed to Gettler. "Let's have my revolver."

Gettler glanced up at him. "Why?"

Jeb nodded toward the jungle. "I'm going in there to that gum tree. We can seal that float with gum and *pita* fiber."

Gettler looked at the blue-grey bark of the tree towering out of the first screen of lianas. He frowned.

"The revolver," said Jeb.

"You going to shoot the sap out of that tree?"

"No telling what's back there," said Jeb.

"Call me if you need help," said Gettler. His eyes looked

glassy, veiled.

"If I don't come back, you'll have to go in there," said Jeb.

"Why?

"I don't see any canoes around here."

Gettler looked at the river. "We should've kept the one I got away in."

"But we didn't."

"No gun," said Gettler. "You won't need it." He began to shiver.

"Okay!" snapped Jeb.

"Be careful when you walk around any big trees," said Gettler. "The Jivaro like to step from ambush and drive a spear up through a man's guts."

"Provided the man *has* guts," said Jeb.

A wild flame lighted Gettler's eyes. "Careful, Logan."

"You may be a great jungle *macho*," said Jeb. "But right now you need me."

"Don't count on it."

"Before you get other ideas, Gettler, ask yourself if you're ready to tramp off through that jungle."

Gettler looked at the wall of green.

"You need me and you're going to continue to need me," said Jeb.

"Arrrrrgh!"

Jeb turned, hefted the machete, crossed to the dark hole of the trail. He felt his back tingling, dared not turn around.

I could kill him now, thought Gettler. But he could not lift the rifle.

Jeb left the beach and entered the jungle in one step. He found himself in an orchid-lined aisle with a path of grey mud laced by tiny roots beneath his feet. The damp gloom produced a first illusion of coolness that disappeared quickly. He moved through muggy shadows, searching for the bole of the gum tree.

There it is.

The tree stood six feet off the trail, but it took Jeb five

minutes to reach it, hacking through a long-spined thorn bush. He chopped a V-shaped notch in the grey bark, propped the bucket in position with a limb. A narrow length of bark went into the base of the notch as a trough. A thin trickle of milk sap ran down the bark, dripped into the bucket.

Jeb returned to the trail.

Pita bark. Where the hell will I find it?

He wet his lips with his tongue, moved on up the trail.

Dirty son-of-a-bitch! Refusing to give me my gun!

The trail climbed steeply, dipped and leveled, and again climbed. The drumming of the rapids grew fainter, the air slightly drier. Around him the jungle was dappled by shafts of sunshine on pollen and dust.

A line of leaf-bearing ants crossed the trail ahead of him on a low vine. The insect caravan wound around a ridged root, struck off into the shadows.

High above him a squirrel monkey suddenly scolded, fell silent. The whistling of *perdices* partridges answered from the hill on the right.

The jungle returned to silence.

Jeb's palm against the machete handle felt slippery with sweat. The rank odor of rotting vegetation crossed his nostrils. He moved forward. Only rare clumps of pale bushes and hanging vines now blocked the avenues between the trees. He stopped, looked around, started forward, withdrew his foot.

A single human footprint slowly filled with water inches away from his boot.

Not a minute old!

The footprint pointed right.

Perspiration flooded Jeb's skin. He looked to the right, expected at any moment to feel the biting thrust of a spear. His back felt naked.

Only dappled green met his eyes.

His mind told him there were other colors present: pale

flowers, grey bark, brown bark, red bark ... and somewhere the copper skin of an Indian. But nothing detracted from the overpowering green: it drew all colors to itself and fused them.

Again he passed his gaze across the jungle: vines, scattered low bushes, ferns, a low clump of ...

He saw the Indian.

Copper skin blended with shadows not fifteen feet off the trail. The native stood hidden from the waist down in ferns. He held a blowgun vertically at his left side.

A woman crouched behind him, and beside her a younger warrior, hardly more than a boy.

A curare gourd and bamboo tube of darts hung over the man's right shoulder. Red string was twisted around his arm just below the shoulder. Red lines of *achiote* streaked his brown face in a pattern of whorls. Both man and boy carried fluffs of kapok behind each ear.

The woman was bent under a woven bark sack.

All wore plain bark breech-clouts.

Jeb recognized the painted symbols on the man: one of the Napo tribes. He stared into the ebony eyes beneath the flat line of bangs. They were cold and untamed eyes.

A family group, thought Jeb. *Traders?*

He nodded his head—a slow, dignified movement, shifted the machete to his left hand, lifted his right hand, palm out.

The man brought his right arm across his body, touched the red string on his upper arm.

Warding off the death finger.

During his first year in Milagro Jeb had taken a short course in Quechua, the language of the Incas that had become the universal tongue of the jungle Indians. Maria mixed Spanish and Quechua indiscriminately. Half the workmen of Milagro did the same.

Jeb dredged the words out of his memory, said: "*Maim shamungui?*" ("*Where from?*")

The man turned his head to the right, indicated the hills above the river. *Beyond the mountains.*

Jeb focused on the curare gourd. *They've probably been buying dart poison from the Jivaro witchmen.* And at the same moment, he realized that the Indian had wanted to be discovered. *Otherwise I wouldn't have seen him. Why'd he want me to see him? Trade?* Jeb motioned for the man to approach.

The Indian came up to the trail—moving almost without sound. Jeb felt in his pants pocket, extracted a clasp knife, passed it into a brown hand. The Indian gravely placed the knife in a monkey-skin pouch at his hip.

Jeb dredged up more of his Quechua. With much rolling of eyes and many gestures, he got across to the Indian that he wished to know if there were Jivaro nearby ... and if the Jivaro were angry.

The man squatted, spat between his fingers for emphasis, drew a curved track in the mud with one finger. *The river.*

He indicated a straight section of channel downstream, held up two fingers. *"Ishcai!" Two days.* The brown hands came close together. *Narrow channel. "Jacaré!" A place of rocks and foaming water.*

"Ti coachat!" Many Jivaro.

Jeb nodded. *"Ari." Yes.*

The native crossed his index fingers before his face, spat between them, said: *"Huasi Huanui!"*

Jeb recognized the crossed fingers and the words: *House of the dead?* He frowned. *House of the dead?* Then he understood: to this Indian, Jeb and his companions already were dead.

The Jivaro had spoken.

The man grinned, exposed a double line of teeth blackened from chewing *sindi-muyu*—the jungle fire seed. Again he pointed downstream, then touched the curare gourd at his shoulder.

"Jambai?" asked Jeb. *Poison?*

"Ari," said the Indian. *Yes.* He held out both hands, fingers extended: *Uncountable numbers of Jivaro with much poison!*

"But we have guns," said Jeb.

The Indian looked at Jeb's waist, peered around. "You have no gun. Only the angry man has guns."

Angry man? He knows about Gettler!

Unconsciously, Jeb hefted the machete.

The man looked at the blade, said: *"Maná jambai." No poison.*

Jeb straightened, unwilling to break off the talk. "Would my new friend help me by leading the way to a fiber bark?"

"To repair the hole in the roaring bird that carries men?

He even knows about the damage to the plane!

Jeb nodded. *"Ari."*

After a moment's hesitation the Indian agreed. But he explained that this was only because no Jivaro were at present in the vicinity—the *immediate* vicinity. And he added as though it were a natural thing that the White man would readily understand: "The Jivaro witchmen have put the death finger on you and on any river tribesmen who try to befriend you. I, of course, am from beyond the mountains—and am not subject to the whims of the Jivaro.

"Why are the Jivaro angry?"

"Because of the White man who was killed."

"What White man?"

"The gentle White man of the rancho. He was the friend of the Jivaro: their brother."

"Who killed this brother of the Jivaro?"

The Indian stared at him, then: "The angry man—the one you saved."

Gettler did kill Bannon!

Jeb looked up. The Indian woman and boy had moved closer. He returned his attention to the man. "I did not know."

"Thus I told my companions."

"Companions?"

"The ones who ran. They were afraid."

Then there were others besides this family. Jeb studied the shadowed avenues of the jungle.

"I stayed because I wanted *cigarillos,*" said the Indian.

The Spanish word caught Jeb's attention. *This one's had contact with civilization.*

"I'm sorry, but I have no cigarettes."

"The woman smokes."

"She is the only one." *The woman!* "She is the wife of the one who was slain," said Jeb. "We did not know that the angry man killed her husband."

"Then it is not magic that the boy has the face of the slain one!"

"He is their child," said Jeb.

The Indian stood up. "The woman and boy are in danger?"

"Yes."

"I will help." The Indian turned, addressed himself in a chatter of words to the woman and boy. They turned, trotted off through the trees. The man turned back to Jeb. "You will need fiber bark? Vines?

Jeb nodded. *The Jivaro are out for revenge! Gettler's right: they won't give up!*

The Indian held out his hand for the machete, nodded off the trail to his left. "Bark there."

Jeb relinquished the machete, watched the Indian go directly to a tree some thirty feet off the trail.

I'm a real babe in the woods, thought Jeb. *I didn't even see it.*

The native worked methodically, stripping off shaggy layers of bark.

He's a plantation Indian from the way he handles the machete, thought Jeb.

The Indian returned with a bundle of bark wrapped in vines. He returned the machete, hoisted the load to his head, moved down trail. The blowgun was carried loosely in his left hand.

Jeb followed. *We've got to disarm Gettler, put him under control!*

He slipped and sloshed down the muddy track. Perspiration soaked his shirt. It clung to his back, twisted beneath his armpits. The grey mud weighted his boots.

Gettler mustn't guess that I know. Jeb glanced around. *The gum tree ought to be close. There it is.*

"Hoy!" called Jeb.

The Indian stopped, turned.

Jeb pointed to the bucket on the gum tree. It looked like an illustration out of the Air Force survival handbook.

The man nodded, retrieved the bucket.

Jeb hesitated, looked at the blowgun. *We could kill Gettler from the screen of the jungle! But curare doesn't kill instantly. Monti and the boy might get hurt. She could even think it was an Indian attack and kill herself! No.* He chewed at his lip, waved for the Indian to go ahead.

The beach loomed up like a bright cave mouth at the end of the trail. Jeb fell farther behind, making heavy work of slogging through the mud. The Indian stepped from the trail into the sunlight.

There came the roar of a rifle. A bloody patch appeared as though by magic in the middle of the Indian's back. He staggered backward.

Jeb screamed: "No! Wait!" even as the Indian collapsed.

In the taut silence that followed he heard Gettler shout: "Come on, you bastards! I'll kill you! I'll kill you all!"

Monti screamed.

"No!" shouted Jeb. "That Indian's helping me. It's all right!" He disregarded his own safety, stumbled out onto the sand, knelt beside the fallen figure.

The Indian was dead.

Jeb looked up, saw Monti clutching Gettler's rifle, struggling. Gettler hurled her away. His eyes looked wild, frightening.

"No!" screamed Monti. "It's Jeb!"

Gettler quieted, glared at Jeb.

He would've killed me, too!

Monti was sobbing hysterically.

If it hadn't been for her, Gettler would've killed me! Jeb looked down at the dead Indian. *This is my fault. I should've thought. Christ!*

A violent frustration welled up in Jeb. He lifted his head, looked across at the plane, at Gettler standing beside it, at Monti sitting in the sand recovering from her hysteria.

Where's David?

Then he saw the boy in the front seat of the plane, staring wide-eyed at the body on the sand. David's face radiated the vacuity of numbing fear.

Slowly, Jeb got to his feet, stepped around the Indian's body, crossed to Gettler. The violence trembled in every nerve and muscle of Jeb's body. He found it difficult to speak. "You just killed a friendly Indian!" he husked. "That Indian was ..."

"There's no such thing as a friendly one!" snarled Gettler.

"This one was helping to ..."

"Are there any more of them back there?" He gestured with the rifle.

"Some who ran away ... and this Indian's wife and child."

"You're just like Bannon!" snapped Gettler. "Take up with every stinking native in the brush!" He took three quick, uneven breaths, backed toward the shelter of the plane.

"There're no Jivaro here," said Jeb.

"They're all alike, I tell you!"

"The Jivaro are waiting for us two days downstream, Gettler."

"How d'you know?"

Jeb hooked a thumb toward the body on the sand. "He told me."

"Probably lying!"

"And maybe not."

"Two days," muttered Gettler. "Where?"

"Rapids."

Monti stumbled to her feet, glared at Gettler. "You utter beast!"

Gettler ignored her. "Rapids. That'll be the place they call 'the cut' ..."

"You trigger-happy madman!" shouted Monti. She brushed a strand of hair off her forehead. "I hope they ..."

"*You* wanted me to kill him!" snapped Gettler. "*You* thought it was an attack!"

"I thought you were jungle-savvy," said Jeb. "Can't you tell a Napo from a Jivaro?"

"They're all alike," said Gettler. "Treacherous, lying ..."

"And deadly when wronged," said Jeb.

Gettler stepped into the protection of the open door of the plane. "So fix this pontoon before some more of them show up!"

"We oughta just sit here and let them come and get you!" snarled Jeb.

The rifle centered on Jeb's head. "Fix the pontoon."

Monti touched Jeb's arm. He shook her off.

"Kill me and you face them alone, Gettler!"

"They may blame all of us," said Monti.

"Fix the pontoon," repeated Gettler. "Don't make trouble or ..."

"You've made all the trouble I want for one day!" said Jeb.

A curious smile flitted across Gettler's mouth. "So do what I say." He frowned.

"First, you should know just what you've done," said Jeb.

"Yes?"

"The Jivaro witchmen have put the *death finger* on anyone who helps us. All of the river tribes'll hear how this Napo died. It'll convince them all the curse is real. Any who might've been inclined to ignore the curse and help us sure as hell won't ignore it now!"

"We don't need help from these treacherous bastards," growled Gettler. "Get busy on the float!"

Jeb returned to the sprawled body, recovered the fibers, vines and gum, carried them to the plane.

David slid down from the cabin. "Is that Indian dead, Mr. Logan?"

"Yes."

"The dead ones are the only safe ones," said Gettler. He climbed into the rear of the cabin, sat with the rifle across his knees.

Jeb found a rock, squatted by the damaged float, began pounding out the torn edges of the hole. It was slow work. Gum stuck to his hands and arms. Flies and sand accumulated on the gum.

The finished patch looked bulky—a thick scab of bark lashed with vines to the outboard edge of the pontoon. It dripped with sand-coated gum. Trapped insects buzzed in the sticky mess.

David collected sections of cane poles Jeb had cut.

"Put those behind the floats for rollers," said Jeb.

He took the machete, crossed to the jungle edge, cut four long cane poles, returned to the plane.

Monti wiped sand from her hands. "What're those?"

"To help guide us after we get going."

She looked down at the pontoon. "Think that'll hold?"

"It should." He found a section of green leaf, wiped at the mess on his hands and arms, took up one of the poles.

"The rollers are ready!" called David.

"Get aboard," said Jeb. "You, too, Monti."

"What about him?" she asked. She looked at the body on the sand. "It seems so callous to ... well just leave him there."

Gettler leaned out the door. "What's the delay?"

"There's nothing we can do," said Jeb. "Get aboard."

"Shouldn't I stay out here and help?" asked David.

Jeb looked at the plane. "Okay. You push on this side. It

shouldn't take much once we get it going on the rollers."

"Yes, sir."

Monti climbed into the plane.

Abruptly, Gettler said, "Wait!"

Jeb straightened. "Why?"

"What if it sinks?"

"You can wade ashore and build us a canoe," said Jeb. "Sit down." He turned to the boy. "Okay, David. On the count of three. Rock it onto the rollers."

David bent to the float. "I'm ready."

"One ... two ... THREE!"

The plane rocked back, moved about six inches.

"Wouldn't it be easier if we got out?" asked Monti.

"No." Jeb wiped his forehead, straightened his flying cap. "Again, David. One ... two ... THREE!"

The pontoons grated on sand. Slowly, the plane rocked back. It tipped down, gathered speed, splashed into the river.

Jeb caught the grapnel line, snubbed the plane up short. "Climb aboard, David."

The boy jumped onto the float, made his way into the cabin. Jeb waded out to the float, studied it. He tapped the metal, rocked the plane.

"It is holding?" asked Monti.

"Seems to be." Jeb unscrewed the cap on top of the float, felt inside. "It's dry." He replaced the cap.

"Aren't we going to bury that dead man?" asked David.

"Hush." said Monti.

"Let the ants do it," said Gettler.

"Fine thanks for warning us about the Jivaro!" said Jeb. And he thought: *When'll I get a chance to tell Monti that our suspicions were right? That Gettler murdered her husband? And maybe it'd be better if she didn't know.*

"Shove off," said Gettler.

Jeb collected the cane poles, wedged them against a strut, brought up the grapnel and put it on the left float. The current tugged at the plane. He leaped aboard, pushed off with one of the poles.

A line of vultures began settling to the beach behind them. Jeb heard the wings, looked back, shuddered. The vultures hopped toward the coppery body at the jungle edge. A bend in the river shut off the scene.

Jeb looked to the west. The sun hung low above the peaks.

"Another hour to sunset," said Jeb. He felt suddenly weak, drained by his exertions. It seemed to take his last energy to climb into the cabin.

Alto cirrus clouds hung above the peaks. Sunset poured color through them until they became red waves in a sea of sky.

The plane swept around a sickle-shaped bend, drifted almost due north along a widening channel. Along the eastern shore the water became silver tinted with mauve, metallic and luminous.

A deep booming of jungle doves sounded from the hills.

Dusk siphoned in its flow of tiny insects. The whine of cicadas increased in the still air.

The sun dipped behind the peaks, rimmed them with fire that was quickly extinguished. The nightly patrol of bats flickered overhead—swooping and soaring. Noises of the evening birds gave way to night sounds; far off a jaguar's coughing growl (followed by sudden stillness), the rustlings and quiverings, an unseen splash nearby.

An amber moon climbed over the jungle. The plane drifted down the moon path like a giant dragonfly crouched on the water. A great skeleton butterfly fluttered across the pale light, waved the filigree of its transparent wings briefly on the plane's cowl, departed.

Gettler mumbled and growled to himself. Once he raised his voice: "Kill them! Kill them all!"

He felt dizzy, as though he were many persons at once. The river reminded him of a barge trip he had taken on the Rhine when he was twenty. He looked to the fuzzy spread of moonlit hills for the familiar outline of castles.

Part of him seemed to cling to the fabric in the ceiling of the plane's cabin—peering down. This part of him whispered in his mind: *"Tell them what's wrong with you before it's too late!"*

Monti retreated into her corner. She could see the moon through the overhead curve of windshield. It was an alien moon—like none she had ever seen. The earth-lighted circle looked far too big, the melon slice of sun reflection far too bright. It was a Hollywood moon: unreal. It frightened her, made her feel small—dwindling away to nothing, a tiny spark lost in the infinity of the universe.

She pressed her eyes tightly closed.

I mustn't think like that or I'll go crazy! God! When will they find us?

David curled into his corner behind Jeb, studied the shadowy outline that was Gettler. The Aussie hat had been thrown back. Gettler's head bulked thickly above the craggy nose and beard-softened curve of his chin.

He's crazy, thought David. *I should be afraid of him, but I'm not. I feel sorry for him.* An adult thought burst into the child mind: *I remind him of someone. That's why he wants me to like him.*

"Killers!" muttered Gettler.

"Was that Indian one of the ones who killed my dad?" asked David.

"No," said Jeb.

"How d'you know?" roared Gettler. "You don't know! They're all killers!"

Silence pressurized the cabin. Jeb heard the cautious sound of Monti's controlled breathing. Slowly, the pressure bled away.

David announced: "I'm going to sleep." He twisted into a new position. His foot bumped Jeb's back through the seat.

"Gettler?" said Jeb.

A grunt answered him.

"You know the jungle, Gettler," said Jeb. "What'll the Jivaro do? We should get ready for them."

Gettler's voice surprised him by coming out calm and remote. "If they're at 'the cut' that's a canyon. They may drop boulders ... or they could run a net across the river to spill us into the rapids."

"That last's what I'm afraid of," said Jeb.

"Are you sure this plane won't fly?" asked Monti.

"Even if I got it off, it wouldn't stay up," said Jeb. "The motor's sure to overheat."

"I hope we don't meet them in the dark," she said.

Gettler chuckled softly. "The things we meet in the dark are always worse, eh?"

Jeb found himself puzzled by Gettler's tone. It was though the man had been transformed into a pleasant stranger—someone entirely different from the wild-eyed killer. A word he only half understood popped into Jeb's mind: schizophrenia—split personality.

"We're always more afraid of what we can't see or understand," said Gettler.

Again he chuckled. By its very difference and tone of sanity the sound was frightening.

Monti sat up straight beside Jeb.

Gettler said: "I keep thinking of Cardinal Newman's 'terrible aboriginal calamity.' That's what we're headed for down there: a meeting with original sin."

David stirred, sat up. "I can't get to sleep."

"I keep listening for a plane," said Monti. "Oh God! When will they come?"

"Keep your fingers crossed," said Jeb.

"What were you talking about, Mr. Gettler?" asked David. "What calamity?"

"I've never prayed so hard for anything in my life," said Monti.

"Well, son," said Gettler, "you've asked a philosophical question about good and evil—original sin. That was the cardinal's calamity."

"What's philosophy?" asked David.

"That's the dreamers interpreting their dream," murmured Gettler.

Monti leaned toward Jeb. "What's he rattling on about?"

Jeb shrugged.

"Good and evil are part of the dream," said Gettler.

"Two days," muttered Jeb. "Jesus! If we only had the radio!"

"Good and evil are man-made opposites," said Gettler.

David shut out the murmurous conversation in the front seats, listened to Gettler. The words falling from the man's lips seemed to have special meaning—something that would suddenly fill out and answer every uncertainty.

"Men anchor their lives between good and evil," said Gettler. "They try that way to stop all motion—to end the flow of life toward death—keep everything as it is. They don't realize that when everything stops: that's death."

Monti began humming softly.

"Everything in the universe flows like this river," said Gettler. "Everything changes constantly from one form into another. Nothing can stop this—nothing should stop it: no anchor, no philosophy, no man or god."

Monti's humming grew louder.

"Everything flows like a river," said Gettler. "Nothing is static, nothing's ever twice the same. Not good! Not evil! Even the Ten Commandments have their exceptions."

"You mean the Bible?" asked David.

Gettler gripped David's arm. "The good-and-evil book! The only thing a man has is his own ability to make decisions from moment to moment. Good and evil can only confuse him."

Jeb heard this last, thought: *What's he feeding David?*

Monti said: "Would it be better to anchor and wait for rescue?"

"We can't be sure of rescue," said Jeb. "We have to take

our chances on the river. We have to!"

"Never let yourself be submerged in the herd," said Gettler. His grip on David's arm became painful. "You do and you have to accept the herd's judgments. Be your own judge. Don't lose any sleep over what the herd thinks!" He relaxed his grip.

Did that Indian tell me the truth? wondered Jeb. *Yes. Christ! That's a killer back there! I have to keep reminding myself.*

Jeb turned, glanced back into the dark shadows.

Just go to sleep, Gettler. Let me get my hands on that revolver!

"Are you sure we shouldn't wait?" asked Monti. "Somebody's sure to miss us."

"Who?"

"The people at Ramona."

"They won't even begin to ask questions for another week."

"But what about the army when that radio station doesn't answer?"

"They may think it's a mechanical failure. Happens all the time. And what's to connect us with the failure of a radio station?'

"But we know they're downstream waiting for us!" She rubbed at her forehead. "They're going to try and kill us!"

"That's the problem," said Jeb. "The river's carrying us toward both danger and safety."

"Somebody's sure to come," she said.

"Just like waiting for the Second Coming!" said Gettler.

"Take it easy, Monti," said Jeb. "We'll fight our way through all right."

But he didn't feel that confident.

Monti looked at Jeb. His angular features looked hard, almost metallic in the reflected moon glow. *He's so strong,* she thought. *And I'm so tired ...* She lowered her head onto Jeb's lap like a small child seeking comfort, burrowed her left hand behind him, under his shirt, caressed his back.

Jeb stroked her hair. A fluttering aliveness pulsed within him ... the delicate beginning movements of desire. He tried to force his attention onto the night around them, the dangers ahead.

Monti's hand became quiet against his back, her breathing deepened. She relaxed into sleep.

She's like a little girl, he thought.

The plane drifted down a lane of glittering water. A cold glow of fireflies danced in the dark shadows of the forest. A sense of eternal corruption came from the jungle.

It pressed in upon the tenuous moon path.

Gettler's words came back to Jeb: *"Everything in the universe flows like a river."*

And he thought, *Maybe Gettler's right. I exist through a flowing of moments ... alive only in my own memory. Everything's changing. You can't say something eternally absolute at this moment and have it be true at the next heartbeat ...*

Introspection came hard to Jeb and brought feelings of anxiety that moved toward terror.

Time is on the jungle's side, he thought. And he experienced an abrupt feeling of detachment, as though he had suddenly come upon himself like a reflection in a mirror ... or heard about himself like an echo ... and he was both the original voice and the echo—the substance and the reflection.

Jeb felt that he existed at this moment in an ultimate awakening where everything around him unfolded before an inner mind—and the only part of himself that he knew became a memory, like a perfume lingering behind a strange passion. He saw *everything* as related to totality, dancing and weaving in a thin plane of reality like a fabric coming off an endless loom.

Reality and illusion were through the same cloth.

And he knew that he would never again be the same.

It was a feverish sensation accompanied by an inner

trembling.

The world around Jeb—the darkly flowing jungle—began to intrude. A wind arose, gave the plane an uneasy shifting motion. A curious damp nutrient in the wind fed Jeb's awareness. He looked up. The stars were sharp points of light that stabbed through rushing clouds.

Something flickered like a firefly on the right bank.

And again. Red streamers of fire wavered in the forest: a bobbing, dancing lacery of light.

"Gettler!" hissed Jeb.

"Heh?"

"On the right bank."

"Torches!"

Monti sat up. "Wha's happening?"

"Torches along the right bank," whispered Jeb.

"How far away are they?" asked David.

"A hundred yards at least," said Gettler.

"Half that," said Jeb.

"Do they see us?" asked Monti.

"Can't miss us," said Jeb.

"What're they doing?" she asked.

"God knows."

Something thudded against a wing. Again. A pellet-rattling of taps sounded along the fuselage.

"Darts!" said Gettler. "Start the motor and get us the hell out of here!"

Jeb primed the engine, snapped on the ignition, pulled the starter. It caught on the second revolution, coughed, belched orange flame around the cowling, settled into its off-beat banging. The plane surged down the dark water. Jeb snapped on the wing lights. They punched two round holes out of the nights, caught up a grey fog of insects.

"Turn off that light!" roared Gettler.

"Can't!" shouted Jeb.

"Turn it off!"

"Shut up and leave me alone!"

They pounded around a slow bend into a wider stretch of water.

Jeb throttled back.

"I thought that Indian said two days downstream!" snarled Gettler.

"Those could've been Napos after revenge for the man you killed," said Jeb.

"Wrong shore!" snapped Gettler.

"You can't be sure."

Another bend. The river grew even wider. Jeb shut off the motor, slapped the light switch. They plunged into darkness, coasting slower and slower.

"Why're you stopping?" demanded Gettler.

"I'm not sure that patch will take this." He looked at the right shore. "They couldn't send a dart this far." Jeb turned. "Check that float patch, Gettler."

"Check it yourself!"

Jeb shrugged. "Excuse me, Monti." He opened her door, climbed across her, down to the float, removed the cap by feel, probed inside.

"How is it?" whispered Monti.

"So far so good."

He replaced the cap, climbed back into his seat.

"It's awful dark," whispered David.

"Going to rain," said Jeb.

"Are we likely to run into rapids at night?" asked Monti.

"Any time—day or night," said Jeb. "As long as we're just drifting we can hear them in time—I hope."

Jeb opened his door, slipped down to the pontoon. The fitful wind imparted a dipping-swaying motion to the plane. He gripped the strut, peered ahead, listened.

"What're you doing?" whispered Gettler.

"Looking for a place to anchor."

"Not yet!"

"It's getting too dark."

"We're too close to them! They'll ..."

"They'll expect us to drift all night. So we won't."

"Can't they still see us?" asked Monti.

"Can you see either shore?" asked Jeb.

"No."

A hissing sound intruded: the noise of the current soughing around an obstruction. Jeb saw a darker shadow against the blackness ahead. It drew nearer. There came the rhythmic lament of water against a broken limb.

Jeb freed the grapnel, tossed it into the dark shadow.

"What is it?" asked Gettler.

"A water soaked tree caught in shallows."

"Did you hit it with the anchor?"

"Yes."

Jeb held the line, felt the anchor catch, twist. The plane swung around downstream, snubbed up short at the end of the line. It began sawing back and forth in a slow, persistent pendulum.

"Where are we?" asked Monti.

Jeb climbed into the cabin, snicked his door shut. "Somewhere in midstream."

"I'm dying for a smoke," she said.

"No lights!" snapped Gettler.

"I know it!"

"I'll take the first watch," said Jeb. And he thought: *Maybe Gettler's tired enough to fall into a deep sleep. Let him do it just once! I'll have my gun back!*

Gettler turned uneasily. "I'm not sleepy."

Son-of-a-bitch! thought Jeb.

"You get some rest," said Gettler. "I'll watch."

If I argue he'll get suspicious, thought Jeb. *Well, let him get even more tired. I'll have a better chance.*

"Okay, Gettler."

Jeb leaned against his door. He still felt feverish, strangely weak and light headed. *I'd better take a pill in the morning.*

Sleep invaded his mind like a rolling fog.

The plane sawed back and forth ... back and forth.

Let him sleep, thought Gettler. *He's no danger to me when he's asleep. The boy can take the watch when I get tired.* He bent to peer at the luminous dial of his watch: eleven minutes to one.

Jeb awoke to rain sounds, and darkness slowly creeping into grey dawn. Light increased. Steel lines of the downpour slanted against the pale green jungle. It was a rain of monotonous violence. It thundered against the plane, pocked the river in countless tiny craters.

"This is the third day," said David. "I'm keeping count."

Monti looked out at the rain. "How long's this going to last?"

"Four or five months," said Gettler.

She sat upright. "Just like that ... like that out there?"

"More or less. There may be a few breaks at first ... and maybe not."

Jeb looked up at the clouds hovering low above the trees that lined the shores.

"How could they see us down here?" demanded Monti. "I mean from a rescue plane?"

"They couldn't," said Jeb. He looked at the riverbank, realized that he could actually see the water rising against the gnarled roots. "But that's not our first problem."

Abruptly, the tree snag that held their anchor shifted, bumped a few feet downstream.

"What's that?" demanded Monti.

"Our first problem," said Jeb. "This river's going to turn into a raging hell." He clambered out, pulled in the line, released the grapnel. Rain felt warm and fresh against his face. He stood on the end of the pontoon enjoying the freshness. Shoreline twisted across his vision: greenery dimmed to pastel by the torrent.

Jeb returned to the cabin feeling refreshed and hungry. "Let's try that fish line, Gettler. I feel lucky."

"I don't," said Gettler.

"What do we have for bait?" asked Jeb.

"Rotten lizard guts," said Gettler. "I wrapped them in an empty K-ration carton." He turned around, groped in the luggage compartment.

"Is that what's smelling up the cabin?" demanded Jeb.

Gettler handed him a reeking package.

Jeb nerved himself to bait the hook, tossed it into the mud yellow river. Dirty suds of foam swirled around the edges of the floats, were beaten flat by the rain when they strayed into the current.

Nothing struck the bait.

The morning wore on through slackening rain. A warm, misty feeling permeated the air. The mildew smell of the cabin grew stronger.

Clouds of gunmetal cotton lifted until they brushed the hilltops above the river. A beaded drapery of raindrops hung on every tree along the shores.

Jeb began to pull in his fish line to examine the bait, suddenly jerked the line, hauled it in frantically.

"Fish!" he shouted.

He lifted it out of the muddy current—a blue and silver flat-nosed catfish that flopped violently on the floor of the cabin where Jeb threw it.

Gettler dispatched the fish with a knife. "Clean it out there," he said. "I'll set up the pellet stove on the back of your seat to cook it."

The fish tasted flat and faintly muddy, but they ate every morsel and wished for more.

A slack, barely moving stretch of river held them. It began to get warmer. Bees hummed about the plane, departed. The rain became an occasional random drop from the rising clouds.

Jeb climbed into the cabin, leaned back, drowsed.

A buzzing insect sound invaded his torpor. He brushed at his face, suddenly snapped upright: wide awake.

"What's wrong?" asked Monti. "You ..."

"Quiet!" He held up his hand, cocked his head to one side.

Gettler leaned over the back of Jeb's seat. "Plane?"

"Yes, by God!"

Jeb lowered himself to the pontoon.

"Could it be more rapids?" asked Monti. "It sounds ..."

"Gettler!" snapped Jeb. "In that slotted pocket under your seat—see if there's a rocket flare!"

Gettler fumbled in the pocket. "They'd never see it."

David scrambled out of the way.

"Are you sure it's a plane?" demanded Monti.

"Sounds like one of the government amphibians from Quito," said Jeb.

Gettler handed out a thin red tube about a foot long. "This it?"

Jeb grabbed it. "Yes!" He tore at the end wrapping.

"Are they hunting for us?" asked Monti. "Will they come down along the river?"

"No!" Jeb threw away the end wrapping. "Match? For Christ's sake, somebody give me some fire!"

Monti brought out her cigarette lighter, leaned out, flicked it. Flame mounted on the third spin of the wheel. Jeb held a tiny grey fuse to the fire, saw it sputter, whirled away and scrambled out of the shelter of the wing. He steadied himself against the cowling, pointed the flare toward the clouds.

The motor sound grew louder: a pulsing roar.

"Phu-u-u-ust!"

A round red fireball hissed upward through the clouds. And another ... another. Six in all.

"Please, God," whispered Monti. "Please!"

The pulsating counterpoint of twin engines echoed along the hills. Jeb turned his head to follow the path of the unseen plane. The sound grew fainter upstream, blended with the soft river noises.

"They didn't see it," said Gettler.

"Clouds are too thick," said Jeb.

"Won't they come down and look for us?" pleaded Monti.

"They're coming to investigate why the army radio doesn't answer," said Jeb. "And they won't be able to make it until that overcast burns off."

"Will it?" she asked. "I mean burn off? Will it?"

"Who knows?" Jeb stared up at the clouds. "It could clear upstream, stay cloudy here—or vice versa."

"Won't they miss us?" she asked.

"How? They believe at Ramona that you were coming for a week or more. My boys at Milagro know about the gas problem. They could figure I stayed over to bring you out."

Monti wet her lips with her tongue, brushed a wisp of red hair back from her brows. "If that search plane gets down on the river, and sees the ruin of the army post, won't they ..."

"They may figure we got ours, too," said Jeb. "Or they may not even think about us at all."

"But they know about the rancho up there and ..."

"I don't think they're going to get down through that overcast," said Jeb.

"Then won't they send a launch?" she demanded.

"Maybe."

"They'll search for us," she said. "I know they will. They'll miss me, and they'll ..."

"This is kind of pointless," said Jeb. "The rainy season's started. There may be speculation that we crashed somewhere—or that the Jivaro got us—but the weather won't permit an aerial search."

She shook her head. "Doesn't the government care if ..."

"This is another country," said Jeb. He remembered his thought of the preceding night. "And time's on the jungle's side."

Monti straightened, stared upstream at the cloud-capped hills. "Jeb, tell me the truth: What're our chances?"

"I don't know. If we don't lose the plane and get stranded on ..."

"I still say we'd be better off in a dugout," said Gettler.

"How'd you like to've been in an open dugout last night when the darts started flying?" asked Jeb. He patted the fuselage. "She may not be much, but she'll stop darts."

Monti said: "Jeb, don't let them capture me. I mean ..." She swallowed. "Don't let them take me alive."

"Oh, stop being so damn melodramatic!" Jeb cleared his throat.

"Another hundred and fifty miles tells the tale," said Gettler. "Then we hit Zaparo country."

"If we get through that ambush downstream," said Jeb.

"That stupid Indian was lying!"

"Why would he lie? And what the hell difference will it make when we reach Zaparo country? They're scared witless of the Jivaro! Sure! And don't forget the curse!"

"Arrrrrgh!" said Gettler. He opened the right hand door, spat over the side, sat back.

"Do they torture?" asked Monti.

"Shut up!" snarled Gettler.

Jeb pointed at the door beside Monti. "Keep yourself busy and you won't have so much time to worry. You can start by getting down and checking that pontoon to see if our patch is leaking. You saw how David did it."

"I'll do it," said David.

"Let me," said Monti. "He's right."

She opened her door, slid down to the pontoon. Presently she straightened. "It's dry."

"Good. Make sure the cap's put back tight."

"Can I fish for awhile?" asked David.

"Go ahead," said Jeb. "Drop the line out that door on your side." He turned to Gettler. "Were there any more flares in that pocket?"

"No."

"Sonofabitch!"

"Were there more?" asked Monti.

"Yes. They were probably pilfered to celebrate

somebody's saint's day." Jeb turned away, stared downstream.

"I think I hear rapids," said David.

Jeb cocked his head. "No." He looked back upstream. "It's that plane coming back."

"Maybe they saw the flare!" said Monti.

"No. They're just going home. And they haven't had time to land upstream."

"Have they been all the way to the army post already?" she asked.

"Sure."

"But we've been two days on ..."

"Three days," said Jeb.

"That's what I meant. It couldn't ..."

"We made it that fast," said Jeb.

Monti sat back.

The returning plane passed to the east of them. Its sounds disappeared.

Monti began to laugh almost hysterically.

"Stop that!" said Jeb.

She shook her head. "I flew over this jungle without understanding it. And there's the story of my life: I flew over everything without understanding anything."

A rock escarpment loomed downstream at a bend in the river. The black outline of it stood out sharply in the rain-cleared air.

"Lava rock," said Jeb.

"I'm not getting any bites on this fish line," said David.

"Maybe the bait's gone," said Jeb. "Take a look."

David coiled in the line, held up an empty hook.

"Knock it off for awhile," said Jeb. "The river's too muddy."

"I thought I'd at least catch a piranha," said David. He wound the line on its stick.

"If you fell in they'd have you in a minute," said Gettler. "But they're never around when you want them."

The plane drifted closer to the lava escarpment. Jeb stared at it. Clouds almost touched the rock. They lowered across the ebony face as he watched.

"You see something up there?" asked Gettler.

"I dunno. Did you?"

"Something moved, but the clouds covered it."

"Could this be the place?" asked Monti. "I mean where that Indian said the ambush was?"

"I don't think so," said Jeb.

"Well, what moved?" she asked.

"Probably a tree," said Jeb.

"Or Jivaro keeping track of us," said Gettler.

"The river's too wide along here for an ambush," said Jeb.

The yelping cry of a toucan sounded from the jungle on their left.

"What was that?" demanded Monti.

Jeb told her.

"I noticed that all the birds went away when it began to rain," said David.

"But the bugs didn't," said Monti. She scratched at a row of welts on her arms. "Don't they ever leave?"

Jeb glanced around, experienced a feeling of surprise when he saw that he had been ignoring a cloud of mosquitoes that drifted with the plane.

"You'll get used to them," he said. "I hadn't even noticed them until you mentioned it."

Monti shuddered. "How can you get used to bugs?"

Gettler smiled to himself. He had been watching the mosquitoes. Their droning accompanied every movement of the plane—and they increased as the day wore on. Gettler studied the sound. The incessant humming seemed to come sometimes from inside his skull—echoing and throbbing.

One mosquito for every memory out of my past, he thought. *The swarming presence of the dead. Noisy ghosts.*

The cloud-filtered sun settled toward the hills. Darkness

built up its hold on the river. Still a gauze curtain or mosquitoes hid the banks.

Then the clouds parted briefly in the west, and they saw the sky like a sheet of burnished turquoise that drifted swiftly into yellow, then a deep wine color as red as a bishop's cloak. And the river surface became black and oily looking.

There came the soft muttering of wings as a flock of small birds fled over them in the gathering night.

Boiling clouds surged back across the red hem of sunset. They were dirty grey clouds, shading to black. A jagged fire plume of lightning etched itself against the black sky.

And the rain took up its endless stammering on the cabin top.

The group sat in the airplane cabin, secretively separate with their common fear.

Jeb groped on the floor, found the flashlight, probed the rain-crystal darkness.

"What're you doing?" demanded Gettler.

"Looking for a place to tie up tonight."

"Won't the Indians see the light?" asked Monti.

"They're huddled in their huts tonight," said Jeb. "What's that?"

"Looks like an island," said Gettler. "The damn rain reflects the light so it's hard to see."

A misty, grey-green mounding appeared to drift toward them while they remained motionless.

"It's an island," said Jeb. "See? There's current on the other side."

A tangle of logs, darkly wet and dripping, came into the flashlight's beam. Jeb loosed the grapnel, tossed it into the logs. There came the "chunk" of metal striking wood. He felt the grapnel bite into something, snapped off the light. The plane swung around into an eddy, hissed through reed grass, stopped.

A din of frogs arose around them: creaking, chirruping,

croaking. The rain seemed to quicken its pace—subduing all other sounds.

Not even the faintest glow of moonlight penetrated the clouds. The four humans existed in a world of beating rain suspended between the frog sounds and the faint wash of the river beneath them.

"Don't anybody talk about food," said Jeb. He tightened his belt.

"God, no," said Monti.

"We'll have to make a real effort at hunting tomorrow," said Jeb.

"While we're being hunted," said Gettler.

Monti began to shiver. "I'm ... afraid ..." she quavered.

Gettler cleared his throat. "Sorry I frightened you." And again his voice was the voice of a stranger with the soft and strangely frightening tone of sanity. "You started to tell us about the movie world the other night. Maybe it'd help if you talked."

"What's there to tell about a job?" She sounded petulant.

"Tell us about the easy life: smooth things to feel all around you—never any rotten smells or sweaty, sticky clothes against your skin ..."

"Where'd you ever hear that fairy story?" she asked.

"The movies I've seen all seem so clean and ..."

"The audience just sees the polished surface on the product," she said. "They should get a look at the strain and sweat." She sighed. "Sometimes the lights are so hot you think you're actually melting. I've worked one whole solid day just smoothing out one phrase in a new song ... or getting one scene right." Her voice became almost harsh: "Huh! No sweaty clothes!"

Gettler said, " But aren't there times when ..."

"Oh, dry up!" she snapped. Then: "I'm sorry. It's just that everything seems so hopeless tonight."

Silence enclosed them.

Monti began to hum, and the throaty voice lifted softly in

minor key:

"Sometimes ah feel like a motherless chile ... Sometimes ah feel like a motherless chile ..."

The beat of the rain carried the rhythm: an endless falling of tears.

"... a lo-o-o-ong wa-a-ay from home."

She broke off with the curious unfinished lilting that was her trademark.

Gettler took a deep breath like the beginning of a sob.

"You are truly an artist," he whispered.

"No." She shook her head. "I've just got a good setting and the right mood music."

"Unhappiness," said Gettler. "It can be beautiful, too. Curious. I never thought of that before."

"That's what we like about the soul!" quipped Monti.

"Stop that!" said Gettler. "You're trying to hide how you feel."

"That's what my psychoanalyst always said," she agreed.

"I don't care who knows how I feel," he said. "You know what your song says to me? It says I was born alone ... that I had to do it for myself. And I'll die alone ... for myself. Nothing can subtract from loneliness."

"It's just association," said Monti. "Negro music equals Negro spirituals equals God equals the hereafter equals ... What does it equal?"

"I'm not very religious," said Jeb. "So I don't know."

"There's God-consciousness in every song the Negroes ever created," said Gettler. "Even the jazz."

"Well, I'd rather sing a spiritual than go to church, all right," said Monti. She sniffed.

"God probably appreciates your singing more than your church attendance anyway," said Jeb. "I know I do."

"Next thing we'll be holding a prayer meeting," said Monti. "Come to Jesus!"

"Nothing like having someone after your head to make you feel religious," said Jeb. "That I agree."

Gettler snorted. "Thou hast being, God!" And his voice had recovered all of its insane wildness. "The universe is God's mistake!"

David stared into the darkness that spouted this wild voice. He felt suddenly alone, lost and numbed by terror.

"There wouldn't be any God without Man!" snarled Gettler. "God wouldn't know he existed if it weren't for Man!"

"I wish the rain would stop," said Monti.

Jeb sighed.

David tried to work saliva into his dry mouth. He found his voice: "Mr. Gettler, one of my teachers said that every human being has to look for his *own* religion." He swallowed. "Isn't that right?"

"If the rain would just stop long enough to let through a rescue plane," said Monti.

"You're not asking much," said Jeb. "Only a miracle."

"It's a problem in courage, son," murmured Gettler. "It doesn't take any courage to *look* for something. But sometimes it takes the courage of the greatest hero to *find* what you're looking for."

"I don't understand you," said David.

Gettler patted his arm. "You will, son. You will."

"But ..."

"Take your mother's song," said Gettler. "A person cries out against life because it's lonely, and because it's separated from whatever created it. But no matter how much you hate life, you love it too. And you know that if you find ... whatever It is ... you may lose the thing you love. You'll go back into the caldron for pieces to make something new."

"We've been on this river a century," said Monti.

"Will it hurt?" whispered David.

"Probably not," said Gettler.

Jeb wondered at the quietness in Gettler's voice.

Whenever he talks to David, thought Jeb.

A burst of rain hammered against the wings and cabin

top, faded into the familiar muttering.

"Mother?" said David.

"Yes?"

"You haven't sung *my* song for a long time."

A deep warmth suddenly filled Monti's voice. "So I haven't." She hummed softly, almost to herself, then:

"Come on along and listen to ... the lullaby of Broadway ..."

David sighed, settled back into the seat, let the music go all through him. "She used to sing me to sleep with that song," he whispered. "When I was just a little kid."

She sang softer and softer.

David's breathing deepened.

The song trembled away into silence.

I almost scared the poor kid, thought Gettler. He reviled himself: *And for no better reason than that I'm scared myself!*

Monti leaned against Jeb's shoulder. Her hair gave off a musk odor that filled his senses.

"Do you have a girlfriend back in Milagro, Jeb?" she asked.

He cleared his throat. A memory picture of Constancia Refugio became very vivid in his mind: lush figure in a tight bodice, doe-like brown eyes hiding a distant look of mysterious cunning, dark hair framing understated features—everything speaking of descent from a Moorish harem beauty.

"Well, do you?" asked Monti.

"I guess so."

"What's that mean?"

"There's a girl."

"What's she like?"

He shrugged.

"Is she beautiful?" persisted Monti.

"Yes."

"One of those dark, full-breasted types?"

"I guess you'd call her that."

"Have you had her to bed yet?"

Gettler snorted.

And Jeb thought: *Well, I guess the Bohemian types don't think anything of that kind of talk, but ...*

"A gentleman," said Monti. "He refuses to answer."

"She's the mayor's daughter," said Jeb. "A very old family in Ecuador."

"Do you want to marry her?"

Again, he shrugged.

Monti straightened. "Have you ever been married, Jeb?"

"When I was a punk just out of college. It ... it didn't turn out very well."

"Divorce?"

"Yes."

"Well, don't feel badly about it. Sometimes things just don't jell, and sometimes ..." She fell silent.

What was it with Roger? she asked herself. *I don't want to miss him. God knows everything wasn't sweetness and light between us.* She put her face in her hands. To hell with it! It's past! Done! Finished! To hell with it!

"They're very strict with their women down here," said Jeb. "It reminds you of mid-Victorian customs that ..."

"It's a wonderful night to dig up the past," said Monti. "Roll out the old dead bones! Line up the corpses!"

"You're tired," said Jeb. "Things'll look better in the morning."

"Now there's a fancy platitude for you," she said. "The countryside swarming with Indians trying to kill us, and you say ..."

"Stow it!" he snapped.

David stirred restlessly.

"So I tried to pat you on the head and tell you we'll do our best to get you through," said Jeb. "So I haven't learned how to use four-letter words in mixed company. Well, I'm doing my best to get us out of a mess!"

"Go ahead! Say it," she said. "You warned me against coming."

Gettler chuckled. "Is this the way you talked to your husband?"

"What's it to you?"

"I wondered what chased him down here," said Gettler.

Monti whirled, glared into the blackness. "What made an animal out of you, Gettler?"

"I was born that way. Same as every other animal."

"Weren't you ever human, even for a day or so?"

"I only pretended."

"For whom? A woman?"

"Shut up!"

"What happened? She give you the old heave-ho?"

Gettler's voice was like a tiger growl—deep and menacing: "Stop ... pushing ... me!"

"So you know what it is to lose someone!" she said.

"Shut up or I'll kill you!"

Jeb grabbed Monti's arm, pulled her around.

And now Gettler was certain about Monti's voice. Even in anger, it carried the same throaty earthy quality as Gerda's voice. It ...

He retreated in terror.

I mustn't think about Gerda!

Do I know what it is to lose someone?

Gettler felt that he swayed on a precipice of memory, that he might topple at any moment—head foremost into the jaws of chaos.

Gerda!

For one shattering instant he saw Gerda: dead and bloody—a naked, twisted corpse with the S.S. officer standing over her.

The muscles of his back quivered and tingled with the effort to reject the memory. He dug his fingernails into his cheeks, bit down on his lower lip to keep from crying out the way he had cried out beneath the lash.

"Animal," said Monti. She pulled away from Jeb's hand.

Gettler drew in a quavering breath, hissed: "Leave me alone! Leave me alone! Leave me alone!"

The darkness trembled with suppressed violence.

"I'm sorry," whispered Monti.

And she couldn't explain to herself why she'd said this. It was just that Gettler's voice carried such desperation.

But to Gettler it was Gerda's voice. He turned his face into the corner. Tears burned down his cheeks. He wrestled with an indigestible fragment of experience, seeing it for what it was: the incident of terror out of his past had broken off an entire layer of his being—and this insane fragment was his own enemy, the enemy of everyone.

Calmness took a long time returning to him, but then he felt cleansed, relaxed.

"The trouble," whispered Gettler, "is that everybody's afraid of everybody else. Cowardice makes us beasts."

And that's what killed you, Rog, he thought. *Cowardice. And a Nazi sadist with a whip. A man you never knew.*

"Maybe you're right," said Monti.

"I know I'm right," said Gettler. "Cowardice killed ..." He stopped, overcome by a feeling of confusion.

"Killed?" asked Monti. "Are you trying to tell me that Roger ..."

"Oh, no ... no," said Gettler.

That was too close! he thought. Cunning swelled in him tensed his nerves. His lower lip trembled uncontrollably.

"Roger was one of the bravest men I ever knew," he said. "Even when he was trapped."

"What were you saying then?" she asked.

"I was only going to say that cowardice kills the human half of us."

Jeb felt that he had missed part of the conversation. Monti had crowded Gettler almost to the point of ... The point of what? A confession that he killed Roger Bannon?

Cowardice? Trapped?

And Jeb suddenly recalled a scene out of his childhood. He had been David's age, just turned twelve. And with a new .22 rifle—a birthday rifle. Hunting quail along a fence line of his uncle's ranch in Eastern Oregon. Two of his uncle's mismatched brindle hounds had burst over a rise in pursuit of a scrawny bitch coyote. The coyote had seen the boy and swerved left only to be trapped in a fence corner.

In the corner, the animal that was a symbol of cowardice had turned and slashed the two dogs into bloody ribbons. And the child Jeb had watched in awe, allowing the coyote to escape.

Now—remembering that scene—Jeb felt that here encapsulated was a summary of all human problems: some people were hounds, and some were the pursued and the trapped.

"I will take the first watch," said Gettler.

Is he coyote or hound? Jeb asked himself. *He's hound. As long as he holds the guns. Maybe tonight we can reverse our roles ...*

But sleep overcame him: a were-slumber peopled by animal-faced women who hurled poisoned spears at him. Jeb ran and dodged the whole night through. And he awoke at dawn as stiff and cramped as if the dream has been reality.

The sonofabitch! He let me sleep again!

Jeb straightened.

A restless drapery of fog cloaked the river.

David leaned forward. "This is the fourth day," he whispered. "How far've we come?"

"Something over three hundred miles," said Jeb. He looked at the altimeter: eighteen hundred and fifty feet.

"Have the Indians followed us for three hundred miles?" asked David.

"Yes."

"Won't they ever give up?"

Jeb chuckled. "They'll give up."

Gettler straightened. "Let's get moving."

Jeb nodded, looked out at the shrouded island. The river had risen in the night to cover everything but the tips of bushes and the matchstick pile of logs that held the grapnel. Flooded remnants of bushes and grass bent downstream, vibrated with the current. The plane rested solidly against one of the logs.

"What're we waiting for?" asked Gettler.

"You're awful damn anxious to head for ..." Jeb nodded downstream. "Them."

"We can't run away from them," said Gettler.

"We're trapped, so we turn and fight," said Jeb. "Okay."

Monti stirred, rubbed her eyes. "I dreamed that ..." She looked up at the fog, the ghost-smoke along the island. "A plane came in my dream."

Jeb opened his door, slipped down to the float, wrenched the grapnel out of its log, pushed off. The current seized the plane. The river held a new feeling of power, a swifter flow.

"When did the rain stop?" asked Monti.

"Just before dawn," said David.

"Will it clear today?" asked Monti. She looked up at the platinum-colored sky.

Jeb hung the grapnel on the strut, coiled the line. " I dunno. What do you think, Gettler?"

"Maybe."

"If it clears will a plane come and get us?" asked David.

"Quien sabe?" said Jeb.

"What's that mean?" asked David.

"Who knows?" said Jeb. "That's what it means."

He tightened his belt another notch, found the fish line, baited the hook with a damp beetle he caught resting on the strut.

"I'm hungry," said David.

Jeb tossed the hook into water that was dirty brown, turgid and roiling. The thought of a fish made him tremble: a fat, juicy, wriggling fish ...

Flooded banks rushed past them, with the jungle beyond

growing clearer as the fog lifted. The river lapped at gnarled, obscene roots.

"Is it going to clear?" demanded Monti.

A fat drop of rain splashed against the windshield in front of her. Another and another.

"That answer your question?" asked Jeb.

Monti leaned back, closed her eyes. *Why? Oh, God! Why?* She thought about the Indians downstream. *Why can't we wait? Just tie up and wait?*

A barrage of rain whipped against the windshield. The plane turned, dipped and wavered.

Jeb tied the fish line to the strut, hastily re-rigged the sea anchor, threw it into the heaving current.

Another blast of wind and rain shook the plane. It slacked off, then came in stinging sheets that blotted all color from the banks, left the four humans drifting in a grey world. The wind died, but the rain still fell so thickly that it appeared to move about horizontally.

Jeb recovered the sea anchor, hung it on the strut.

There seemed no separation between wet and dry. Through the rain pall they saw a mottled granite shore pass silently like a surrealist backdrop.

Something tugged at the fish line.

Jeb jerked at the line.

"Have you got something?" asked Gettler.

"I dunno."

Another jerk.

Violence exploded on the other end of the line. Jeb held it grimly, gained two feet, lost one foot, gained another two feet.

Monti watched him. She wet her lips with her tongue.

"Careful," whispered Gettler. "Don't lose it."

"What's he got?" asked David.

Gettler shook his head.

A green shape almost three feet long broached beside the pontoon, spattered water over Jeb, and sounded. The line burned through his fingers.

"It's a *palinche*!" said Gettler.

"What's a *palinche*?" asked Monti. "Is it good to eat?"

"It's the native name for a kind of tarpon," said Gettler. "It's boney but edible."

Again, Jeb brought the fish alongside. It rolled. Abruptly, the water around the fish erupted to darting forms: piranha. The *palinche* threshed, tried to dive, but Jeb hoisted it out of the water. Two piranha fell from it. Others leaped vainly out of the river. One fell across the float, vibrated its tail against the metal, splashed back into the water.

Jeb dropped a ragged, tailless remnant of *palinche* onto the floor of the cabin. The piranha were gone before he could free the hook and drop it back into the water.

"They left us a little bit of it," said Gettler.

He set up the pellet stove.

"Aren't you going to try for piranha?" asked David.

"This is a meal," said Gettler. "Leave the little cannibals alone." He cut out a section of fish liver. "Save this for bait. We can make a good meal on what the bastards left us."

They ate the fish half raw, searching out every crumb.

"I never thought I'd like the taste of mud," said Monti.

"They do taste a little on the dirt side," said Jeb.

"Delicious," said Monti. "Catch another one."

Jeb took the fish line. "I'll ..."

The plane lurched. He slipped and clutched at the seat in front of him.

"What the hell?"

"Shallows," said Gettler. "We're out of the channel."

Jeb dropped the fish line onto the cabin floor, grabbed up a cane pole. Gettler swarmed down to the other float, took a pole.

The plane rocked and scraped, swung free in a new current.

Jeb looked around. The river appeared a mile wide, spotted with clumps of trees, floating islands of sedge, drifting logs.

"Do you want me to fish?" asked David.

"Leave it alone," said Jeb. "We're in trouble."

"What's wrong?" asked Monti.

"River's over its banks," said Gettler. "We're liable to get hung up."

Again the plane skidded across shallows.

Jeb felt every movement against the patched float as though a sore on his own body were being scraped. But the patch held.

They pushed and fended with the cane poles, found more deep water. The work with the poles became a steady thing, keeping the plane out of the random currents that coursed into the drowned jungle.

Once, they hung up tail first where the river poured between two trees. Another time, they bumped and thudded over a twisting, water-logged snag that paced them downstream—rolling and diving like a live thing.

And the rain poured endlessly out of a leaden sky. Birds and animals disappeared, but the insects remained, and even increased. They hovered under the wings, invaded the cabin.

Monti slapped at her arms, neck.

"These bugs are driving me crazy!"

"They're working in relays now, said Jeb. "There's a fresh crew out here under the wings waiting to get in at you."

"It's not funny!"

"Take it easy, Monti."

She pressed her palms against her face. "I hate them! I hate them!"

In the middle of the afternoon the rain slackened, fell off to an occasional plopping drop that spattered against the river, thudded on the plane. Pale avenues of blue opened in the clouds.

"It's clearing!" said Monti. "Oh, my God! It's clearing!"

"Don't get your hopes up," said Jeb.

They poled the plane onto a sodden mud bank by an

open savannah. Jeb stared across the rain-flattened grass at the oily green jungle wall some two hundred yards away.

"See anything?" asked Gettler.

"Something moved. Could've been a leaf shedding water ... or an animal ..."

"Or an Indian?"

"Dunno."

Jeb leaned against the fuselage, closed his eyes. "David."

"Yes, sir."

"Watch the jungle."

"Sure."

Gettler crawled into the cabin, sprawled in the rear seat. "We've got to find a canoe," he panted. "This thing's too heavy. It's a man-killer."

Monti leaned out the door above Jeb. "Do you hear something?" she asked.

He brought his attention out of his weariness, opened his eyes, concentrated on listening. Above the dripping aftermath of rain he heard a faint roaring like a distant wind through trees.

"Is it rapids?" asked Monti.

"Sounds like it."

Gettler aroused himself, leaned out the door on his side, cocked his head. "Yeah. Rapids." He sat back, began checking the rifle.

"Is this the place?" whispered Monti.

"What place?" asked David. "You mean ..."

"Hush!" she said.

"What do you think, Gettler?" asked Jeb.

"It's probably the place."

Monti stared at the jungle. "Jeb!" she hissed.

"Huh?"

"I saw something move ... over by those trees."

They focused their attention on the jungle.

"What'd it look like?" asked Gettler.

"Just movement. I couldn't see what it was."

"We'd better shove off," said Jeb. "Gettler, come down and hold us with a pole until I get the motor started."

"Wait," said Gettler. He looked downstream.

"What for?" asked Jeb. "Time's on their side."

Gettler swallowed, shook his head. The immediacy of fear clogged his mind. Ahead, nauseous violence! The pendulum that ruled him hurtled far out into anger.

"Let 'em come!" He began to tremble. "I'll cut their guts out!"

"I can hold the plane," said Monti.

Jeb glanced at the jungle. "Okay." He clambered into the seat as Monti slid down to the opposite float.

At that moment, a gap opened in the clouds. Sunshine hammered down upon them, set the world to steaming.

"The sun!" said Monti.

Jeb looked up at the blue avenue opening overhead.

Steam began to mist the river surface. It hovered in soft eiderdown patches whirling a few feet off the water. The interior of the plane began to fog. Vapor condensed on the windshield.

"A plane could see us now," said David.

Jeb nodded, glanced again at the jungle. Something moved the tall grass halfway to the green wall of trees.

"Monti," whispered Jeb. "Give a very gentle push and climb inside."

"But you haven't started the ..."

"Do as I say!"

She leaned against the pole.

Immediately, bronzed figures leaped from the grass, charged toward the plane. A current gripped the floats, turned the plane. Darts thudded into the fuselage.

Gettler screamed, slammed open the door beside Jeb, began firing the rifle. David pulled his mother in the other door.

"I'm all right!" she shouted.

Jeb pulled the starter. The engine coughed twice, died.

He pumped the primer, and again pulled the starter. And again the motor failed to start.

Gettler re-loaded the rifle.

A circling current whirled the plane around a bend. The sound of the rapids grew louder.

Again Jeb pulled the starter.

"Baby," he prayed. "Come on, baby. You can do it."

The motor suddenly caught, coughed and backfired, settled into its banging roar. Oil fumes began to choke the cabin.

"Close the doors!" shouted Jeb.

They were slammed.

"You okay, Monti?"

"Yes." She began to shake.

"Fasten your belts." He locked his with his left hand.

Another bend: and ahead—no more than a quarter of a mile—the flooding river plunged off between glassy walls of black rock. Water tumbled and leaped in crazy violence, like a wild thing trying to escape.

The plane skimmed across a glossy pool, and a slithering current shot them sideways—a hundred feet closer to the smooth black wall.

Spray filled the air.

And the vast pulsing roar of the chasm overcame all other sounds.

The plane shot over the brink of white foam.

Something geysered the water beside them. A staccato rattling shook the right wing: an insect sound beneath the overpowering thunder of water.

All in one flickering moment, Jeb saw the quick violent motion of Indians along the rim of the canyon. A line of boulders thundered down the rock walls above the plane. And it was like a slow-motion movie. Everything stretched out ... everything except his own responses. He slammed his hand against the throttle. The motor banged and leaped as though it would break out of its mountings.

The plane slammed down against a curling wave, and a new current rushed them forward. River and straining motor combined. The little plane surged ahead in the plunging current ... and they were airborne!

Jeb fought the controls in the raging air of the canyon. In three pulsing seconds they were out of it, and thundering over a line of trees ... then back across the river channel. Another tree-spiked hill shot beneath them, and a long straight avenue of river opened out ahead. It looked like turbulent brown oil.

He became conscious of Gettler pounding his shoulder.

"Go, man! Look at us go!"

Monti was crying and laughing beside him.

"We made it!" she shouted. "Oh, thank God! We made it!"

But the controls felt heavy under Jeb's hands. He saw downstream a great bend in the river—and lowering beyond that a wide, island-broken lake of flooded land. He eased back on the wheel, trying to gain more altitude. The plane began to stagger at the edge of stalling. He tipped the nose back down, inches below level flight, nursing it for distance.

"How long to Ramona?" shouted Monti.

Jeb shook his head. He glanced at the oil pressure gauge, the temperature. The temperature needle climbed inexorably toward the red zone. Oil pressure was falling away.

Gettler said: "Man! I thought you said this thing wouldn't fly!"

"It's not going to fly much longer," said Jeb.

The river curved off to the right through more drowned land. A thin furrow of turbulent water marked the main channel. Jeb followed it.

The temperature needle hovered on the edge of the red.

He became conscious of a heavy smell of gasoline, looked left, then right, and fought down a surge of terror. A multi-barbed spear, its tip glistening with shards of aluminum, protruded through the wing. Gasoline whipped away from the spear hole in a spray.

Jeb yanked back on the throttle, cut off the motor.

A whistling sound filled the cabin.

"What's wrong?" shouted Gettler.

Jeb pointed to the right, kept his attention on the river.

"Jesus!" whispered Gettler. "Skewered!"

The plane yawed sickeningly. Jeb fought the controls, brought the plane down in a splashing, rocking dead-stick landing.

An eddy turned the plane.

Monti spoke in a dried out voice: "How far'd we come?"

"Maybe ten miles," said Jeb. He looked at the spear tip jutting from the wing, glanced up at the gauge on the wing tank. It read empty. A last few drops of gasoline dripped from the spear, made rainbow circles on the muddy river.

"No smoking, Monti," said Jeb. He nodded towards the spear. "Right in the tank! The bastards!"

He looked at the gauge on the left wing tank: three quarters—twenty to twenty-five gallons.

"How much gas does that leave us?" asked Gettler.

Jeb told him, turned to David. "David, get down and check the patch on that float."

"Yes, sir." He crawled over Gettler's knees.

Monti held the door handle. "What about Indians?"

"We've left them behind," said Jeb.

"For a little while," muttered Gettler.

Monti opened her door. David clambered down to the float.

"Will they try again?" she asked.

"As soon as they discover that we're down," said Gettler. "And they'll be twice as mad because we escaped their ambush."

Jeb nodded.

David leaned in the door. "It's dry inside. I felt the patch under water, and it seems to be all right."

"Once that gum sets it holds like iron," said Jeb. "Okay,

David. Put the cap back on tight and get in."

David obeyed.

"What'll they try next?" whispered Monti.

"Your guess is as good as mine," said Jeb.

The current swept the plane across a flooded island.

"Here go the Volga boatmen," said Jeb. He opened his door, slid down to the pontoon. The cane pole was gone, lost in the wild flight through the canyon.

Gettler went out the other door, stood on the opposite pontoon. He placed the rifle on the floor in the rear with the butt ready at hand.

"Is your pole gone, too?" asked Jeb.

"Yes."

Gettler turned, stared at the spear tip.

Jeb reached for the machete under the front seat, hesitated. A rough, leaf-wrapped object about two inches long and an inch in diameter lay on the floor by the machete handle. Jeb glanced up. They were all looking at the spear. He palmed the object, slipped it into his pocket, slid out the machete.

"Look for a stand of *caña brava*," said Jeb.

"Right." Gettler nodded, studied the drowned shore.

Jeb took the machete in his left hand, slid his right into his pocket, fumbled off the leaf wrappings. The thing inside felt hard, glassy. He risked a glance at it in his cupped hand., jammed it quickly back into his pocket.

A raw emerald! And Christ! What a monster!

Jeb's mind began to fill out details of his suspicions.

There's why Bannon was murdered. They found a mine! Maybe one of the old Inca mines! And Gettler wants it all for himself!

The plane rounded another bend, twisted along an eddy toward a shallow mud bank. A line of cane trees screened the jungle beyond the mud.

Jeb knelt, paddled with the machete, saw Gettler crouch on the other pontoon, paddle with both hands.

A tongue of current pushed them onto the mud. The plane swung around with its tail pointing downstream. Jeb tossed the grapnel over the cowl, saw it catch in matted grass. He slid off the pontoon, slogged across to the canes.

Gettler stared at the jungle, one hand on the rifle butt.

Jeb cut four poles, passed them to Gettler, then stepped down and worked the spear out of the wing.

A short stream of gasoline flooded out behind the spear handle, dwindled to random droplets.

Behind two of the spear barbs a dark brown gum remained. Jeb touched it with his fingertip, tried to smell it, but was defeated by the overpowering odor of gasoline.

"Curare?" asked Gettler.

"Looks like it."

"The sonsofbitches!" snarled Gettler.

"Is it really deadly?" asked Mont.

"An alkaloid," said Gettler. "It paralyzes the muscles."

"Isn't there any cure?" she asked.

"A stuff called prostygmine helps," he said. "Any in your kit, Logan?"

"Four ampoules," said Jeb. He stared at the gummy substance on his finger, wiped it against his pants.

Monti shuddered.

"It kills by smothering," said Gettler. "So artificial respiration helps. The Indians force down big doses of salt water, and that seems to ..."

"Stop it!" she cried. "I don't want to hear about it!"

Jeb recovered the grapnel, sloshed back to his float, clambered aboard, scraped the mud from his shoes. He wedged the spear against the strut beside a spare cane pole.

"Why're you keeping that spear?" demanded Gettler. His eyes looked wary.

"It's a weapon," said Jeb. "We may need it."

"It's no good against a gun," said Gettler. He leaned into a cane pole, pushed the plane off the mud.

I read you, thought Jeb. And his mind returned to the

emerald in his pocket. *What happened if Gettler misses this rock?* He glanced across at the bulges in Gettler's jacket. *Maybe he has enough that he won't miss this one. Would he kill us if he finds out I have the emerald?*

Jeb pushed on his cane pole.

The plane moved toward mid-river. A whirling current caught the floats, swept the plane along on a brown tide.

Gettler rested.

What'll it take to turn him into a raging killer? Jeb asked himself.

The uneasy truce between them filled Jeb with a sudden fearful anxiety.

We've got to get the guns away from him!

The plane coursed around another bend.

Downstream, on a flat elevation behind the left bank, a squat grouping of thatched huts huddled behind a thorn wall. Two lines of fire-blackened stumps reached out toward the jungle like rows of rotten teeth. No canoes lined the river bank. Nothing moved in the huts.

A dog yapped in the jungle behind the village, and was silenced in mid-yelp.

"Jivaro village," said Jeb.

Gettler studied the scene. "Jivaro," he agreed.

"Where are they?" asked Monti.

"The fighting men are all back at the canyon," said Jeb.

"There'll be nothing but women, children and old men here," said Gettler.

"Where?" asked David.

"Hiding in the jungle back there."

The plane drifted closer, and the pungent odor of freshly ground cassava root wafted across Jeb's nose. It started a swift, stomach-gripping pang of hunger.

"Where're their canoes?" asked Monti.

"Some of them are hidden," said Gettler. "The others are upstream at the ambush."

They drifted past the village, watched the blank

doorways. A plantation of cassava and pineapple came in view below the village.

Gettler pointed, said: "Christ! Look at the pineapple!"

"Enough to last us a month," said Jeb.

"Don't I know it!" snapped Gettler. He lifted out the rifle with a sudden, violent anger, sent a bullet smashing into one of the huts. "That'll teach you! You dirty bastards!"

Jeb felt a quick affinity with the gesture.

"Why don't they come after us in their canoes?" asked David.

"They're vulnerable on the open river where we can outshoot them," said Jeb. "And as long as our motor holds out, we can out*run* them."

"But there're so many of them."

"They're not the kind to commit suicide," said Jeb.

David shook his head. "*They* have guns, too!"

"But they aren't very good with them," said Jeb. "It was a lucky fluke shot that got us."

"What if they snagged us with something?" demanded Monti. "A net or something?"

Gettler's voice arose in screaming fury: "Shut up!"

Monti fell silent.

Another bend hid the village.

Jeb could feel Gettler's hysteria dissipate. "How about checking that pontoon again?" he asked.

Gettler nodded, bent over the cap. Presently, he stood up, said: "Still dry."

"The sky's clear," said Monti. "Why doesn't a rescue plane come?"

"They probably don't know there's anybody to rescue," said Jeb. He pushed his cap back, wiped at his forehead. A sudden wave of nausea swept over him. The sun glare off the river hit him with what felt like an actual physical pressure. His head throbbed.

The plane floated through a great silence of trembling heat. A damp pressure of warmth and unnatural stillness enclosed Jeb. He shook his head against a momentary dizziness. And for a brief second he saw two shorelines, one above the other. It left him strangely out of breath. Another wave of dizziness passed over him. The river rose and fell nauseatingly before his eyes like waves of the sea.

Monti leaned out the door above him. “Jeb? Is something wrong? You look pale.”

“Just the heart,” he whispered.

“Maybe you’d better rest awhile.”

Gettler frowned across the cowling. “You sick, Logan?”

“The heat’s getting me.”

A brief compassion touched Gettler. “Then take a rest.”

And he snarled at himself: *Sure! Let me do all the work! I’m the strength by which we survive!*

The thought of resting caressed Jeb’s mind. He wedged the cane pole against the strut, dragged himself up into the seat. How good the seat back felt against his neck. An electric current of fatigue tingled through his body. The sensation drained away into sleep.

Monti studied Jeb’s face. A bristly matting of reddish beard softened the angular chin line. He breathed in a shallow, choppy rhythm. Perspiration dotted his forehead. He appeared almost drained of vitality.

She shook her head, turned away, and for the first time allowed herself to examine the possibility that there would be no rescue. The river stretched out endlessly in her mind: a track that carried them along curves of burning light and crawling darkness.

Her own words came back to her: *“I flew over this jungle without understanding it.”* And she thought: *That’s the way it’s been with all my yesterdays. I flew over everything and never looked down.*

The river and her own life underwent a subtle fusion in her thoughts. It was a decadent pilgrimage on a current that narrowed everything down to its one track. And she floated on it so carefully inert ... so static, willing everything under the surface to remain undisturbed. But something was going on beneath her frozen surface, and the currents that boiled up to tear at her consciousness filled her with a mind-clotting dread.

We can't possibly make it, she thought. *There's too much against us. We're going to die.*

She pressed the knuckles of her right hand against her teeth. The air around her throbbed with heat and fear. The river was a great serpent that would devour them.

Gettler leaned in, cleared his throat. "Is he sick?"

Monti shuddered, focused on the question. She put her hand on Jeb's forehead. "He feels feverish."

"Christ!"

Gettler withdrew, fended a log with the pole.

Let him die then! he thought. *One less to feed. And I'll have the woman to myself.* He glanced at Monti. There was a female grace to her even in the repose of fatigue. Jeb beside her was drained out, sprawling like a sack.

The plane drifted past a long tendril of muddy land.

Gettler poled away from it.

Jeb climbed out of a black pit into semi-awareness. Faint sounds intruded: a splashing, the soft creak of metal, an unintelligible whisper. He hung suspended in a place that had no shape or size, no orientation, no relationship to himself. There was an odor of mildew.

Damn plane's rotting apart under us!

Plane!

River!

He opened his eyes, and his first impression was of violent colors: sunset splashing across the peaks directly ahead. He lowered his gaze to the shoreline. It appeared blurred by grey fuzz.

I'm not awake yet.

Jeb shook his head. But the fuzz remained.

Can't be rain.

He looked to the right. Gettler stood on the pontoon, a

cane pole gripped loosely in his left hand. There was no fuzziness to Gettler's outline ... only the shore beyond.

"Are you awake?" asked Monti.

Jeb swallowed, spoke past a dry tongue: "Yes. How long have I been sleeping?"

"About three hours." She pressed her hand against his forehead. "You had a fever, but you feel okay now ... cooler."

Jeb straightened against a pulling of torpor. Still that feeling of clarity and detail about everything except the shoreline.

"Can't seem to make out the shore."

"Ashes," said Gettler. "Been falling all afternoon."

"Fire?"

"Volcano," said Gettler. "Caught a glimpse of it awhile ago." He looked across the cowling. "Sky's darker down there. Smoke."

"Is it dangerous?" asked Monti.

"The river doesn't go close enough to it," said Jeb. He looked back at David. "In the medicine box ... bottle of terramycin ... give me two pills."

David turned, dug behind the seat. Presently, he handed Jeb two tablets.

Jeb washed them down with a splash of warm water from the canvas bucket. He handed the bucket to Monti, leaned back, closed his eyes. *I can't get sick,* he thought. *I don't dare!*

He heard Monti drinking from the water bag, the gurgling slosh as she put the bag on the floor.

Gettler came along the float, leaned in the door. "Logan."

Jeb opened his eyes, turned his head without raising it from the seat back. "Yeah?"

"How far d'you figure we've come?"

Jeb closed his eyes. The question seemed to have no reference to reality. A heavy weight just behind his eyes obstructed thought. He struggled against the weight without success, shook his head.

"The high water's giving us a boost," said Gettler.

He reached out with the pole, fended off a snag that turned in the brown current beside them. A root lifted, rolled, submerged.

"How far've we come from that village?" asked Jeb.

"Maybe twenty-five miles."

It was an unintelligible figure ... a zero added to zero.

"Don't you have a map?" asked Gettler.

Map?

Jeb opened his eyes. "There's a home-made one with the others in the seat pocket behind Monti. Not accurate except for some of the altitudes I recorded myself."

"Over three hundred miles anyway," said Gettler.

"Won't the Indians from the village follow us by canoe?" asked Monti.

"They're with us," said Gettler. "Canoes or afoot."

Jeb sniffed at the odor of mildew in the plane, the clinging sourness of perspiration. *We're starving,* he thought. *Got to find food.*

"Will they come in the dark?" she asked.

"Probably not," said Jeb. "Superstitious. Can't see the *death finger* at night."

"What's the death finger?" asked David.

"They think death's not natural," said Gettler. "They think it comes only when a witch doctor points his finger at you."

Jeb opened his eyes. The forest skyline was a blurred ridge against the saffron hem of sunset. The sky overhead was tawny with falling ashes. Darkness washed over them with an abrupt feeling of purity, dissipated as a wind arose to swirl ashes into the cabin.

Monti coughed at the touch of the sulphurous dust.

The moon came up to draw a yellow trail along the water. A rush of wind shook the plane, hummed through the trees. The wind increased, and they saw the air become clearer, the moonlight more whitely brilliant. The light spilled out over the dark forest and onto the river.

Jeb found the flashlight, directed it against the shore.

"What're you doing?" demanded Gettler.

"Checking the height of the water. It's up again."

"More rain behind us," said Gettler.

Jeb turned off the light.

Moonlight flooded over them: a milky, impersonal glow. And an enormous silence enclosed the drifting plane. It stretched from the silvered peaks ahead into every jungle shadow, reaching out in all directions as far as the mind could imagine.

Jeb leaned forward, looked up. The stillness spread straight up to the stars. He found the Southern Cross on their left, looked back to the moon.

Gettler came in from the pontoon, sank heavily onto the seat, grunted.

Again the silence enfolded them.

"A place like this could drive you crazy," said Monti. "It makes you feel that ... you don't matter."

"We have to solve the food problem," said Gettler.

"Some kind of meat," said Jeb.

"But how can you hunt?" asked Monti. "Isn't it too dangerous ... out there? I mean ... with the Indians?"

"Just being here's dangerous," said Jeb.

"Just being *alive* is dangerous," said Gettler. And again it was as though darkness temporarily erased his madness. The low voice carried a weary note of calmness.

But Monti was caught up in a new fear: *What if something happened that left me alone here? If they go hunting* ... She could not even face the thought.

"The jungle terrifies me," she said.

"The unknown," murmured Gettler. "The jungle's the omnipresent unknown that ..."

"Oh, stop playing with words!" she snapped. "We know you're educated."

"That's the difference between us and the savages," said

Gettler.

"Gosh, the moon's bright," said David.

"We've tangled ourselves in a snare of words," said Gettler.

"He drives me nuts!" hissed Monti.

Jeb patted her arm.

"But the words are empty of everything except a kind of vacant ritual," said Gettler. "They're refined past all meaning. They're like the finest pastry flour: capable of making a sickly sweet civilized cookie with no nourishment."

"Words?" asked David.

"Yes, words."

"Won't anything shut him up?" whispered Monti.

"Then what are words?" asked David. "Shouldn't we talk?"

"Filling David full of that crap!" hissed Monti.

"Words are actually little tags like they put on your luggage when you travel," said Gettler. "They label something that's moving ... something that's changing. They mark a position on a circle. They tell you where it starts, and where it must return."

"Crap!" said Monti.

"Just another label," chuckled Gettler.

"Don't the Indians use words?" asked David.

"Yes, but they still know how to talk with their bodies. And they still read nature directly without man-made noise in the way."

"Do they really cut off your head?" asked David.

Gettler choked on a gasping breath.

Christ! I'm talking like damned-good Bannon! he thought.

A nerve twitched at the corner of Gettler's mouth. He chuckled: a cold sound. "See! It takes a child to cut through the sham. How simple the difference between savage and civilized: a matter of cutting off the head!"

"Will you shut up!" cried Monti. She pressed her hands

against her mouth, stared at the moon trail ahead.

"They kill us and take our heads," said Gettler. "They believe they subjugate our *spirits* that way. Do you ..."

"Please!" said Monti.

"Knock it off," said Jeb. "You're frightening Monti."

"But don't you see it?" demanded Gettler. "Don't you see the difference? The savage tries to conquer the spirits of the dead. Civilization tries to conquer the spirits of the living!"

"Knock it off, Gettler," said Jeb. "You're being morbid."

"I'm being a realist!" barked Gettler. "The world's not what our labels say it is! Nothing says what I am! Nor you!"

"Don't you believe in anything?" demanded Monti.

"I believe in myself!"

Again silence blotted up their voices.

The plane turned slowly in an eddy.

The sonofabitch, thought Jeb. *Scaring Monti. Mixing up that poor kid.*

"Do you understand what I said, David?" asked Gettler.

"I don't know, sir. You say things aren't what we call them. That's funny talk. I ..." He fell silent.

"Go ahead," said Gettler.

"Well ... what am I, then?"

"Ahhh," said Gettler. "What is the self? The eternal question."

"I'm more interested in where we're going to find food," snapped Monti.

"The female nourishes," said Gettler. "But David's question fits our present situation, too. Here we are—isolated, lost in the omnipresent unknown that I ..."

"Oh, for Christ's sake!" said Monti. She turned sideways, pressed her cheek against the seat back.

"Where's the flashlight?" asked Gettler.

"What do you want with it?" asked Jeb.

"I want to answer the boy's question. Give it here."

Jeb found the light, passed it back.

Gettler pressed the switch. Light stabbed the darkness.

"What am I doing, David?" asked Gettler.

"What am I doing, David?" mimicked Monti.

"You're shining the flashlight," said David.

"You're shining the flashlight," mimicked Monti.

Jeb pressed her arm for silence. Gettler's actions and words suddenly fascinated him. *A madman might just know!* he thought.

"See how the light reaches out there," said Gettler.

"Yes, sir."

"That's the self."

"You mean like that light shining there?"

"Yes. The self's a projection from something else. It has no other reality. The self's an image ... another symbol."

He turned off the light.

"Crap," said Monti. But she sounded defensive.

David spoke into the darkness: "Is God shining the light, Mr. Gettler?"

"Who knows?" said Gettler.

"Come to Jesus!" said Monti.

"Everyone strives for consciousness of God," said Gettler. "And do you know what frightens me? I'm afraid I'll see the hand on the light switch ... and it'll be my own hand."

The plane drifted in and out of moon shadows. A darker shadow suddenly swept across the river. Jeb looked up to see shreds of sky torn out of rushing clouds.

"It's getting cloudy," he said.

A silver-rimmed thunderhead erased the moon. They heard the wind stirring in the jungle. The plane rocked, turned. Again the moon appeared.

"We'd better tie up for the night," said Jeb. "That looks like an island ahead ... that dark place."

"The river's full of islands in the wet season," said Gettler.

Jeb opened his door, slid down to the pontoon. Gettler clambered down to the opposite pontoon. The plane drifted closer to the mound of darkness.

“Looks flooded,” said Gettler. He began poling toward the island as a current tugged them away.

Jeb readied the grapnel. His knees felt weak and trembling. He gripped the strut with his left hand. There came a soughing of water through bushes and grass. Jeb threw the grapnel into the shadows, felt it grab. The plane swung downstream, dragging and scratching through drowned bushes and grass, stirring up a fog of insects. Jeb ducked a reaching limb, prayed that the patched float would hold. He could see the darker shadows of the jungle shore close on the right. The other shore was farther away.

Jeb dragged himself back into the cabin, sprawled in the seat. The door remained open. He willed himself to pull it closed, and again sank back against the seat.

Gettler crawled into the rear, grunted as he settled himself comfortably.

“How’re you feeling, Jeb?” asked Monti.

“Weak as a kitten. I better take a couple more pills.”

She found the medicine, helped him with the water.

Gettler said: “I s’pose this means I’ll have to stand all the watches, too.”

David said: “I can ...”

“I’m feeling weak, but I’m wide awake,” said Jeb. “I slept all afternoon.”

Gettler sighed, a heavy sound filled with weariness.

He’s tired, thought Jeb. *He’ll probably sleep like a log, now that I’m too weak to jump him!* A sense of impotence surged through him.

Wind and current tugged at the plane, set up an uneasy rocking motion that stopped when the wind died.

“All right,” said Gettler. “Take the first watch, Logan, but I’ll sleep lightly. Remember that.” He turned, grunted.

“Shall I stay awake, too?” asked David.

“No need,” said Jeb.

“Go to sleep, David,” said Monti.

David leaned back, closed his eyes. *Why’s Gettler so*

afraid of everyone? he asked himself. *He lied to me about why he's holding onto all the guns.* David opened his eyes, looked toward Gettler. But without the moon there was only a vague darkness without details. *Should I try to get one of the guns? But what if he caught me again?* David's nose smarted at the memory of Gettler's blow.

Gettler turned restlessly.

What a funny man, thought David. And he recalled the whispered conversation between his mother and Jeb Logan—their suspicions about Gettler. *Aw, he wouldn't really kill a friend!* But another part of David's mind argued: *He's crazy, though. And he did kill that Indian Jeb said was helping us!*

David leaned forward, whispered: "Mother?"

Gettler snapped upright. "What're y'doing?"

"I just wondered what time it was," said David. He stared fearfully at the hulking shadow beside him.

"It's night time," said Gettler. "Go to sleep so you'll be alert when it comes time for you to stand watch."

"Try to sleep, David," said Monti.

David retreated into his corner, closed his eyes. *He sleeps too lightly! There's nothing I can do.*

Gettler settled back to his restless dozing.

David's breathing deepened. He sank into a nightmare that jerked at his muscles: a spectral Gettler chased him through a black jungle, crying: "Help me! Help me!" And each time the dream-David stopped, hideous laughter filled his head, bullets crashed around him. And again he ran, sobbing, panting. It went on without end.

Monti leaned toward Jeb, put her head in his lap.

I need a man, she thought. *I need his strength.* And she laughed silently at herself. *So I pick one who's burned out by fever!*

Jeb stroked her hair, almost a mindless reflex.

But there is strength in him, thought Monti. *Man means strength.* She lifted her left hand, caressed his neck.

Jeb's fingertips touched her cheek.

Sex is like a drug, she thought. *You should commune with your body ... and the sound drowns out everything fearful. Your bodies say the darkness isn't really there. Nothing can really hurt you. There's no such thing as death!*

She lifted her face, pulled his lips down to meet her own. Danger sweetened the kiss ... drew it out, long and clinging.

I haven't forgotten you, Roger, she thought. *This man's like the strong part of you I loved. And I need that now. Oh, God! How I need it!*

Desire pumped strength into Jeb. He crushed her against him. And their danger became an academic thing to him ... drawing far away into the warm night. He slipped his right hand beneath her shirt, caressed her back.

Monti found his hand, guided it up, pressed it against her breast.

Oh, God! if only we were alone! she thought.

Jeb kissed her neck, and his beard burned against her cheek, but she felt no pain. And again their lips clung.

Abruptly, a cold part of her mind leered up at her: *But you aren't alone! So you'd better stop while you can!*

She pulled her lips away, whispered in Jeb's ear: "They'll hear us." And even while she whispered she sensed her mind searching for words to deny reality, for excuses to prolong this moment.

Jeb's hand fumbled across her breast. She pulled his hand away, kissed it, clung to it while she straightened and retreated into her corner. Jeb tried to follow, but she held him with a hand against his chest.

"Please," she whispered. And then softer: "I'm sorry."

Jeb swallowed, tried to quiet the panting swiftness of his breath.

David—in his nightmare—thrashed convulsively behind them. Gettler mumbled, turned.

It was like an icy shower to Jeb. Reason returned. The night and its peril flooded through his senses. He drew back, sneered at himself. *Jesus Kee-rist! How'd I get sucked into that tornado?*

Monti reached out, found Jeb's hand, held it. He wanted to push her away, but couldn't.

Okay, so I want her, he told himself. *What's abnormal about that?*

Jeb turned the watch over to David at two a.m.

But even after that it was a long night for Jeb and Monti—their minds tormented by the dream that came from frustration.

Jeb awoke to the nervous voice of the jungle dawn. He listened to the twitterings and scrabblings, the sudden silences. His mind felt clear, tingling with awareness. Weakness still drenched his muscles, but it was weakness in retreat.

He straightened, looked out at the river, yellow with its burden of mud. The river in flood lost itself amidst vegetation on all sides, and there was no real shoreline. Jeb glanced upward. The night's clouds were gone. An opalescent mist hung just above the water.

The sun climbed over the hills, bleached all color from the rim of the eastern horizon. The mist burned away.

Jeb glanced at Monti asleep in her corner. Blue shadows darkened the skin below her eyelids. Her cheeks were sunken, pale.

David coughed.

Gettler rumbled: "We better get moving."

Monti awoke, rubbed her eyes, pushed the flame-colored hair away from her forehead. She caught Jeb's gaze upon her, and for a moment their eyes locked.

"Day number five," said David.

"How many more?" whispered Monti.

Jeb shook his head.

"Live them one at a time," said Gettler. "It's easier that way."

Jeb opened his door, slid down onto the float. His knees

felt rubbery from the fever, but his muscles obeyed his will.

Fungus blotches spread across the leaves of the drowned trees on the left. In the gloom beyond, Jeb discerned the fairy-lace foliage of a tree fern. He moved his attention to the right, pointed while trying to find his voice. A papaya drooped over the current, its limbs heavy with fruit.

"Papaya!" husked Gettler. He lowered himself out the door on the right, took up a pole.

Jeb loosed the grapnel from its bed in the flooded bushes.

They guided the plane across to the papaya, hunger lending a desperate strength to their muscles.

"Is it good to eat?" asked David.

"Yes," said Monti.

The plane buried its nose in bushes beneath the papaya. Gettler grabbed a vine, held it. Jeb climbed onto the cowling, passed the fruit down to Monti. Limbs freed of their burden snapped out of reach.

"That's all of it," said Jeb.

Gettler released the vines, pushed off. The current caught them.

Jeb slid down and into the cabin.

They gorged on papaya. The fruit eased their hunger pangs, but there was no real satisfaction in it.

"We still need meat," said Gettler. He studied the rushing shoreline.

A hissing eddy swirled them toward a wall of trees where yellow water foamed around submerged trunks. Jeb and Gettler scrambled down to the pontoons, fought the cane poles until the plane was back in the central current.

Again they drifted on open water—a wide, moving lake—but the swollen river stretched wild fingers out into the forest. They could only guess at the true channel, a precarious thread to civilization.

A stupor of heat settled over the plane as the sun climbed the sky. Heat shimmered off the river in coiling vibrations.

Every air current carried its torturing stream of insects.

Monti wrapped her face in the silver scarf, and huddled in the front seat. David leaned across the seat back above her, staring downstream with a glassy-eyed expression, as though his mind had ceased all motion in the heat.

Gettler sat on the right hand pontoon, cane pole across his lap, the rifle butt ready at hand on the cabin floor above him. The small eyes glittered with a fearful alertness from beneath the brim of the Aussie hat.

Jeb on the left pontoon leaned against the strut in the glittering metal shadow of the wing, stared at the passing shore.

Time's like this river, he thought. He felt the swelling pressure of this thought ... and he had the idea that somewhere he had dived into Time, and had become trapped in Time's current without the means to escape.

A half-drowned island split the flow ahead of them. Jeb and Gettler stirred to action, fought the plane into the left hand current. Their cane poles vibrated in the surging water. They came out below the island only to confront another division of the current. Now, they took the channel on the right, working with desperate speed as the river gained speed. They whirled past another island, rounded a sweeping bend. And the river widened, slowed.

But still vagrant currents poured off through walls of trees on every side.

Jeb saw the current ahead swelling across a submerged island: the waters pregnant with dipping bushes, grass and tangled flotsam. He leaned against the cane pole to change course, felt the blisters burning on his palms.

Then they were past the obstruction.

Jeb sighed with weariness.

Monti sat up, and suddenly spoke in a strange flat tone of fear: "Jeb ..."

He looked in at her. She was staring at the floor, every muscle frozen, her attention hypnotically fixed.

Even before Jeb lowered his eyes he knew what he would see. There was an electric message in Monti's attitude that said: "Snake!"

The half-opened door blocked Jeb's view. He inched back along the pontoon, took a half breath, held it. The brown-hooded head of a fer-de-lance swayed not six inches from Monti's leg. Its body lay coiled across the barrel of the rifle.

An essence of every story that Jeb had ever heard about this snake flashed through his mind: the bite was almost certain death.

"Don't move!" whispered Jeb.

Gettler appeared beyond Monti. "Something wrong?"

"Snake," breathed Jeb. He looked at the machete beneath the seats. The blade rested within an inch of the snake's tail.

Gettler lowered his head, peered under Monti's legs, drew in his breath. "Careful," he whispered. "That's a fer-de-lance—pit viper. Deadly."

David stared across the seat back. "Can't you shoot it?" he whispered.

Gettler moved slowly to one side. "I can only see part of it. There's no room for a good shot."

"I'll try for the machete," said Jeb. He spoke just above a whisper. "Whatever you do, Monti, don't move or jerk away. Just keep your ..."

"I think I'm going to faint," she whispered. Her attention remained locked on the snake.

"No you're not!" hissed Jeb. He moved his hand toward the machete.

The snake's tongue vibrated toward Monti. It drew back an inch.

"If I had that little revolver I could shoot it from here," whispered David.

Jeb hesitated, wet his lips with his tongue. *Will Gettler trust the kid with a gun? And if he does ...*

"Are you sure you can shoot it from there?" asked Gettler.

"Yes, sir."

Gettler reached across Monti's shoulders with the twenty-two. "Here it is, son. Move slowly. Don't attract its attention. Aim for the head."

"Have you ever shot a gun like that, David?" whispered Jeb.

"Yes, sir." David rested the gun barrel on the back of the seat beside his mother, put his tongue between his lips in concentration.

"Squeeze the trigger very slowly," breathed Jeb.

The snake suddenly stretched upward. Its tongue flickered in blurring motion.

"David, wait!" hissed Jeb. "Let me get the machete. Then if you miss ..."

"Hurry!" whispered David. "It looks like it's going to bite!"

"Please *do* something," prayed Monti.

She stared at the snake's flickering tongue in complete fascination.

Jeb moved his right hand closer to the machete ... slowly ... slowly. His hand passed an invisible point where it came within striking range of the snake. He touched the machete handle, slipped his fingers around it. His gaze centered on the snake's head. Gently ... gently ... he lifted the handle, then the blade.

The fer-de-lance turned, looked at the glinting metal. There was deadly grace in its movement. The tongue flickered. It swung around to face Jeb not two feet from him.

Jeb locked his muscles into immobility, felt cold perspiration on his forehead. And he thought: *If it strikes it'll get me right in the face! I won't have time to move!*

David said: "Mr. Logan, I'm going to shoot."

The gun's roar filled the cabin. The snake's head smashed against the floor from the impact of the bullet. A thrashing, flailing violence exploded beneath Monti's feet. She leaped onto the seat, then over it and into the rear.

Jeb lifted the machete, chopped twice at the writhing coils.

He stepped aside, pulled the snake into the river with the flat of the blade.

Piranha came to the blood. They surged half out of the water beneath the fuselage, tearing and cutting at the snake. Jeb tore his attention away from the water, looked into the cabin.

Monti hugged David. Hysterical sobs shook her. David glanced across her shoulder at Jeb, looked at the revolver in his hand. There was a question in the boy's eyes.

Jeb's attention shifted to Gettler.

The big man filled the opposite door. His bearded chin jutted toward David; the magnum revolver was held ready in his right hand.

"I'll take the twenty-two now, David," said Gettler. He reached toward it with his left hand.

David continued to stare at Jeb as though waiting for a signal.

The kid doesn't have a chance, thought Jeb.

"Now!" snarled Gettler. A nerve twitched his check.

"Give him back the gun," said Jeb.

A cloud seemed to pass across David's eyes. He turned, handed the little pistol to Gettler.

"That was good shooting, son," said Gettler. He slid the twenty-two into one of the bulging pockets of his jacket.

"Oh, David!" sobbed Monti.

"It's all right, Mother." David patted her shoulder. "The snake's dead."

"I was paralyzed," she whispered. "I've never been so frightened." She pulled away from David, slumped back in the seat beside him, put her hands over her eyes.

Gettler took up his cane pole, fended off a floating island of sedge. Every touch of the pole aroused a cloud of insects.

"Where'd you learn to shoot like that, David?" asked Jeb.

"My ... Dad showed me. Then one of Mother's

bandleaders. He ..."

"Howard," said Monti. She lowered her hands.

"Yes," said David. "He had this target range in his basement where ..."

"I'd almost forgotten about that," said Monti.

"They used to leave me ... alone there ... well, not alone exactly. They ..."

"There was always someone around," said Monti. "Julio never left the place." She spoke defensively, then to Jeb: "Julio was Howard's houseboy."

"I see," said Jeb, but he failed to understand her sudden defensive attitude.

"One night I shot up a whole case of ammunition," said David. "Julio said I was even better than him." He shrugged. "Heck, this was really an easy shot. So close. And I even had an arm rest." He smiled.

And for one fleeting moment Jeb saw past the smile to the father, and realized that Roger Bannon's quiet strength had been transmitted to this boy.

Jeb glanced at Monti, said: "You don't have a thing to worry about with a man like this to protect you."

A brief hint of a smile touched her lips. She took a quavering breath, patted David's arm, then spoke abruptly: "Could there be another snake? I mean, how'd that one get in the plane?"

"They don't often travel in pairs," said Jeb.

"Wrong season," said Gettler. He spoke without looking up from his pole.

"That one probably came aboard from those bushes back there where we got the fruit," said Jeb. He pushed the machete back under the seat, looked lingeringly at the rifle on the floor. It was too far away and pointed the wrong direction. He took up his cane pole, studied the brown current around them.

The plane drifted almost in the center of a wide reach of water dotted by floating sedge islands, each with a hazy cover of insects. A petrified glaze of heat rebounded from the river, inflated the air beneath the wings and in the cabin. There was an immensity about the river in flood. It was a great broad surface glistening darkly in every open place—as flat and glassy as a pool of dirty oil. There might have been no current at all. The air felt muggy, stagnant—filled with droning insects, strange dank odors and the omnipresent smell of mildew.

A line of yellow bubbles and foam laced about the pontoons.

Jeb found the water bag on the floor of the cabin, drank, replaced the bag.

All around him the silence trembled in the heat.

Abruptly, the plane rocked. Gettler cursed, and the pontoon beneath him boomed like a drum as he stamped on it.

Jeb stooped, peered under the fuselage. "What's wrong?"

"Piranha!" snapped Gettler. "I dipped my foot in the water to cool it." He bent over his left foot, looked at it with something like astonishment. Blood dripped from a gash above his ankle, ran off the float into the river.

"Are you okay?" asked Jeb.

"David, get the first aid kit out of the back," said Monti.

"Water's all muddy," said Gettler. "I had no idea they'd still be with us."

"They must've been drifting along with us ever since we fed them the snake," said Jeb.

"Here's the first aid kit." David handed it out the door.

"Need any help?" asked Monti.

"No." Gettler pushed the kit aside. "Hold that thing there. I'm coming inside." He climbed into the front, took the kit. "Burns like fire!"

The water beside Gettler's float suddenly erupted as piranha arose to the dripping blood.

Jeb snatched the fish line from the floor of the cabin, tossed the bare hook into the boiling mass of fish. The hook was seized immediately. He jerked it back. A frenzied piranha—blunt headed and wild eyed—banged against the strut. Jeb grabbed the machete, dropped the fish onto the cabin floor, smashed it with the flat of the blade.

In the next few minutes he caught five fish; then the school vanished as abruptly as it had appeared.

Gettler finished dressing his wound. "Vicious little bastards! Saw them take an Indian once on the Urucú. Canoe tipped over. One yelp and he was gone. Nothing but a big red spot on the river and those fish flashing all over."

Monti leaned across the seat back. "If you'll clean them, I'll set up the pellet stove and cook them." She wet her lips with her tongue.

"Losing your squeamishness, I see," said Gettler. He handed the first aid kit back to David, slid down to the float, began cleaning the fish.

Again the water boiled with piranha.

"They're hungry," said Gettler.

"So'm I," said Monti, then: "David, help me with this damned stove. I can't seem to get it going."

"Use some of your lighter fluid," said Jeb.

Presently, the smell of cooking fish was added to the other odors in the cabin. They ate every scrap of the meat, shared a papaya.

Gettler leaned back against the strut, belched. "River's getting pretty damned high," he said.

Jeb moved to the front of his pontoon, rested a hand on the cowling, stared ahead. About a half mile downstream the river split off between—he counted them—eight islands. Nine channels.

"Look down there," said Jeb.

"I've been looking," said Gettler.

Jeb swung up onto the cowling, scrambled onto the wing above the cabin, turned and looked downstream. The river spread in all directions. Little mounds of green were isolated in the water on every side.

"Which one's the right channel?" asked Gettler.

Jeb shook his head. "Dunno. What'll we do—go eeny, meeny, miney, moe?"

"Look behind us," said Gettler.

Jeb turned, looked upstream.

Like a grey sheet hanging between the river and a low line of puffy clouds—a rain storm swept down upon them.

"Rain!" shouted Jeb.

He slid down to the float and underneath the wing, rigged the sea anchor, dropped it into the brown water.

The rain hurled itself upon them. Wind shook the plane, skidded it across the floating drag until it swung around pointing upstream.

Jeb crouched behind the open door, looked into the rear seat at David and Monti.

"What'd you see from up there on top?" asked David.

"It looks like a big lake with little islands all over it," said Jeb. "Channels going every which way."

"How do we know which one to take?" asked Monti.

Gettler leaned in the other door, said: "We don't."

And Jeb thought: *Any one of those channels could be a dead end ... trailing off into some swamp. And if the river falls, there we'd be: stranded.*

"I think this is an area I've heard about," said Gettler. "If I'm right there's a swamp on our ..." he paused, squinted in concentration "... on our right. Yes. It'd be on the left when you're coming upstream." And he spoke Jeb's thought: "We could get lost and stranded out there real easy."

The wind faded to a series of fretting gusts, died off to stillness that left only the stuttering chop of rain. Jeb straightened, looked around. The plane freed of the wind swung around to the pull of the drag anchor in the current. Again they faced downstream.

Gettler faced right. "There's where we don't want to go."

Jeb took up his cane pole, began guiding the plane to the left. When the sea anchor interfered he lifted it from the river, hung it on the strut.

A drowned island came under the floats. Bushes dragged at the metal. The two men poled across the obstruction, holding steadily to the left through runneled currents flattened by the monotonous pocking of rainfall.

Jeb paused, listened to the drumming fall of water on the wings. A sodden depression of spirits touched all four in the plane. They drifted through a hissing ghost world saturated with warm, damp vapors.

An avenue of half submerged trees opened before the plane. The current furrowed over, quickened, hurled the plane through into a maze of narrow channels. No time for decisions. The swiftest current took them—and the men with the poles could only fend off bushes, trees. A tangled wall of vegetation loomed directly ahead. Brown water poured through, foaming around piles of debris, over logs caught in the matted growth. The plane swept headlong into the tangle, snagged, tore free. Vines caught at the wings, broke away, trailed in the water. They scraped and bumped their way into another open reach of boiling current that swept them inexorably toward a solid barricade of trees.

Jeb tore vines and bushes from the propeller, clambered into the cabin, primed the motor. It caught on the third roll of the starter, coughed and snorted, belched a thick stream of oily smoke. He swung the plane left, quartering against the current until they won their way around the trees into another channel.

The gauge on the wing tank wavered toward the half mark.

Jeb shut off the motor, returned to the pontoon.

The current slowed, but the maze of channels appeared endless.

What if Gettler had his directions wrong? Jeb asked himself.

And Gettler stared about with a worried frown, wrestling with the same doubt.

Again the plane swept toward a line of trees. This time they won around the obstruction with only the poles. Another dead end appeared. Green walls towered on three sides.

They leaned into the cane poles, thrusting the plane against the flow. A new channel opened before them only to run out in another dead end within twenty minutes.

Again, Jeb used the motor ... and again they poled across the current. He lost track of direction and the number of blind channels they probed.

Late in the grey afternoon the rain slackened to a random dripping.

The two men worked like punch-weary fighters, nosed the plane into a grassy, log-mounded hummock: all that remained of an island. Insects clouded the air the moment the floats slipped into the flooded grass.

Jeb tossed the grapnel onto the hummock, leaned against the cowling, stared exhaustedly at the tangled pile of grey logs on the opposite end of the island. He felt too tired to slap at the insects settling on him.

Gettler took the rifle, jumped ashore, made his way toward the logs.

Monti slid down to the float beside Jeb. "You look bushed," she said.

David leaned out the door. "Couldn't I help with the poles?"

"You're not heavy enough," said Jeb.

"What's he doing?" asked Monti. She nodded toward Gettler.

Jeb turned, looked down the island.

Gettler had taken off his hat, and was collecting something in it from the underside of a log.

"I dunno," said Jeb.

Presently, Gettler returned, held out the hat. "Snails," he said.

Monti shuddered convulsively, then: "How do we cook

them?"

"Boil them," said Gettler. He looked up at David. "Bring down some papaya and the little pan from the pellet stove."

David turned to obey.

Jeb took the machete from the cabin, joined Gettler on the shore.

"I think there's some dry rotten wood in those logs," said Gettler.

Jeb nodded, pushed his way through a fog of insects across to the piled logs. The center of one gave up dry fuel for a fire. Jeb carried it back to Gettler. Monti joined them, contributed a splash of lighter fluid to start the blaze. David brought the fruit and pan.

"These are kind of dull eating," said Gettler. He dumped the hatful of snails into the pan, held it over the flames.

Monti moved around into the smoke to escape the insects. "Who cares a long as its food?" she asked.

Jeb squatted in a sodden torpor, stirred only when Gettler handed him a leaf bearing four snails and a quarter of papaya.

They ate in a kind of despairing silence.

Gettler finished, stood up, looked downstream. "How far d'you figure we've come, Logan?"

"A little more'n a third of the way," said Jeb.

"Christ!" Gettler looked back upstream. "We've got to find us a dugout. That metal monster will kill us if we have to horse it through many more days like this one."

Jeb shook his head.

"Have we gotten away from the Indians?" asked David.

"Not a chance," snarled Gettler. "*They're* in canoes."

Night fell across the island: a black pall, warm and dripping, and full of biting insects. A frog chorus swelled around the four humans. From somewhere came the delicate flower scent of orchids. A great crashing sound thumped the dark as a tree—undermined by the flood—toppled into the water.

The dying fire remained like a single orange eye.

Jeb suddenly recalled the crazy fallen look of the radio tower at the army post, and he wondered what it had looked like as it dropped.

Then he thought, *In the long run, everything falls.*

And he felt a terrible indrawing need to find some kind of happiness, to accumulate a few biting pleasures against the darkness. He looked up at the shadowy figure of Monti standing in the smoke.

"We'd better stay here for the night," said Gettler.

Jeb nodded, turned his attention to the plane, saw it glinting red in the firelight. Shadows hid the slow deterioration of metal.

Quite abruptly, Jeb was shaken by a great affection for his plane. Despite its crippled and patched condition, it still contained the essence of a tremendous symbol: It stood for safety, for the gregarious security of the swarming civilization that had spawned it.

He spoke brusquely to cover the sudden emotion: "We should get back aboard. Douse the fire, David. Just scatter it with a stick. The rain'll put it out."

"Yes, sir."

"We need a canoe," said Gettler.

And even though he knew that his own reaction was most likely foolish—that Gettler had logic on his side—Jeb shook his head. "I'm sticking with the plane."

"Arrrrrgh!" snarled Gettler. He crossed to the plane, lifted his shadowy bulk onto the float and into the rear of the cabin.

Jeb hesitated, thinking: *Is Gettler tired enough that he'll dope off into a deep sleep? If we could only get the guns away from him!*

Monti stepped close to Jeb. "He's tired," she whispered. "He'll sleep. Maybe we could get the guns tonight ..."

Jeb shook his head. "Sure he's tired. But he's living too close to the edge of panic. He'll sleep on his hair trigger."

"If he'd only get sick," whispered Monti.

"Yeah."

And Jeb wondered: *Shall I tell her what I learned from that Indian? That Gettler did murder her husband?*

David came up to them, and the moment was lost. "Is that scattered enough, sir?"

Jeb glanced back at the embers. "That's fine, David."

The boy threw a charred stick into the water, went across to the plane, climbed into the cabin beside Gettler.

I don't dare tell her, thought Jeb. *She tends to get hysterical, and she might give it away to Gettler that she knows. He'd kill us for sure.*

"Don't trust anyone," she murmured. "Why doesn't that beefy sonofabitch trust anyone? Does he think he's kidding us—the way he's sitting on the guns?"

"He's ..." Jeb shrugged. "... jungle happy."

"He's more dangerous than that snake," said Monti. "I don't know how, but he had something to do with Roger's death."

And again Jeb wondered: *Confirm it or deny it?*

He took a middle ground: "There could be other explanations for the way he's acting."

"Name one!"

"He's nuts."

"There we agree."

"David has some kind of control over him," said Jeb.

"I noticed." Intuitively, she added: "He had a son once, Gettler did." She shook her head. "Something terrible happened to that man somewhere, Jeb. There are moments when I almost ... feel sorry for him."

"He's going to get curious at what we're talking about," said Jeb. "We'd better get inside."

She stared pensively at the plane. "I suppose you're right."

Jeb looked down at the dim outline of her silhouetted against the last glow of the dying embers. "You're still the best looking bug-chewed woman I've ever seen."

"You've been in the jungle too long, man." She gave a chopping, brittle laugh, rubbed the welts on her left arm. "They're getting worse. Let's go in."

They crossed to the plane, clambered inside.

"Get everything all decided?" asked Gettler.

"We're lost, aren't we?" asked Monti.

"Everyone's lost," said Gettler. He sounded drunk.

"We've lost the main current in this flood," said Jeb. "We could be way out in the middle of a swamp."

"How far've we come today?" asked David.

"We're no more'n twenty miles overland from where we stopped last night," said Gettler.

"Thirty at least," said Jeb.

"It'd been seventy-five miles if we had a canoe," said Gettler.

"And we'd be out there in that rain," said Jeb.

"You didn't seem too anxious to come inside," said Gettler.

"The bugs are better company!" snapped Monti.

"Perhaps I should come up front and change your mind about that," said Gettler. "I grow on people."

"No doubt!" she said. "Like a cancer."

"The plane has its advantages," said Jeb.

"And you've the blisters on your hands to prove it," growled Gettler. "We need a canoe!"

Jeb stared out into the night. The last embers of their fire had died, leaving utter blackness. The rain had increased and its incessant rhythm mingled with the humming of insects, the washing swirl of the river against the floats, to create a womb-like somnolence within the plane. He inhaled deeply of crusting odors that surrounded them: rotting fruit, the musky creeping of mildew, perspiration, the smell of cooked fish—and a distant hint of perfume.

"Maybe we've lost the channel," said Jeb. "But as long's we float we're pretty sure to find it again."

"If the Jivaro don't find us first," said Gettler.

"This water all goes down to the Amazon," said Jeb.

"Can they find us in the dark?" asked Monti.

Gettler made an odd whimpering sound, whispered: "They're with us every minute ... waiting."

Jeb looked at the firefly lights of the instrument dials in front of him. "If we stick with the plane we'll make it."

"This is their country," husked Gettler. "We don't stand a chance!"

"For Christ's sake! Stop it!" cried Monti.

"Sure," said Gettler. "For Christ's sake."

Jeb slammed a palm against the control wheel in front of him. Metal creaked. "We can make it! I know we can!"

And Gettler laughed: a pure sound of enjoyment. "You *know*!"

"Yeah, I *know*!"

"Maybe a little of your blood will drift past Ramona," said Gettler. "In a very diluted form."

"Do you *like* to scare people?" demanded Monti.

Gettler sighed. "Okay, I'll talk about *knowing*. The only way you *know* something is by experience. I've experienced the jungle ... and I don't trust any of it. I *hate* it!"

"Then why'd you stay?" asked Monti.

"Because it's the only honest place left in the world."

"No," said Monti. "You're lying."

And Gettler chuckled. "Maybe you're right, come to think of it."

"I saw some fungus on one of those logs out there," said Monti. "Suddenly the fungus flew away. It was a moth or a butterfly or something. Yesterday, there was a bug on the windshield that looked like a dead stick."

"There's deception here," agreed Gettler. "Maybe deception's the real key to survival."

Monti said: "These damned philosophers and their phony pretentions!"

"I see lights out there!" hissed David.

"Fireflies," said Jeb.

"Honest!" sneered Monti. "The world's a jungle, yes. But one part's no different from another." She stretched.

"We just wander around until we find the brand of dishonesty that suits us."

"Mr. Gettler," said David. "The other night when you said I was like the light shining from the flashlight ... Well, I've tried to understand that, but ..."

"David! Drop that!" snapped Monti. "Christ! I won't have you turning into one of these word-twisters, too!"

"Leave him be," said Gettler. "He's come upon the paradox of identity at an early age. That's good."

"Men!" said Monti. "It's in their blood. I swear."

The plane tugged abruptly at its mooring, turned, grazed some bushes.

"River's rising again," said Jeb.

Monti leaned against the seat close to Jeb. "Maybe they'll send a boat up to look for us," she whispered.

"Who?"

"Somebody'll miss us. They're sure to."

"Mr. Gettler," said David. "What's a paradox?"

"Something that seems foolish, absurd, but which happens to be true nonetheless."

"Listen to him!" whispered Monti.

Jeb touched her arm, patted it.

She put her hand in his, leaned her head against his shoulder.

David said: "But how can ..."

"Look out there," said Gettler. "What do you see?"

"Those fireflies."

"No you don't."

"But I ..."

"You *think* you see the fireflies," said Gettler. "*Think* is the key word."

Monti said: "I'd like to close my eyes and wake up to find this was just a horrible nightmare."

Jeb squeezed her hand.

"What you actually *see*, son," said Gettler, "is your own body responding to the light. It's all inside you."

"Or wouldn't it be wonderful if this was actually some little river ... in Georgia, say," murmured Monti, "and damp here like it'd be in Georgia. We might just be drifting along a safe, clean little river."

"We have only our senses," said Gettler. "Nothing else. We just *think* we sense things outside us, but all the time we're only feeling our own bodies."

"And somewhere out there the Negroes'd be singing," murmured Monti. She began humming to herself, low.

"The trouble," said Gettler, "comes when we mistake this pattern of feeling things ... we mistake that for ourselves ... for our own identity. And we start acting like the things outside us were inside us."

David suddenly had the sensation that he lived inside a thin and imperfect shell that was filled to the bursting point with confusion ... but that if he gave everything just the right kind of a shake it'd all settle into something understandable and safe.

"How'd we get this way?" he asked.

"It's the way we learn about words," said Gettler. "That sets us into habits that fool us. We group things together for convenience: trees, birds, dogs, houses ... Very useful. But that gets us into the habit of thinking that somehow these things are identical—something has to be the *same* for them to be called by the same label. See what I mean?"

"I think so."

"Well, son, if you enter any problem with a preconceived idea of how to solve it ... and the problem doesn't happen to fit your idea, you may never solve it. You'll see things that aren't there ... or not see things that *are* there—all because your mind is prepared for something different from the reality staring you in the face!"

Monti said: "Roger used to ramble on like that for hours.

Drove me mad!" She pulled her hand out of Jeb's, straightened.

Christ! What's wrong with me? she asked herself. *When I had a live husband I didn't hesitate to enjoy whatever came along. Now that he's dead I have to develop a moral compunction!*

Her anger turned abruptly on Gettler. "Why'nt you shut up back there?"

"Leave us be," said Gettler. He turned toward David in the darkness. "See what I mean, son?"

"You go to sleep, David!" barked Monti.

"Look," snarled Gettler. "I leave you alone with the irresistible ladies' man up there. You leave me alone with this boy who wants to learn something!"

"You don't know anything he needs to know!"

Gettler lashed out, slammed the hinged back of the seat, hurled Monti forward. "Watch your tongue, woman!"

Jeb whirled, uncertain of what had happened, thinking that Gettler had hit Monti. "Just a damn minute!" he shouted.

"I'm all right," said Monti.

There came the sharp click of a gun hammer being cocked.

Gettler said: "You've no refinement, Logan. A woman might think she prefers you to me."

He's going nuts! thought Monti.

"But give her five minutes with me, and she'd see how wrong she'd been," said Gettler.

"Lay off that, Gettler," said Logan. He tried to wet his lips with a dry tongue.

Gettler shifted his position, chuckled—an emotionless, deadly sound.

"No," whispered Monti.

Gettler put out his left hand, touched Monti's hair. She tried to pull away, but he clutched a lock of her hair, held her.

Monti gasped.

Jeb braced himself to leap over the seat at Gettler. *If he's going to kill us he'll have to do it the hard way!*

"Mr. Gettler, please don't argue with her," said David. "I still don't understand what you've been explaining to me."

Slowly, Gettler released Monti's hair, sat back. Wildness drained out of him, and he thought: *Now, why was I angry? What'd she say to make me angry?* He couldn't remember, and another thought arose in his mind: *Her hair doesn't feel like Gerda's.*

"I don't understand how words can be the same as a problem," said David.

Monti, held her breath, exhaled when Gettler spoke.

Gettler eased down the hammer on the revolver, said: "Our words are preconceived notions about the world ... the universe. The problem is in understanding. Do you see that?"

"Ye-e-e-ess."

"You sleep on it," said Gettler.

Jeb silently turned around in his seat, faced forward. He felt that the crisis had not been solved—only extended.

Gettler patted David's shoulder, "Maybe after you sleep on it, the whole thing'll become clearer to you."

That was too close! thought Monti. *We've got to disarm him! We've just got to!*

"G'night," said David. And he thought: *Why'd mother have to go and make him angry? He's all right as long as he's just talking. What harm can talking do?*

He went to sleep to dream about a succession of words that weren't exactly words: more like the irregularly shaped blocks the psychologist at the school had made him play with once. Only ... he knew they were words, and he had to fit them into holes of peculiar shape. But none of the words would fit.

"Take the first watch, Logan," whispered Gettler.

"Yes, *sir*," said Jeb.

"I'll be sleeping very lightly, in case you need anything,"

said Gettler. And he chuckled softly—with only the faintest hint of madness.

The sonofabitch! thought Jeb.

He heard Gettler turn, settle himself for sleeping. Presently, there came the shallow, cat-rhythm sound of Gettler sleeping.

Jeb settled himself to staying awake. He sensed the tense, watchfulness of Monti beside him. The phosphorescent glow of instrument dials held a hypnotic fascination for Jeb. He found he could not look at them without having his eyelids droop. He forced his attention onto the surrounding darkness, listened to the monotonous drumming of rain against metal, the restless skirt-swishing of water beneath the floats.

Abruptly, Monti leaned across facing Jeb.

There came a momentary break in Gettler's breathing, and the rhythm resumed.

She put her left hand behind Jeb's neck, her lips found his. He pulled her against him with a rough strength, and for a long minute they were an island of isolated awareness in the sea of night. Monti pulled away, brushed her cheek against his beard, whispered: "Thank you."

Jeb stroked her hair, acutely aware of the warm softness against him.

"I was so afraid," she whispered.

"Shhhh," he said.

And he thought: *The poor kid. Nothing ever prepared her for an emergency like this.* But something about that thought struck him wrong, and Jeb sensed that all the rest of them might die while Monti survived because of some mysterious strength a man couldn't understand.

Monti shifted in his arms, cradled her head in Jeb's lap.

He continued to stroke her hair, wide awake now in spite of his fatigue ... keenly aware of every sound in the damp darkness: the slow sloshing of a limb in the current, the close drum of rain on the plane ... and now the soft, even breathing of Monti as she slept.

Far off there came the soughing and rumbling of trees in the wind. The sound grew.

A new storm coming, he thought.

The wind was a live thing talking in the jungle—shuddering against the plane in a pellet-rattle of rain, hissing and whispering.

Jeb tried to put meaning into the wind sounds, aware that it was an insane thing to do, yet fascinated by the thought that the wind could talk. And it made the time pass quickly.

Gettler stirred, said: "I'll take over, Logan." He cleared his throat, and Monti moved restlessly in Jeb's lap. "Any signs of trouble?"

"Nothing I could identify," whispered Jeb. He glanced at his wristwatch. Midnight. And he thought: *Gettler must have a built-in clock.*

The weariness that had been building up in Jeb flooded over. He suddenly felt that nothing could be as important as sleep. He tipped his head against the seat back, and the dark overcame him.

Gettler rubbed his left elbow to restore circulation where he had been sleeping on it. The warm dampness of the night felt very familiar, as though this moment were the thing he knew best of everything in the universe. But it was tinged with melancholy: the inner balancing emotion that told him he had only a small part of control over a small part of his destiny. And he re-experienced a sense of regret, thought: *I'm sorry, Rog. Sorry I killed you. But you shouldn't have tried to play God!*

Jeb awoke to a wetly dripping dawn. A gauze curtain of rain blurred the drowned forest. The river was a desolate emptiness that reached everywhere into the greyness. Countless rain craters repeated themselves endlessly on the surface.

Monti still slept across Jeb's lap. He lifted her gently to a sitting position. She opened her eyes, smiled at him with sleepy half-awareness.

Gettler shifted heavily, mumbled something in his sleep.

Jeb glanced around, and again wondered if he could grab the revolver jutting from Gettler's belt.

But Gettler opened his eyes, muttered: "We've got to find a canoe." He straightened. "Today."

"Then go find one!" snapped Jeb.

"Watch your lip, fly-boy," said Gettler. He turned to David. "Everything quiet in your watch?"

"Yes, sir."

Jeb opened his door, slipped down to the float, breathed deeply to swallow his anger. Moisture saturated the air. It felt warm and damp in his nostrils and against the back of his throat. He freed the grapnel from the island, lifted it aboard with its trail of dripping reeds and grass. The current pulled the plane around until its tail pointed downstream. Jeb braced himself on the float, set his cane pole into the flooded underbrush, pushed. Bushes grated under the pontoons, and the river took them. Grey shapes of trees swam into view and passed through the misting rain. Everything beyond a hundred feet appeared ghostly, without real outlines.

Gettler lowered himself onto the opposite float, pushed his hat back from his forehead, trailed his pole in the water. The jacket hung more loosely on him. Deep stains of perspiration blotched the fabric under his arms.

He never takes that coat off, thought Jeb. No matter the heat. *How many more emeralds is he carrying?* And he felt the gem in his own pocket. *Sure as hell! That's what caused the break-up between Gettler and Bannon.*

David leaned forward against the seat above Jeb. "Day number six," he said. "Almost a week."

"It seems more like a lifetime," said Monti.

"It may be all the lifetime you'll have," said Gettler.

"Oh, go feed yourself to the fish," said Monti.

Jeb stared ahead through the pall of rain. A half-submerged island loomed through the greyness. Jammed logs tangled across its top, mingled with the debris of another flood.

The two men grunted at the poles, forced the plane to the left around the island. A new current caught them, rushed them headlong down a torrent between lines of overhanging trees. Pieces of the river swirled away on both sides around flooded tree trunks and submerged roots.

Jeb called across to Gettler: "We've got to work our way farther to the left! Hug the bank!"

Gettler stared across the cowling with red-rimmed eyes. "What's the difference? We'll never get out of this maze as long as we stick with your pile of tin!"

Jeb choked down an angry reply, whirled away, found bottom with the pole, began thrusting the plane toward the left bank. There was a violent rocking motion to his actions.

Gettler hesitated, then began helping.

The current slowed. Trees and drowned banks receded into the moist greyness. The two men poled the plane across tugging eddies—keeping to the left. A sodden shoreline lifted out of the grey: a mist-washed landscape that seemed to take on motion while the plane hung suspended in muddy water.

"David, bait the fishhook with a piece of that fish skin, and see what you can catch," said Jeb.

"If you hook a piranha don't just jerk it into the cabin," said Gettler.

"Mr. Logan did."

"Yes, but he was ready to smash them with the machete. Those damn cannibals are as dangerous out of the water as they are in it."

"What'll I do?"

"Just haul it out of the water and hold it there until one of us can stun it," said Gettler.

David baited the hook, dropped it over the right side. "Won't I be liable to lose a fish if I just lift it up and let it hang in the air?"

"Well, you could lose a finger if you dropped it into the cabin without being ready."

"Just do as you're told, David," said Monti.

"But I want to know why."

"That's a special carbon steel, long-shank hook on that fish line," said Gettler. "Do you know why?"

"No, sir."

"It's made to catch anything in these waters, including piranha. And those fish can bite clean through an ordinary hook."

"Gol-lee!" David swallowed. "Did that one take a big chunk out of your foot?"

"No. It just scraped me because I was pulling my foot out when it hit."

David stared at the point where the fish line disappeared into the water.

"Maybe you'd better let one of the men fish," said Monti.

"He can do it," said Jeb. "Just as long as he's careful."

"I'll be careful," said David. He crouched by the door, waiting, listening. Every sound had come to have a special and familiar meaning: the hissing of the rain, the soggy dripping and scraping of the cane poles, grunts of effort from the two men, an occasional snapping creak from the metal of the plane.

And the ceaseless humming of insects.

They came whining through the rain as though it were not there—following charmed avenues through the curtain of water. They were a constant torture: biting, stinging, fluttering around every inch of exposed skin.

Monti buried her face against the seat, covered her neck with the scarf. Still they found her. When it became unbearable, she lighted a cigarette. The smoke gave a limited and temporary relief.

Jeb suffered the attacks in silence. His mind became lost in a circle of actions that had to be accomplished with minimum effort: lift the pole, drop it to the bottom ahead, wait for the current to overtake the new position—push.

And again ... and again ... and again ...

"I think I've got a fish," whispered David. He pulled on the line.

Instantly, everyone became alert following the boy's movements with hunger-sharpened senses.

David brought in another foot of line.

"Have you or haven't you?" demanded Gettler.

"There's something on the line," said David. He began hauling it in hand over hand. A brown shape about two feet long came up beside the float without a fight.

"Is it dangerous?" asked Monti.

"Hell, no!" barked Gettler. "Haul it in!"

David jerked the fish into the cabin. It gave several flaps of its tail.

"What is it?" asked David.

"A sucker of some kind," said Jeb.

"Who cares?" said Gettler. "Start cooking it."

"Get the little stove, David," said Monti.

He moved to obey. "I knew I had something."

They ate the fish in a kind of ravenous stupor, bolting chunks of half-cooked meat. One papaya remained. They finished this—as though eating, once started carried through with its own momentum until there was nothing else to be consumed.

David re-baited the hook with a fresh piece of fish, cast it into the current.

A kind of digestive lassitude came over them.

Gettler put down his cane pole, climbed into the rear beside David.

"Let her drift," he said.

Jeb leaned against the strut, peered into the veiled mist.

"I think I hear something," whispered David.

"What?" asked Monti.

"Listen!" hissed Gettler.

A rhythmic grunting gained volume above the muted constancy of rain and river. It came from beyond the shrouded trees on their left, passing left to right: downstream.

Gettler put a hand over David's mouth, leaned forward to whisper in Monti's ear: "Don't make a sound!"

Jeb stood frozen in a half crouch on the left pontoon.

The grunting passed out of hearing.

Jeb made his way cautiously back to the open door, peered in at Gettler. "Jivaro?"

"That's their paddling chant."

"There must be another channel beyond those trees," whispered Jeb.

"Yes. Now they're ahead of us again."

"Are they hunting for us?" sobbed Monti.

"They're going down to set up another ambush," said Jeb. "Sure as hell!" He looked downstream.

"Do they know where we are?" asked David.

"Probably not," said Jeb. "Visibility's too poor, and there's too much river with this high water for them to search all of it."

"They don't need to search all of it!" snarled Gettler. "All they need's a narrow place where we have to go through!"

His voice climbed: “Christ! Did you hear them? All that noise! Like they owned the river!”

“They do,” said Jeb. “They own it.”

“What can we do?” moaned Monti.

“They own this river,” repeated Jeb. “And they’d know where the main channel is. That must be it beyond those trees!”

“We’d better go back to the right,” said Gettler.

“Why?” asked Jeb. “The weather’s on our side. You can’t see three hundred feet through that rain.”

“We could stumble right into the middle of them before we knew it!” barked Gettler.

“Or before they knew it,” said Jeb.

A current twisted the plane around until it drifted backward.

Gettler slid down to the pontoon on his side, checked the rifle, placed it on the cabin floor ready at hand.

A line of flooded trees climbed out of the rain downstream. Fingers of brown current surged off around the trunks. Jeb and Gettler grunted at the poles, but the current was too strong. It swept the plane into the trees, and the wings caught. Water swirled around the pontoons.

Jeb worked his way to the rear, leaped onto an exposed root system, strained to push the plane out of the trap. It moved upstream by inches. Gettler helped from the opposite side, pushing with the pole, staying near the rifle.

There came a moment when Jeb faced the necessity of risking the river and the threat of piranha.

All the experts say they avoid fast water, he thought, and he stared at the muddy current rushing beneath the plane. *Oh, hell!* And he stepped off into it. The water came up to his waist, a surging brown pressure.

“Jeb!” shouted Monti. “Those fish!”

“He’s okay,” said Gettler. “Water’s too swift for them here.”

Jeb shoved at the pontoon, pushed himself against the

current.

Slowly, with a tearing and rustling of vines, creaking and scraping of metal they worked the plane along the barrier and into a new channel. Jeb hauled himself onto the float as the current took them.

Monti slid down, helped him.

"Jeb, that's too dangerous," she whispered.

He stared at her, a strange exhilaration filling his senses. "I'm all right, Monti."

"I thought my heart would stop," she said.

"Everything's okay. Go back inside."

She shuddered, turned, climbed into the cabin.

The plane drifted past a high mud bank gnawed by the river and eroding rivulets of rain water. Two alligators slid off the mud and into the water at the approach of the plane.

A great whirling back eddy caught the plane below the mud bank, swept it in a wide circle to the left.

"Look!" said Gettler. He pointed with the cane pole at an island of flotsam caught in the upper turn of the eddy.

A long dark mound—perhaps eighteen feet in length and no more than three feet wide—protruded from the flotsam.

"Canoe," said Gettler. "It's overturned."

He pushed his pole into the river bottom, checked the plane's side drift, sent it toward the canoe.

Jeb stared at the overturned dugout. His exhilaration of a few minutes before drained away like water from a punctured skin. And all of the black terror that he had suffered on the morning of his nightmare premonition came rushing back.

Gettler hooked the canoe with the pole, brought it under the wing beside him.

"High water must've swept it away from its mooring," he said.

"I'm sticking with the plane!" gritted Jeb.

Gettler ignored him knelt by the canoe, caught it on the far edge with one hand, swirled it over. Water sloshed from one end to the other.

"David, give me the extra canvas bucket," said Gettler.

"What're you going to do?" asked Monti.

"Bail this thing out."

Monti looked down at the rifle on the floor beneath her feet, glanced up to see Gettler watching her. He shook his head once. She reddened, whirled away.

Gettler took the bucket from David, began bailing. A black-charred bottom came into view as he cleared out the muddy water.

Jeb spoke louder: "I'm sticking with the plane!"

Gettler swung the canoe around behind the pontoon, brought it under the fuselage.

"David, give me a length of that fish line," he said.

David obeyed.

"What *are* you doing?" demanded Monti.

"Now we've got a lifeboat," said Gettler. He tied it to the pontoon with two lengths of the fish line, stared across at Jeb. "Any objections, Logan?"

Angry words started to rise in Jeb's throat. He fought them down. *The bastard's right. We could lose the plane anytime: a leak in that pontoon with no place to land for repairs.* Another thought flooded Jeb's mind: *But that sonofabitch could force our hand now by wrecking the patch on that pontoon!*

Jeb spoke tentatively: "The canoe's just some more weight for us to push around with ..."

"Look around you," said Gettler.

Jeb raised his attention from the canoe. They had drifted out of the eddy on a slowly angling current to the right. Through the blurring rain he could just make out a sloping line of hills on the left, more rising ground on the opposite shore.

"We're back in the main channel," said Gettler.

The sight gave Jeb a brief emotional lift. He looked downstream. The swift current was sweeping them toward civilization, toward Ramona and *mama-cocha*: the great salt ocean that was only a legend here in the jungle.

Then he thought about the Jivaro war canoe that had passed with its grunting paddlers ... and of the certain ambush that waited ahead.

Monti waved a fluttering cloud of insects away from her face with an absent-minded movement of her hand. She, too, stared into the rain mist downstream.

"Are you sure those were Jivaro who passed us?" she asked.

"Who else'd have guts enough to make that much noise in Jivaro country?" asked Gettler.

"Won't they ever give up?" she demanded. "Why can't they leave us alone?"

"Because we're here," said Gettler.

The plane turned, drifted sideways downstream, angling closer and closer to the right shore. The forest wall darkened from grey through mottled granite to the deep shadowy green, the tumultuous overpowering green of violent jungle growth. They swept close to the fluid meeting point of water and forest: a place full of swishing and sucking sounds. Trailing vines caught at the tail assembly. Gettler fended them off, and the current dragged the plane toward mid-channel.

Time dragged out in runnels of river current.

The rain slackened. Vagrant scratches of blue sky began to appear through the clouds. The river took on a smooth grey lacquered surface broken by parallel currents like grains in wood. Then the setting sun came under the clouds like a single bloodshot eye staring directly upriver at them. The hills devoured the sun, and in the sudden darkness the plane rode a ribbon of oily black velvet toward patches of glittering stars that shone like wet diamonds through the broken clouds.

A sedge island with its inevitable curtain of insects loomed dark on dark in the dank night.

"What do you say?" asked Jeb.

"Is it floating free or hung up?" asked Gettler.

"Current's going around it," said Jeb. "It seems to be caught in some shallows."

"Let's tie up," said Gettler.

"Lots of insects," said Jeb.

"And it's getting darker," said Gettler.

Jeb threw the grapnel, felt it bite into the sedge.

"You can't get away from the bugs anyway," said Gettler.

The plane twisted around against the anchor line, grated into the sedge. Thick swarms of insects buzzed upward at the disturbance.

Jeb and Gettler retreated into the cabin, closed the doors.

And now there was a new sound to the night: the scraping bump-bump-bump of the canoe against the float as the plane sawed back and forth at the end of the anchor line.

Monti leaned her head against Jeb's shoulder.

Gettler saw the faint shadow of movement, interpreted it. A biting pang of jealousy dug into him. *I should force her to come back here,* he thought. *These fools couldn't resist me. It'd be nice to have a woman snuggled against me. Jesus! How long has it been?*

"We've got to see that we stay in the main channel," said Jeb.

And he realized that he was talking out of his fear that they would be forced to abandon the plane. The realization brought a sudden need to defend himself.

"We'll make better time," he said, and immediately realized how asinine the words sounded.

But Gettler had not focused on the words. He felt himself trembling with something deeper than rage.

"There's going to be a change tonight," he said.

"What'd you say?" asked Jeb.

"David's going to trade places with his mother," said Gettler.

Monti tensed, clutched Jeb's arm.

"Thing's are all right the way they are," said Jeb.

"For you," said Gettler. "David, go up front, and let your mother come back here."

"I'm happy where I am," said Monti.

"This is not a request," said Gettler. "It's an order."

"I don't take your orders!"

"Oh?"

"I prefer staying right where I am!"

"You think the fly-boy is a better man than I am?"

"For Christ's sake, Gettler!" barked Jeb. "Leave her alone!"

Gettler felt that little pinwheels of light rotated in his mind directly behind his eyes. He spoke softly: "Stay out of this."

"Jeb's at least a gentleman!" snapped Monti.

"Why do women think they prefer gentlemen?" asked Gettler. He addressed the darkness where David crouched in terror.

"Your type are all alike!" said Monti. "When something doesn't come your way naturally ... you take it by force!"

"Force is natural," said Gettler.

"Drop it, Gettler!" said Jeb.

"I could kill you right now," said Gettler, and the softness of his voice carried a more intense menace than if he had shouted.

Monti shuddered, pressed closer to Jeb.

"Every woman thinks she wants a gentleman until she's tasted a little decadence," said Gettler. "Logan, you will wait outside."

"Wait!" cried Monti.

She felt terror overwhelming her, and yet beneath it there was a fascination, a feeling that Gettler could be right: that the touch of him might overpower her senses with an ecstasy that she could never again resist. She felt herself on the brink of an addiction ... like a person about to take a lethean drug.

"We've waited long enough," said Gettler.

It's come to this, thought Jeb. *I'm going to get myself killed over a woman.* He pushed Monti away, tensed himself for the moment of struggle.

And David acted out of instinct.

"Don't you like me anymore, Mr. Gettler?" asked David.

Gettler sensed himself dissolving in a frenzy of warring fragments. *Why can't the boy shut up?*

"I thought you liked talking with me," said David.

"Sure I do, son," said Gettler. "It's just that ..."

"Then why can't I stay back here with you?"

Something waited at the edge of Gettler's consciousness. He weighed David's question as though it were a crisis point for the entire world. The spinning pinwheels behind Gettler's eyes almost blinded him.

Should the boy stay with me? Why shouldn't he stay?

The answer came through the pinwheels whirling in his mind, spiraling up out of a far darkness, and Gettler spoke in a kind of trance-like voice: *"You can't stay because you aren't real. They tortured you and killed you to make your mother obey them."* A sob caught in Gettler's throat. *"Poor little Peter. One day the world was so good ... and the next day it was a horror—full of screams and ..."*

There rose up before Gettler's eyes a picture of a child's body, naked and spread-eagled on a table—the skin laced by the dark weals from a smoking poker. He glared at the memory image as though it had actual substance. And his mind reacted as to the reality—in the same pattern of the original event: it rebelled in revulsion, horror and denial. He put his hands up, pushed against the night.

"No!" The sound was torn out of him, filling his silent audience with a surge of panic.

"You killed him!" screamed Gettler. "What did he do? He was just a child! What could a child do? He was just a child ... he was just a child ... he was just a child ... HE WAS JUST A CHILD!"

And Jeb suddenly felt that he was watching a soul unravel before him. Monti was almost overcome by an urge to whirl, and grab Gettler ... to comfort him.

"Nobody's killed me," said David. "I'm right here."

Something shattered the contact with the present, plunged backward in time to the moment of utter denial. He whirled, crushed David against him. A bit of the present filtered back followed by a moment of utter clarity. He spoke tenderly across David's head, spoke down the pinwheel corridor of time to the distant dead: "I'm sorry, Peter. I should've taken you away. I knew they were monsters." He lapsed into German: *"I knew. I knew. I should've taken you and your mother to safety."*

Tears scalded Monti's eyes. She shook her head. The picture of Gettler was becoming plainer in her mind. She spoke past a throat that ached with repressed sobs: "Who killed your son?"

But to Gettler her voice was Gerda's voice, and it drove him back into hysteria. He raged in German: *"It was my fault! We should've run away! But I didn't know they'd suspect me so soon! Gerda! I didn't know! GERDA! Please forgive me!"*

And he repeated himself in English: "Please forgive me, Gerda."

And again in Spanish, as though he were forced to explore every pattern of communication in his mind for a magic formula that lay the ghost of the past: "*Por Dios, Gerda! Tu perdón!*"

"Was Gerda your wife?" asked Monti.

Gettler's hysteria melted. He realized that he had been raving. A painful clarity came over him. He pushed himself away from David, retreated into his corner.

"Did they kill your wife, too?" asked Monti.

And Jeb sensed a feeling like embarrassment within himself. He wanted to shout at Monti: *"Christ! Leave him alone!"*

Gettler spoke in a low, tired voice: “They ... made her ... watch. She got the knife from one of them ... fell on it.”

Monti shuddered uncontrollably.

“The Third Reich *ate* them,” said Gettler. “One gulp. Just like they’d never been.”

“You called me Peter,” said David.

“I’m sorry if I disturbed you,” whispered Gettler.

“Was Peter ... was that your boy’s name?”

“Yes.”

“Were you really a professor?” asked Monti.

“Huh!” It was almost a coughing sound from Gettler. “What I was ... I was a set of muscles in a labor battalion.”

“But why?” demanded Monti.

“I was an enemy ... an enemy of the state.”

“But what did you do?” she asked.

“Monti, leave him alone,” said Jeb.

“No. I like to find out what makes people tick.”

A growl rumbled from Gettler. “You lie!”

“What?”

“You are a torturer,” said Gettler. “You create pain. You hope my pain will force me to betray the secret of life. All you want from me is an answer that will stop your fears. This is why there are sadists.”

“All I wanted to find out is why they killed your wife and child,” said Monti.

“Let the dead bury their dead,” said Gettler.

“Didn’t you even try to get revenge?” she asked.

“Ha-ha!” Gettler roared. “You use a pretty word there.”

“All I mean is ...”

“You don’t know what you mean!”

And Jeb thought: *She’s set him off again!*

“Let’s change the subject,” said Jeb.

“No!” barked Gettler. “She asks about revenge. To her it’s a slap on the wrist. Not even that! His voice lowered. “Me, I understand this word. It goes down into my guts. Revenge! You hang your enemy by his toes. You skin him with hot pliers ... with exquisite slowness, you ..."

"In heaven's name!" cried Monti. "What did they *do* to you?"

"Ahhhhhh ... they taught me to appreciate the jungle. This lesson I learned: the philosophy of the jungle. You cannot take *that* from me!"

"How old was ... Peter?" asked David.

How old? Gettler pushed his memory down the path that repelled it. *Thirteen? Yes. Thirteen.*

"He was thirteen."

Gettler nodded to himself. *Yes. It was Peter's birthday. I had his present under my arm—the telescope. Yes. I had it under my arm when I came home to ... to ...*

His mind recoiled in panic, bringing back only the image of a face: a man's face, grinning, heavy-jowled and square beneath the black uniform cap. And the glittering eyes: the sadistically delighted eyes, the little pig eyes with their gleam of power and joy at his horror.

"They rubbed the blood on my hands," whispered Gettler. "And when I screamed ... they laughed."

"God in heaven!" whispered Monti.

"There's no God!" muttered Gettler. "In heaven or hell! I've seen the proof. There's no room for our God in a jungle."

A tortured silence invaded the tiny cabin.

Monti crept close to Jeb, pressed against him for comfort.

"All that kept me alive," whispered Gettler, "... all that kept me alive was the planning in my mind. What I would do to Oberst Karl Freuchoff when ... It is very funny what happened. All the lovely tortures I imagined. For nothing. He was killed in the war. At Stalingrad. Oh, I asked. I looked. And his family ... the bombs. All gone. It was very funny ..."

David breathed softly, silently: fearful that he would be heard.

Monti shuddered, pressed her face against Jeb's arm.

"So I went away," murmured Gettler. "Yes. That is what I

did."

Again, silence closed in upon them ... with only the rain and wind outside—the bump-bump-bump of the canoe against the float like a frightened heartbeat.

There was a gradual descent to calmness. Monti drew away, and without thinking, began to hum: low, plaintive. Then she sang—so subdued that the sound almost lost itself in the gusts of wind and rain.

"None but the lonely heart can know my sadness ..."

Presently, Gettler took it up, singing in German while hot tears scalded his cheeks.

"Nur wer die Sehnsucht kennt, weiss, was ich leide! Allein und abgetrennt von aller Freude! ..."

Jeb's eyes smarted. He rubbed them, thought: *My God! No wonder the poor sonofabitch is crazy!*

In the first platinum light of dawn they cast off on a rain-shrouded river. It was a rain of monotonous violence that created a liquid world all around them. Rain lashed the river. The windshield ran torrents.

Jeb dropped down to the float, tossed the sea anchor into the current.

Wind-hurled lines of rain slanted beneath the wings. Each gust tightened the line to the floating drag. The plane dipped and swayed with an uneasy shuddering motion.

The four humans sat in dampened, submissive torpor while the muddy current pulled them between vaporous grey lines of hills.

There was a new emotional atmosphere in the plane: a subdued tolerance, a softening that fitted their growing physical weakness.

Gettler appeared withdrawn after his outburst in the night. He rubbed at his beard, sighed and shook his head repeatedly.

"This is the seventh day," said David. "A week."

Jeb returned to the pontoon.

"Where's the fish line?" he asked.

"Here's what's left of it," said David. He passed it out the door.

"There's enough," said Jeb. He rubbed a shred of rag in the snake blood on the cabin floor, tied the cloth to the hook, tossed it into the water. Within seconds a piranha gobbled the hook. Jeb flipped it onto the pontoon, held it beneath his foot while he killed it with the machete. He tossed the fish into the cabin, caught another ... and another.

"I'll clean them," said David. "I know how."

He leaned over the seat, reached for one of the fish.

"Careful!" shouted Jeb.

But David's hand had already touched a fish's nose. The jaws snapped convulsively. The boy jerked his hand back, and the end of his little finger dangled from a bloody stump just below the second joint.

"But it was dead," said David. He spoke in a tone of shocked disbelief.

"David!" screamed Monti. She reached for the boy as he sat back in the rear, holding up the welling red end of his finger.

"It was dead," repeated David.

Gettler already was bringing the first aid kit from behind the seat. He opened the kit in his lap, brought a clasp knife from his pocket, cut off the dangling fingertip, painted the end with disinfectant, bandaged it.

David kept repeating: "But it was dead."

"You never put your hand anywhere near the teeth of one of those things until the head's cut off," said Jeb. "We warned you."

"Even when the head's off, you're careful," said Gettler. He tied off the bandage.

"The whole end of his finger," whispered Monti.

"Be thankful it wasn't his entire hand," said Gettler. "How's it feel, son?"

"It throbs."

"Keep that bandage out of the river," said Gettler. He stared at the white wrapping, and a dull moroseness crept over his features. Slowly, he sank back in the seat, turned to gaze at the passing shore.

Monti closed the first aid kit, put it on the floor.

"Does it hurt badly, dear?"

"It's a little worse than it was." He bit at his lower lip.

"There're a few codeine tablets in the kit," said Jeb. "Give him one if the pain becomes too rough, but it'd be better to save them for tonight."

One bite! thought Gettler. *That's how the jungle kills. The flies and the ants come for what's left. The worms. And there's not even a ripple, nothing to say you were here. Or the piranha take you—and your bones dissolve in the ooze.* He shivered at the passionate encounter with his own fear. The whirling pinwheels returned behind his eyes. He could see them even with his eyes open.

Grey-green banks rose higher around the plane. The current picked up speed, and the channel narrowed.

Jeb wrestled with the cane pole.

"Hey!" he called. "Give me a hand!"

Gettler snapped around, startled.

The plane had surged to the left around a narrow island. Vines snagged on the wings in the constricted channel. The plane whirled and lurched, pulled in lunges and starts by the floating drag anchor. The canoe bumped and scraped against the pontoon.

Gettler scrambled down to the right hand float, took up his pole, once he bent to check the lashings on the dugout.

"We're in another side channel!" shouted Jeb.

The plane broke through another writhing growth of vines.

"If it gets any narrower we'll have to abandon the plane," said Gettler. "We'd never get back up against this current."

Jeb's lips thinned into a grim line.

The plane's wings bowled headlong into flooded cane stands that lined both banks. Whiplashing fronds cut at the two men. Cane bent, crackling and scraping as the current tore the plane through.

"Christ! I hope that patched float holds!" prayed Jeb.

They broke into the clear, swirling across an eddy at the juncture of another channel. The plane rounded a bend, and the river widened between overhanging walls of dark jungle that dropped to thin reaches of drowned saw grass. Rain hissed in the water, pounded against the metal of the plane.

The falling drops were so thick they seemed suspended in the air, performing crazy jigs.

Another river bend dropped away behind them ... and another. The damp heat mounted, and as it increased the rain slowly eased off to a heavy mist that hung from the sky like a grey gauze curtain. Abruptly, the rain stopped. The river reflected the clouds as on a polished surface. Then vapor curls began forming above the current.

The plane parted the mist, rounded another river bend.

A dark line appeared downstream surging toward them. The wind returned, bringing new sheets of rain that raked across them with fierce, biting slashes.

Jeb peered at the left shore dimly visible in the downpour. He turned to Monti.

"Know where we are?"

She roused herself from a sagging torpor.

"Where?"

"This is where we came down to refuel on our way in."

She stared past him at the mottled grey shore.

"The beach's under water," said Jeb. He pointed. "It was right along there. See that candelo tree?"

"Yes." She nodded numbly.

And Jeb thought: *It only took us an hour and a half to fly upstream from here. We've been more than a week coming back.* He turned, looked into the rain-veiled reaches downstream, thought about the twisting, turning river ahead.

The current took them around another bend to the left. An eddy swung the plane out toward the darkening right shore.

Abruptly, David pointed to the right. "What's that?"

Jeb glanced around, snapped: "Tapir! Gettler, shoot that before ..." He broke off in the act of lifting the cane pole to push them toward the animal.

The tapir stood on a completely flooded island, brown water lapping at its stomach. The animal's actions arrested

Jeb's voice.

A lurch backward, and the tapir stared myopically upstream. It snuffled, wriggled.

Water erupted in savage violence around the animal. Flashing silver forms of piranha leaped completely clear of the river to slash at the tapir's sides.

The animal squealed once, sank into a rolling turbulence of red water.

Jeb felt a sudden premonition as deeply ominous as the one he'd experienced on the morning that started this flight. A heavy certainty sank into him that death was sure to strike them. He glanced from David to Monti to Gettler to Monti, stared down at his own hands on the cane pole.

Which one of us? Maybe all of us.

His stomach felt leaden.

A slowly curving river bend hid the jungle tragedy.

Gettler suddenly slammed his hand against the strut, raged: "It stinks! Everything stinks!"

"Take it easy," murmured Monti.

"Arrrrrgh!" snarled Gettler.

"Were those piranha?" whispered David.

"Yes," said Jeb.

David swallowed.

Monti looked down at the three fish on the cabin floor.

Jeb followed the direction of her eyes. "I'll clean them if you feel like cooking them."

"I'm ..." She shuddered.

"Eat or be eaten!" snarled Gettler.

"I'm hungry," said David.

"There's the spirit," said Gettler, and lower: "Eat or be eaten."

Another river bend passed beneath them.

Jeb gestured downstream where the current split around a grey-green mound, fuzzy-edged in the hissing rain.

"Island."

The two men labored with their cane poles, guiding the

plane into a grassy stretch at the upper end of the island. An inevitable cloud of insects poured out of the disturbed grass, swarmed around exposed flesh.

Jeb ignored them, stared down the island.

The full length of it was open: no more than twenty-five yards long. It was covered with low scrub that bent before the driving rain.

"Something moved in that scrub," said Gettler.

"That's what I thought," said Jeb.

"Looked like a little monkey," said Gettler. He took the rifle from the cabin floor, moved forward along the float, leaped into the grass, sloshed through it to the higher ground.

Jeb took out the three fish, cleaned them. He looked in at David.

"See how you're supposed to handle these? By the tail."

"Yes, sir."

"How's the hand?"

"It's ... okay."

Monti unfolded the little heat tab stove, began cooking the fish.

The small game revolver cracked twice from the lower end of the island. The three at the plane jerked around, stared at Gettler. His bulky figure was bent over something in the bushes.

"What is it?" asked Monti.

"Can't see," said Jeb.

Gettler straightened, lifted a small, red monkey. He brought it back to the plane, flopped it onto the end of Jeb's pontoon.

"It's damn near skin and bones from starvation," said Gettler. "It was stranded out here by the flood."

"Uggh!" said Monti. "You don't expect us to ..."

"How hungry are you?" demanded Gettler.

"I'll eat fish," she said.

"Hah!"

"Cut the monkey meat off in strips," said Jeb. "We can cook it with the fish."

Monti turned away.

Gettler bent over the monkey, brought out his knife. Presently, he straightened, handed Jeb a double handful of stringy red meat.

"I've seen more meat on a cat," said Gettler. "Korean cat." He turned to Monti. "You and David share the fish. We'll eat this ..."

"We'll split our fair share of the fish," she said. "Just don't make me try to eat *that.*" She pushed the stove and tin pan toward him. "Here. You cook it."

They ate without civilized reserves, swallowing half-chewed gulps of food.

We get more like animals every day, thought Monti.

Gettler stood in the rain off the end of Jeb's float, stared morosely upstream, then down. Water dripped from his flopping hat, ran in rivulets off his shoulders. He leaned the rifle against a bush, took the hat off, shook it and replaced it.

"Monti, there's a little tea in the kit," said Jeb. "Why don't you brew some?"

Gettler turned. "Tea?" His red-rimmed eyes glared at Jeb. "Why'nt you say you had tea?"

"There isn't much of it," said Jeb. "I've held back, waiting for a time like this when we really need it."

"Why do we need it now?

"For a lift. For morale."

"And you decide about it."

Jeb looked at him. "What's eating you?"

Gettler trembled with rage, focusing his attention on the tea with a feeling that he had just discovered in it all the truth he needed to know about Jeb Logan.

"So *you* save the tea?" snarled Gettler.

"It's not that important," said Jeb.

"You don't like me, eh?" asked Gettler.

Good grieving god! Is he going to blow his stack over a

stupid mess of tea? wondered Jeb.

"You don't trust me?" pressed Gettler.

"Oh, dry up!"

Gettler suddenly raged at him: "You've been hoping I'd die! Leave more for the rest of you!"

"It's only tea!" cried Monti.

"The ladies' man decides," snarled Gettler.

"Oh, go to hell!" said Jeb.

"Stop it!" shouted Monti. "This is ridiculous!"

Gettler ignored her, splashed out alongside the pontoon, glared at Jeb. "But I didn't die!"

Jeb stared down into Gettler's eyes. They radiated violence, unveiled savagery.

No sympathy for Gettler complicated Jeb's thinking in that moment. He thought only: *So this is how a murderous madman looks.*

Gettler suddenly lashed out, knocked Jeb backward under the fuselage, hurled himself across the float with hands clutching for Jeb's neck.

Monti screamed.

Jeb rolled in the shallow, reed-clotted water, struggled to evade Gettler's groping fingers. The man's completely uninhibited strength momentarily paralyzed Jeb with fear.

"Kill you!" snarled Gettler.

His hands found Jeb's throat, squeezed. Gettler closed his eyes, called up a memory image of Oberst Freuchoff. Strength coursed through his fingers. They pulsed with a life of their own.

Jeb lashed out frantically with his left hand, banged Gettler's head against the dugout. The terrible choking eased momentarily. Jeb drew in a quick gasping breath, tried to break away. The water and restricted space beneath the plane hampered him. His head was thrust under the muddy flow. Gettler's fingers constricted. Again, Jeb battered Gettler's head against the dugout, heaved himself up, choking.

Dimly, he was aware of Monti screaming.

One of Jeb's flailing hands found a strut. He pulled himself backward across the dugout, dragging Gettler with him like a terrible leech. Jeb dug a finger into Gettler's left eye, kicked him in the groin. The throat grip loosened, broke. Jeb hurled himself backward with Gettler leaping after him, questing hands outthrust.

Then they were out in front of the plane, rolling in the sodden grass, thrashing, slugging, kicking.

If I can only get one of the guns! thought Jeb.

But there was no revolver in Gettler's belt.

The rifle!

Again, Gettler found Jeb's throat.

And from the corner of his eye, Jeb saw Monti out of the plane and scrambling after the rifle that still leaned against a bush.

Spots danced before Jeb's eyes. He felt strength draining from him. They rolled over, and he loosened the choking hands for a short breath that was throttled off.

Gettler felt none of Jeb's blows. An ecstasy filled him. *So long to wait, Oberst!*

Monti swung the rifle butt, caught Gettler alongside the head. He lost his grip on Jeb's throat. Jeb drank in a burning breath, tried to roll away, felt something hard under his side.

The revolver?

Before he could roll away, Gettler dived after him, brought out the hard lump from beneath them: *The revolver!* Jeb grabbed for Gettler's wrist, bent the hand away.

"Thought you'd get away!" snarled Gettler.

They rolled over and over in the soggy grass, struggling for the gun. Gettler grunted, mouthed curses in German. Suddenly, the gun went off, blasted past Jeb's ear, momentarily deafening him. He saw Monti's feet behind Gettler, glimpsed the rifle in her hands. She pushed the muzzle past Jeb, jammed it against Gettler's chest.

"Stop it!" she screamed.

Gettler still fought to bring the revolver against Jeb.

"I'll kill you!" screamed Monti. "I mean it!"

Gettler hesitated, turned his head slowly to look up at her. His eyes were bloodshot, feral. Strength flowed out of him, and his eyes took on a veiled, retreating look.

Jeb maintained his grip on Gettler's gun hand.

"Drop that gun!" ordered Monti.

"You wouldn't pull that trigger," said Gettler.

Desperation tightened Monti's voice. "I will! If I have to, I will!"

Jeb shook Gettler's hand. "Drop that gun!"

"Do as he says," said Monti. She prodded Gettler with the rifle.

Gettler opened his hand. The revolver slipped out of his fingers into the grass.

Jeb grabbed it, drew back, patted Gettler's pockets for the twenty-two, found it and stuffed it into his own belt. He got to his feet, covered Gettler with the big revolver, said, "Move away from him, Monti."

She obeyed, holding the rifle at the ready.

Gettler heaved himself to his feet, backed away.

Monti said: "What's that bulging in his pockets, Jeb?"

Gettler bent forward, hands claw like, clutching at the air. His head moved from side to side like a snake's.

Jeb tensed, said: "Emeralds. Raw emeralds."

"How'd you know?" demanded Gettler, then: "Rog told you. Just like him. He told you."

"Emeralds?" asked Monti.

"There's why your husband died," said Jeb.

"Wanted to cover up the mine," snarled Gettler. "Forget about it! That's what he wanted!"

"Is that why you killed him?" asked Jeb.

Gettler shook his head sharply, closed his eyes. A smile spread across his lips. "*I* didn't kill him."

Jeb glanced over his shoulder, saw David's white face

peering through the plane's windshield. "Bring us the adhesive tape from the first aid kit," called Jeb.

David jumped, then moved to obey.

"What're you going to do?" demanded Gettler.

"Tie you up," said Jeb.

Gettler stumbled backward. "Why? What've I done?"

Jeb stared at him, startled. "What've you ..."

"I won't let you tie me," said Gettler. His eyes regained their wild light. "You'll put the blood on my hands." And he whimpered: "You'll whip me."

"Would you rather we left you here for the Indians?" asked Jeb.

David came up with the tape, handed it to Jeb.

"Did he really kill my dad?"

"No!" shouted Gettler. He looked pleadingly at David. "Don't believe them! Lies! Lies!"

"How're we going to tie him?" asked Monti.

Again Gettler crouched. His head swayed from side to side.

And he suddenly reminded Jeb of the coyote that had been trapped in the fence corner of his uncle's ranch—the trapped, cowardly coyote that had slashed two slavering hounds to ribbons. And Jeb thought: *Now, we're the hounds!*

But Gettler began to cry, destroying the illusion.

Jeb had never before seen a grown man cry. It filled him with a deep embarrassment.

"Turn around!" barked Jeb.

Gettler obeyed.

"Put your hands behind you!"

Slowly, the hands came back.

Jeb jammed the revolver into his waistband, motioned to Monti. "Come up beside me, Monti. If he makes a sudden move ... well ..." He glanced at the rifle in her hands.

"I understand," she said.

David turned away, stumbled back to the plane.

Jeb saw that the boy was crying.

Monti said: "Hurry up. Get it over with."

Jeb crossed Gettler's wrists, bound them around and around with the tape. He emptied Gettler's pockets: clasp knife, eleven cartridges for the rifle, bandanna, fingernail clipper, a bar of soap wrapped in a rag, a small unmarked bottle of pills, pocket compass ... and two more emeralds in leaf wrappings.

Monti gasped when Jeb unwrapped the stones. "They're so ... big."

"Clean!" sobbed Gettler. "No more dirt! Good smells! Sweet smells. Soft things!" He whirled, glared at Jeb.

"Okay," said Jeb. "Into the plane." He herded Gettler along the float, helped him into the rear seat beside David.

The boy turned away, stared out the side window.

"You'll have to keep an eye on him for us, David," said Jeb.

David nodded without turning around.

Jeb sorted the cartridges, stowed the other items from Gettler's pockets in the survival kit on the floor of the luggage compartment.

Monti climbed into her side of the cabin. She looked at David's bandaged hand. "How's your hand feel, dear?"

David glanced at her, looked away. "It's okay."

Jeb brought the grapnel from the island, hung it on the strut, took up the cane pole, pushed the plane into the current.

Hysterical laughter suddenly erupted from Gettler. "Smart guy, Logan!" he gasped. "Now, you have to do all the work!" The laughter rolled from him.

"Oh, shut up!" snapped Monti.

"I could help," said David.

"Not with that hand," said Monti.

"It's all right. Really."

"No."

The plane drifted through the rain—between dense,

somber greyness of jungle walls. It was a ghost world of dull, leaden colors. Sounds took on the same quality. Gettler chuckled to himself intermittently. There was a coffin creaking to the plane's metal. Mosquitoes droned, and Jeb's cane pole scraped against the float, splashed with a muted dullness.

A bird called abruptly from the left shore with a sound like a stick drawn along a board fence. There came the deep booming of jungle doves farther back, and the rain stopped abruptly as though someone had shut it off.

Color returned to the riverbanks, a dark, shiny green. The leaves ran in torrents.

A storm of gaudy orange flowers swept out from the trees to the right, enveloped the plane, crawling everywhere.

Overhead, the clouds began to lift, piling up before sudden gusts of wind that shook plane and forest. Thin streaks of blue appeared, widened. The sun came through, and it was like turning on a furnace. The air above the river vibrated with the heat. Both shorelines wavered as though seen through defective glass.

Jeb rubbed at his throat where Gettler had choked him. The skin burned. A reaction of relief set in, and he felt his knees trembling. He stared out at a sudden spangling of lower ornaments in the tumult of green jungle.

The plane felt as though it were gliding down a long incline, making a transient passage toward a goal that was more instinctive than definite.

My God! We got the guns! Jeb thought.

The plane drifted around a sweeping bend, and a native village appeared downstream along the right bank: dark brown huts of sticks and mud clustered on a flat stretch of high ground.

"Monti, give me the rifle," said Jeb.

She passed it to him.

"Close the door on your side," he said.

She shut the door like a thunderclap in the tense air. The

plane drifted closer.

Nothing stirred in the village.

The plane drifted closer.

"No canoes," said Monti.

Jeb glanced at the far shore behind him. Too far away for a dart attack. He looked back to the village, glanced in at Gettler.

Some of the wildness faded from Gettler's eyes. He studied the village.

"What tribe, Gettler?" asked Jeb.

The reply came in a conversational calm: "Could be Zaparo. But some of those cone roofs in back look like Jivaro make. It's either Jivaro with some huts copied from the Zaparo, or the other way around."

"That's what I figured," said Jeb.

"Where are they?" whispered Monti.

"Hiding in the jungle back there," said Jeb.

"Better release me," said Gettler. "You'll need help if they attack."

"We'll struggle along as we are," said Jeb.

Gettler sank back, turned his head slowly to keep his gaze on the village as the plane drifted past.

A light breeze carried the vegetable-carrion stink of the place across their path.

Another bend hid the village from sight.

"If they were Zaparo, then the curse is working," said Jeb. "We'll get no help."

Gettler began muttering, and his words grew distinguishable only after a moment. "... and such as are skillful of lamentation to wailing. And in all the vineyards shall be wailing: for I will pass through thee, sayeth the Lord."

"What's he saying?" asked Monti.

"The day of the Lord is darkness, and not light," said Gettler.

"Sounds like something out of the Bible," said Jeb.

"The Bible? Him?"

"Shall not the day of the Lord be darkness, and not light?" muttered Gettler. "Even very dark, and no brightness in it?"

David leaned forward close to Monti. "What's he saying, Mother?"

"I don't know, dear."

"He sounds scary."

"But let judgment run down as waters, and righteousness as a mighty stream," said Gettler.

And again his voice sank into an unintelligible mutter.

David sank back, pulled away into his own corner.

Gettler suddenly roared: "Everything's rotting!"

He glared up at a green splotch of mildew on the fabric of the cabin ceiling, began to breathe rapidly in shallow, rocking gasps.

Jeb and Monti turned.

"Mother!" hissed David. He stared at Gettler.

"You're going to let them take my head!" cried Gettler.

"Stop that!" barked Jeb.

"I know what you're planning!" snarled Gettler. He began straining at the tape binding his wrists. The veins stood out like ropes along his neck.

"What'll I do?" demanded David.

Gettler stopped, turned, looked down at David. A nerve twitched in the man's forehead. He frowned, swayed. Abruptly, he spoke to David in a coarse, husking voice: "Don't let me get away! Don't ..." He slumped back, and his head lolled to one side.

David turned toward his mother. Monti looked at Jeb.

"In the Dark Ages they talked about a human being possessed," whispered Jeb. "I never understood it before."

"He's breathing so funny," whispered Monti.

Tears formed at the corners of Gettler's eyes, rolled down into his beard.

Jeb and Monti turned away.

Monti rubbed at her forehead.

Jeb cursed under his breath, slipped the rifle onto the floor beneath Monti's feet, returned to the cane pole.

The day wore on in a crescendo of heat that draped over them like a wet rag. Darkness came as an abrupt feeling of purity. The sun's afterglow fired the tips of the peaks in the west. A first quarter moon bathed the river in cold light. Flitting bats laced the sky overhead. Fireflies danced and jigged at the jungle's edge. The frog roar mounted from the shallows, and there came splashing sounds in the river all around.

Jeb wearily studied the moon path downstream, felt the burning fire of the blisters on his hands. He could see the dark shadow of Monti in the front seat, David leaning close to her.

"How's your hand, David?" asked Jeb.

The boy straightened, looked out at Jeb. "It's all right, sir."

"If it hurts badly you should tell us," said Jeb.

"I can stand it."

Something in David's tone spoke of suffering.

"It hurts pretty badly, doesn't it?" asked Jeb.

"Sure, but ..."

"Give him one of the codeine pills, Monti," said Jeb. "Better use the flash to make sure you get the right ones."

Monti groped on the floor for the flashlight. Presently its beam poked out a cone of brilliance in the cabin.

"Dear, you should tell us when it hurts," she said.

"But, Mother, I'm ..."

"It's all right. We understand. Here. Take this. Do you want the water?"

"Yes."

The bucket gurgled as she passed it back.

Jeb turned away. And now, in the cloak of darkness, he found a moment to wonder how they should guard Gettler during the night. The madman loomed as a constant menace hidden in the black shadows at the rear of the cabin.

Christ! If he broke out of those tapes in the night ...

Jeb shook his head.

A dark blotch of drowned bushes loomed out of the night. Jeb heard the current hissing and swirling over them. He glanced up at the moon, saw a black massing of clouds in the east: another storm.

The flooded island was passing now on the left.

Jeb readied the grapnel, took up the cane pole, worked the plane closer, tossed the iron into the dark shadows. It dragged with a sound of breaking limbs and scraping, then caught. The plane swung around downstream, rasped across the drowned bushes. Insects came up like a living vapor at the disturbance. Jeb scrambled into the cabin, closed the door. Monti was singing softly, her voice like a reverie sound.

"Dee-eep river ... my home is o-ver Jordan ..."

She broke off, looked at Jeb.

"What're we going to do for food?"

"We'll have to find something tomorrow for sure," he said.

Jeb found the flashlight, turned its beam into the rear of the cabin. Gettler stared blankly straight ahead.

"David, check the tape on his hands," said Jeb.

The boy looked back with a doped unconcern, turned, peered down behind Gettler, spoke slowly: "'S all right."

Jeb snapped off the light, settled back into his own seat.

Sounds of the river at night enveloped them: a dipping limb that murmured to itself in the current, the faint rasping of bushes against the float, a whiffling and snuffling from the left shore as an animal drank, the incessant ear-ringing of insects, the croaking of frogs.

Monti's voice came into this background like water filling up a low place: "It's a terrible thing to say," she murmured. "I know it is. But for a while today I was almost happy. Sitting here, watching the river, wondering what the next bend would reveal. Watching you out there on the float. Even the heat didn't bother me. I just felt curious about everything."

"Maybe that's the secret of happiness," said Jeb. "Curiosity."

"So the next bend in the river shows you a Jivaro war party waiting," muttered Gettler. And his voice carried that half-hidden *laughing-at-you* tone of clarity.

Monti cleared her throat.

"Thanks, Gettler," said Jeb. "We needed that warning real bad."

"There's always something new around the next bend in the river," said Gettler. "And finally: the ocean." His voice took on a sudden pleading note: "Logan, cut these tapes off my wrists. They're too tight. They'll cause an ..."

"I checked them. So did David," said Jeb. "They're not too tight."

"And thank you," murmured Gettler.

In the silence that followed, they heard David's deep, drugged breathing. Presently, there came the sound of snoring from Gettler.

And Jeb realized with a feeling of shock that Gettler probably was sleeping in utter exhaustion—his first deep sleep since they'd picked him up at the rancho.

The moon dipped lower across the jungle. Full darkness enveloped them: a thick and oily darkness with clouds blotting out the stars.

A wind arose, mounting swiftly. It shook the plane and the forest around them, humming everywhere like a terrible organ. From both banks came the rushing, slapping sound of leaves colliding in the wind.

And Gettler dreamed. In the dream, he was two people: a student and a professor in a phantom lecture hall. All around them grouped other students without faces.

"When your hands are tied, that defines your limits," lectured the dream professor. *"Happiness comes only through a defining of limits. But it may happen that you do not want happiness that way ... and that you may be*

happier ... paradoxically—without the happiness-limitation."

The dream-student Gettler nodded, and drifted away into a moment of non-identity that opened into himself as the dream-professor.

"But nothing harmful must happen to the boy," he lectured. *"The boy David-Peter-Peter-David is in terrible danger, and you must protect him."*

Gettler turned in his sleep, muttered, resumed his snoring.

The bump-bump-bump of the canoe tied beneath the fuselage arose in the night and faded like a drum sending a jungle message.

Jeb studied the black curtain of night, unable to sleep. He heard David's drugged breathing, Gettler's snores, the restless shifting of Monti. A dancing green line of fireflies bewitched the darkness, and were blotted out by a gust of wind-driven rain that pounded against the windshield.

An ominous flowing of premonition saturated Jeb. He felt the pressure of certainty that one or more of them was marked to die. It was like finding himself high above the earth in a plane without power: no place to go but down, and nothing but sharp peaks below.

Monti leaned toward him, whispered: "You awake?"

Suddenly, he needed a completeness that only she could provide. The sensation exploded in him, sent his arms out, and swept her against him. Their lips crushed together in a torturing kiss—a smothering of fire and agony.

She moaned as his hand groped beneath her shirt.

Something about the danger around them intensified the hunger of their bodies, drove them both to frenzies of passion that neither had ever before experienced.

Monti's hands fluttered against him, responding to every demand. She opened their shirts, pressed herself against him: warm skin to warm skin. There came a soft, uninhibited yielding to her every motion: a warm, sensuous twisting that anticipated him.

She put her lips close to his ear, panted: "Be ... very ... quiet ... ohhhhhhh ..."

Their movements became like the river current: the soft and natural swaying that preceded the chasm and the rapids where the water pounded and flung itself in white violence.

And when the moment was spent, they still clung to each other, tasting remembered sweetness.

At dawn, the rain eased away to a fog-like drizzle.

Jeb slipped down to the left float, retrieved the grapnel, pushed the plane off into the current.

The pocked water around them carried an endless procession of flotsam: islands of sedge, logs, branches, leaves, bits of flower-garlanded greenery.

He looked in at Monti, recalling the night.

She glanced at him, turned away.

A hot flush crept over her skin, and she thought: *For Christ's sake! I'm embarrassed! Why'n hell do I suddenly develop a conscience?*

Gettler climbed to consciousness from a deep, drenched sleep, found himself feeling clear-headed and refreshed. But his shoulders were cramped from the awkward position, and his wrists burned beneath the tape. He yawned.

David's first awakening sensation came as a throbbing at his temples—followed by a sharp twinge of pain in the stump of his finger, and a rasping dryness in his throat.

"Water," he husked.

Monti turned.

"Does your head hurt, dear?"

"'M so thirsty."

She helped him with the water bucket.

"Is that better?"

"Yes. Where are we?"

"Going from nowhere to somewhere," said Gettler.

Monti stabbed a sharp glance at him, settled back in the front seat.

A tearing emptiness of hunger clutched her stomach. The

pang receded, left her feeling weak and desperate. Her mind focused in sudden rage on Gettler, and she whirled. "You dirty, murdering sonofabitch!" she rasped. "I'm sorry I didn't kill you!"

As though at this signal to violence, there came a crash of thunder upriver, and the rain returned to its blinding, drenching equatorial downpour.

Monti slumped back, leaned against her door.

The outburst had shocked Jeb to sudden attention, but Gettler acted as though he had not heard.

Only David continued to stare at Monti, turning her words over and over in his mind.

Murdering? She means he killed my dad. Did he?

The boy turned his attention to Gettler, but the man had closed his eyes, and was sleeping softly like a baby.

The incessant drum roll of rain on the wings and cabin top filled the four humans with a timeless feeling. All around hung the grey vaporous curtain. Dim shapes of trees and hills took form through it, and dissolved as the plane floated past. Everything beyond the wingtips looked out of focus—as though created just that moment and left unfinished.

A spit of muddy land grew out of the rain.

Jeb suddenly crouched, peering at it. The brown shore was lined with rows of alligators drawn up in waiting ranks.

The Jivaro know we're back here somewhere, thought Jeb. *A shot wouldn't tell them something they don't already know.*

He wet his lips with his tongue, dug the pole into the river, sent the plane toward the bank below the alligators.

"What're you doing?" whispered Monti.

"Going to get us some food."

Jeb took the rifle from the cabin floor, gave Monti the little twenty-two, lifted the grapnel from the strut and hurled it ashore as the plane grounded.

Upstream, one of the alligators pushed itself off into the river.

Hunger was like an electric current surging through Jeb. He brought the rifle to his shoulder, steeled himself against trembling, sighted on an eye of the nearest alligator, squeezed the trigger. The gun roared, bucked against Jeb's shoulder.

But there was a blood-spattered threshing monster on the shore, twisting and flopping, hurling mud all around it.

The remaining alligators scrambled into the river.

"Hah!" shouted Gettler. "We eat!"

"What is it?" asked David.

"Alligator," said Gettler.

Jeb exchanged the rifle for the machete, slipped off the float into the mud, slogged through clinging ooze toward the alligator. It had quieted to an occasional twitch, and lay half on its side, head in the water.

The machete dragged heavily against Jeb's hand. It seemed to have doubled its weight since the last time he'd held it. He stopped beside the dead alligator, lifted the blade, swung down: and again ... and again, until the tail lay severed.

Jeb picked up the tail, turned to retrace his steps. Rain poured down the muddy bank, filling his footprints, running away to the river in brown rivulets. He looked around, hesitating, feeling a sudden menace that made him tremble.

Something moved in the greyness of the veiled jungle wall at the base of the narrow spit.

His first thought: *Indian!*

Jeb dropped the alligator tail, put his hand to the magnum revolver wedged in his belt.

The rain-bent saw grass above him rippled, and Jeb stared at two glaring eyes in a cat face: *jaguar!*

His mind came around in a kind of shocked protest, and he told himself: *But jaguar hunt only at night!*

The animal flowed out of the grass and onto the muddy shore, crouched.

Jeb dragged up the revolver, snapped off a shot at the

lowered head. The gun blasted and kicked in his hand as the big cat leaped. Jeb threw himself sideways, firing again as he moved.

The jaguar splashed into the river, jerked from side to side, twitched, shuddered, became quiet with its head under water. Something rippled the current beyond the dead animal. The cat suddenly slipped away, disappeared in an abrupt swirl of water.

Jeb's breathing quieted. He retrieved the alligator tail and slogged back to the plane. He flopped the tail out onto the float, scrambled hurriedly up beside it, slid the machete under the seat.

"That's the first time I ever saw a jaguar hunt a man in the open in broad daylight," said Gettler. "Too bad it was so slow."

"Thanks," said Jeb.

"It was probably old, sick and starving," said Gettler.

Monti leaned out, looked down at the alligator tail.

"Is that good to eat?"

"Sure." Jeb turned toward David. "Get out the pellet stove."

"Yes, sir."

Jeb cooked the meat, cut it into four shares, handed three in the cabin to Monti.

"You going to cut these tapes off me?" asked Gettler.

"David can feed you," said Jeb.

He squatted on the float, began gnawing his share of the meat. It tasted faintly of mud.

A transparent butterfly staggered through the rain, pasted its stranded filigree against the plane's cowling in front of Jeb. A gusting of the downpour washed it off into the river.

Presently, Jeb arose, brought the anchor aboard, pushed off. The plane joined the other flotsam on the rain-cratered current.

The day stretched out like an extension of the flowing

river. Jeb's muscles grew numb with the exertion of keeping the plane out of the side currents. His throat felt thick and swollen where Gettler had bruised it.

And Jeb's thoughts returned to Monti, but with a sense of detachment: *Am I in love with her? Oh, Hell! Love doesn't happen like this! It's just physical. Natural.*

He glanced in at Monti. She was napping, curled back in her corner with her cheek against the seat back. The red hair wisped in disorderly strands from beneath the silver scarf. Deep blue shadows traced the sunken curves beneath her eyelids. Freckles stood out darkly against the translucent paleness of her skin.

Jesus! She's beautiful! he thought.

And he wanted to go into the cabin, cradle her head against him, reassure her.

Am I in love?

In the afternoon the rain slackened, almost stopped. A washed clarity in the air opened up the distances, brought everything into sharp focus. The clouds lifted, but did not break. Birds and animals came out of hiding. A droll-faced monkey chattered at them from an overhanging tree. Jungle hummingbirds darted among the garlanded branches. Pale lemon-green parakeets flocked over the water.

A giant leaf paced them for a time, bearing a long orange-shelled snail on its surface like a Magellan of the jungle world.

The cloud-shrouded sun touched the western peaks, and the forest around the plane began to draw in its night shadows: first the dark greens went to grey, then to black; lighter flowers dimmed.

A velvet smoothness overcame the river, and it was night.

Jeb took out the flashlight, probed ahead: nothing. The dimming yellowness of the light told of weakened batteries. He turned it off.

The plane suddenly grated on an obstruction, lurched, throwing Jeb against the strut. He snapped the light back on, sent its beam around them to reveal a rippling of shallows—*shallows*.

They scraped and bumped downstream.

"What's happening?" demanded Monti.

"Shallows."

Jeb turned off the light, found the grapnel and hurled it into the darkness. He felt it grip as the plane swept off into deeper water. They began the familiar sawing back and forth, back and forth in the current. Jeb scrambled through the cabin, dropped down to the opposite float, felt the patch. It was still in place. He took off the cap, groped inside the float: about two inches of water.

"Is it all right?" asked Monti.

"I think so."

He crouched on the float, feeling inside it. The water didn't seem to be rising.

"David, dig down behind you and give me the pump," said Jeb.

"Yes, sir."

"I hope it sinks," said Gettler.

Jeb ignored him, checked the lashings on the dugout.

"Here's the pump," said David.

There came a sudden scrambling in the cabin's darkness. David cried out, and Gettler began to laugh. Something banged against the float beneath Jeb, splashed in the river.

"You pushed me!" said David.

Monti found the flashlight, shone it into the rear.

Gettler stared back at the light, smiling.

"He made me drop the pump," said David.

Jeb felt weariness without anger. He replaced the cap on the float, leaned into the cabin.

"Did he hurt you, David?"

"No, sir. He just pushed my hand."

"Are we going to sink?" asked Monti.

"No."

Jeb took the flashlight, directed it into Gettler's eyes. The man blinked, but his face held its steady, almost vacant smile.

"Why'd you do that?" asked Jeb.

Gettler chuckled, sank back, closed his eyes.

The pinwheels whirled in his brain.

Jeb handed the light to David. "Check the tape on his hands."

David took the light, peered behind Gettler. "Everything looks the same."

Jeb climbed inside past Monti, took back the light, turned it off.

"Where are we?" asked Monti.

"Some shallows somewhere."

"You're tired," said Monti.

"Yes."

"I can stand watch," said David.

"Okay."

"Maybe we can recover that pump in the morning," said Monti.

"It doesn't make any difference," said Jeb.

And he felt that this was the only truth remaining in the world.

"Nothing makes any difference," he said.

"It's too much for you—handling the plane all alone," said Monti.

"I could help," said David.

Jeb shook his head. "No."

"How's your hand, David?" asked Monti.

"It hurts a little, but it's better."

"You should check the bandages," whispered Jeb.

"It's all right," said David.

"I'll do it first thing in the morning," she said.

Jeb leaned his head against the seat back. It felt so smooth, so restful. He slept, and dreams filled his mind. Creeping green mold spread everywhere around him, crept up his legs, reached for his mouth and nose. The smell of it filled his nostrils. He twisted, moaned.

A small warm hand touched his forehead, and a voice whispered: “It’s all right. Go to sleep.”

Jeb’s dreaming mind swept back through dead years to his mother’s voice; he relaxed.

“Go to sleep dear. Everything’ll be all right in the morning.”

His breathing smoothed, deepened.

Monti withdrew her hand from his forehead.

How like Roger he is, she thought. An abrupt feeling of self-revulsion filled her. *Stop kidding yourself, Monti! He isn’t Roger!* Her mouth shaped into a sneer. *What in Christ’s name am I doing here?* She put her hands over her eyes. *What am I going to do?*

Jeb turned in his sleep, leaned against her.

And Monti’s thought went out to him as though to something forbidden that drew her mind against her will.

Well, what the hell! (And she recognized her father’s expression in her thoughts.) *So I’m attracted to a man. That’s what men and women are for.*

Jeb awoke in the pre-dawn blackness. An acid etching of hunger knotted his stomach. He thought that he could feel the disintegration of the plane around them as he felt the hungry wasting of his own body. Uncounted little working-away noises trembled through the plane as it swung back and forth in the current. The soft *thump-kalump* of the canoe against the float came like a counterpoint to his own heartbeats. Intertwined odors trailed through the darkness: the biting smell of rust, mildew, perspiration and rotting fruit, oil smoke and carrion.

And over it all hung the fetid musk of the jungle: a compound of mud and plants, perfumes and stenches—with endless harmonics between, underneath and over.

Jeb cleared his throat.

Monti stirred.

“You awake?” whispered Jeb.

"Yes." She coughed. "I made David go to sleep."

"All quiet?"

"Yes."

"It'll be daylight pretty soon."

"I know. Everything gets so quiet just before dawn."

"It's stopped raining."

"It hasn't rained all night."

Jeb slapped at an insect crawling on his arm. He became conscious that insects were everywhere in the cabin: buzzing, clicking, fluttering, crawling ...

"God, the bugs are fierce!" he said.

"I had my door open for awhile," she said.

Dawn exploded over the river as though a switch had been thrown. They saw that the clouds were breaking in the east: shreds of sky—a washed grey-blue—widened to reveal the sun.

The waking sounds of birds clamored in the forest with whistles, screeches, coughings, *jib-jib-jibs*—and a distant roar that could have been a long-tailed monkey pretending it was a jaguar.

Gettler mumbled, straightened.

Jeb turned.

"You want me to help you down to the float?"

"Go to hell!" growled Gettler. He glared at Jeb.

David opened his eyes, blinked, said: "This is the ninth day."

Jeb turned to Monti. "Better change the bandage while I'm casting off."

She nodded.

He opened his door, swung down to the float, worked the grapnel off the bottom with the aid of a cane pole. Immediately the plane turned sideways, matched its pace to the brown current.

An iridescent opaline beetle arrowed from the left bank, came under the wing, rested momentarily on the strut, and plunged off toward the opposite shore.

Jeb looked into the cabin.

"How's his hand?"

"It looked awfully red. I put some more of that ointment on it."

"It doesn't hurt as much as it did," said David.

"My hands are falling off," snarled Gettler. "Not that I suppose you care."

"Turn around and let me see them," said Jeb.

Gettler sneered.

"I can *turn* you around," said Jeb.

Slowly, Gettler twisted in the seat, exposed his taped wrists.

Jeb tugged at the bindings.

"Your hands look okay."

Gettler settled back in the seat.

A current pulled the plane toward the right hand shore. Jeb labored with the cane pole until they again floated in the center of the stream.

"Will my door lock?" asked Monti.

Jeb trailed his cane pole in the water, glanced in at her. "That latch there beside the handle. Pull it back. Why?"

"We could turn him loose out there on the right side, and lock my door."

"Why?"

"He could help you."

Jeb looked at Gettler, pursed his lips, glanced through the cabin at the other strut. The spear that had pierced the wing tank was still wedged there.

"Give me that spear on this side," said Jeb.

Monti leaned out, recovered the spear, handed it to him. Jeb wedged it against the strut on his side.

"How about it, Gettler?" he asked.

"How about what?"

"If we parole you on the other side will you help?"

"Why should I?"

"Let me," said David. "My finger's all right."

Gettler shook his head, spoke in a suddenly odd tone of sanity: "You can't make the boy do a man's work! It'll kill him!"

"Maybe I should help," said Monti.

Jeb shook his head.

"The boy didn't do anything to deserve being tortured!" said Gettler. "I saw his hand. There's no reason to torture him." Glittering wildness returned to Gettler's eyes.

"We're not torturing him," said Jeb.

"I'll help," muttered Gettler. "I give you my promise."

Jeb took a pocketknife in his right hand, the revolver in his left, said: "Okay. Turn around."

Gettler obeyed.

Jeb cut the tape between his wrists.

"Out the other side!" snapped Jeb.

Gettler rubbed his wrists.

"Now!" said Jeb.

Gettler clambered across David, dropped down to the float.

Monti slammed her door, locked it.

Gettler took up a cane pole, dipped it in the current.

Jeb turned, looked downstream.

Maybe that was a mistake, he thought. *Gettler might watch his chance to jump ashore and run away.* Jeb shrugged. *Well, what if he did? It'd sure make things easier.*

Clouds piled against the face of the hills in the west. The day grew brighter, and the heat mounted.

Solitude closed in upon them. There came over the river a feeling of timeless immensity: something endless and moving like a place of eternity caught between forest walls.

The jungle cast a spell over the plane.

The four humans surrendered themselves to the smooth gliding of sun and river. They drifted and drowsed along a breadth of warm light between two darknesses.

A roaring sound of rapids pressed in upon Jeb's awareness. He suddenly straightened to attention.

Downstream, the river narrowed like the converging lines of a railroad track, and seemed to end in a feathery green lifting of hills. Jeb read the current, recognized that the river must curve left.

The roaring sound grew louder.

Jeb climbed into the cabin, pumped the primer.

"What about him?" asked Monti. She nodded toward Gettler standing on the float.

"There's time," said Jeb.

He pulled the starter button. The motor kicked over twice without response. Again he tried the starter. It emitted a lifeless, grinding noise.

"Isn't it going to start?" asked Monti.

"Doesn't sound like it's getting any spark," muttered Jeb.

Now, they could feel the cooler airborne dampness that told of violent white water. The sound plunged up the river to them, filling the space between the jungle walls.

Again Jeb pumped the primer, pulled the starter without result.

Gettler shouted, pointed to the right.

"What's he pointing at?" asked Monti.

Jeb studied the shore, hesitated.

"It's a spear," said David. "Hanging from that tree."

"I see it," said Monti. "What is it?"

"Ghost spear!" yelled Gettler.

Monti whirled toward Jeb. "What's he saying?"

"It's nothing," said Jeb.

And again he tried the starter.

"David," said Jeb.

"Yes, sir." The boy leaned forward.

"Give Gettler your pocket knife. Tell him to cut the canoe loose, and have it ready."

David, slid across the seat, opened the door.

Jeb tried the starter.

"I had a jalopy in college that sounded like that when it wouldn't start," said Monti.

The roar of water now dominated the air over the river. Jeb felt the damp coolness of the wind-blown spray.

"Come on, baby—start!" he pleaded.

And again he tried the starter.

"Could it be flooded?" asked Monti.

Jeb fought down a desire to shout: "Shut up!"

He worked the starter, and it ground more slowly with the weakening of the battery.

Gettler leaned in the open door. "You're not going to start it." He held the canoe beneath the fuselage with his foot. "We'd better get in the canoe."

"You know what that spear meant!" snapped Jeb.

Gettler looked downstream.

The plane drifted toward hills that climbed steeply on both sides. Their green faded away to softness like a covering of sage-colored moss.

"What about that spear?" asked Monti.

"What was that white stuff on it?" demanded David.

"Kapok," said Jeb.

"What's it mean?" shouted Monti.

"They've made an offering to their river god, asking him to take us," said Gettler.

Jeb's hands moved with desperate jerkiness as he again tried the starter.

The motor ground with a hopeless slowness.

Gettler crouched on the pontoon, holding the canoe.

Something spanged into the fuselage beside the door.

"Dart!" screamed Gettler.

There came a splashing, scraping sound from beneath the plane.

In that moment, they swept around the bend. The current quickened. Directly ahead—less than one hundred yards away—the water curled over between glistening black lava walls. Deeper and deeper creases furrowed the current as it swept over into the gorge.

A deafening, hammering roar broke over the plane.

The lava flow was split cleanly by the river as though a giant axe had hewed it.

"Gettler!" screamed Monti. "He's gone in the canoe!"

"Hang on!" shouted Jeb.

He scrambled out the door, grabbed up his cane pole. Out of the corners of his eyes he glimpsed the canoe behind them, Gettler crouched in the center, paddling with a pole.

But there was no time to worry about Gettler.

A surging coil of demented water lifted the plane, seemed to hold it poised, then hurled it forward into a terrifying savagery.

Jeb grabbed for the strut, hugged against it.

The left hand pontoon submerged, swept his feet out from under him. Jeb fought his way back onto the pontoon. The plane whirled completely around. Something jerked it forward. Jeb saw that the grapnel sea anchor had fallen overboard. He dared not let go of the strut to recover it, and could only stare at the taut line disappearing into the river ahead.

The canyon walls soared upward into amber spray mist seemingly just beyond the wingtips. Currents slithered along the smooth walls, and whirled back into the central torrent. A mountainous boiling of water loomed ahead as the maelstrom surged over a hidden rock.

Jeb freed one hand from the strut, pointed his cane pole ahead, felt it grate on rock. The pole, bent, snapped. He hurled away the useless stump, clutched the strut.

There was no time for fear. He experienced only a sinking sensation of awe as the pontoon beneath him lifted on the current and cleared the rock. The plane plunged down the other side, and a wave washed completely over them.

Screeching metal could be heard even above the chasm's roar.

The plane tipped backward, bobbed forward, straightened.

And they were out of it! Drifting to the right across a wide dark pool that still boiled with the concealed violence of the rapids.

Jeb took a deep, shaking breath.

"I never thought we'd make it," he whispered. "My God!"

"Look!" screamed Monti.

Jeb straightened.

Monti was leaning out the door, pointing upstream.

Jeb turned.

A dark matchstick hurtled toward them down the gorge with an ant figure moving violently in it.

Gettler!

The matchstick grew larger, resolved into a canoe. And now they could see the cane pole in his hands. Troughs and flumes of insane water tore at the canoe: rushing currents that blundered everywhere.

The canoe shot between two rocks as though squirted. It reared like a horse above the final boiling surge of current, and slapped down in the lower pool.

"He made it!" shouted David.

Gettler poled toward the drifting plane.

The roar of white water grew dimmer. Jeb became aware of straining and groaning sounds in the metal of the plane. Both pontoons gurgled with water inside them. They floated low. The strut shackles had been strained where they joined the float beneath Jeb. There was at least three inches of play at the juncture.

"Hallooooo!" called Gettler.

David looked at Jeb. "The water went right over us!"

Jeb glanced back at the rapids. He could still see one wall of the lava escarpment and the tailrace of white water. He saw no logical answer to how they had survived that violence yet the fact that they had survived it gave him no reassurance. He felt that they were being saved only for a more terrible trial.

Gettler poled the canoe under the wing beside Jeb, grabbed the pontoon.

"Is she going to float?" he asked.

Jeb stared at him.

"You didn't have to come back here," he said. "You abandoned us. Why didn't you ..."

"I couldn't help that up there," said Gettler. "The plane got away from me when I ducked into the canoe to escape the darts."

"Then why'd you come back?"

"You have the guns," said Gettler.

Jeb sighed, then: "Find us some cane poles." He slipped the machete from the floor of the cabin, tossed it into the canoe, put a hand on the revolver at his waist.

Gettler smiled. "Sure, captain." He looked around. "Where?"

Jeb looked around. Thorn bushes, a flooded reach of saw grass, assorted islands of sedge with their vaporous clouds of insects, here and there alligator snouts parting the current in wait for anything the rapids disgorged. Beyond the thorn bushes and saw grass, forests of hardwood climbed upward.

"Now you see why you're not supposed to be able to navigate this river in the wet season," said Gettler.

"We survived those rapids," protested Jeb.

"The river god wasn't ready for us yet."

"And where were the Jivaro?" asked Jeb. "That was a perfect place for an ambush!"

"You saw the spear," said Gettler. "They prayed to the demon of the rapids, then sat back to let the demon take us."

A widening curve of river hid the rapids. The river downstream spread across lowlands like a stagnant lake.

"Animals starve here in this season," said Gettler. "Only the bugs stay active."

"You want us to give up?" asked Jeb.

"We take the canoe," said Gettler. "It's our only hope."

Jeb glanced along the narrow length of the dugout, saw the wash of dirty water in its bottom, the brown bubbles along the cracks in the wood.

The plane creaked and gurgled.

"That thing's sinking," said Gettler.

"Give me your cane pole," said Jeb.

Gettler hesitated, passed the pole to Jeb.

"Swing the canoe around to the other side and tie it up," said Jeb.

Gettler shrugged, obeyed.

"David, get up on top and look for a place to beach," said Jeb.

The boy clambered out, and Jeb boosted him onto the cabin top.

David shielded his eyes with his hand, stared downstream.

"Don't let a sedge island fool you," said Jeb. "Look for current going around both sides of an island."

"Over there to the right," said David. "That one." He pointed at a dark mound.

Jeb recovered the sea anchor, hung it in the strut, began working the plane toward the island. The dark spot grew larger as they approached.

"It *is* an island!" said Monti.

Current whorls billowed away on both sides in a thin lacery of foam.

Less than an inch remained between the top of Jeb's pontoon and the river surface. He dug the pole into the river bottom, sent the plane crabwise into a patch of drowned grass at the upper tip of the island.

"Now what?" demanded Gettler.

"Now you bail out the pontoons," said Jeb.

"With what?"

"With a dipper made from fish line and an end joint of this cane pole. Get busy."

Jeb passed him the pole beneath the fuselage.

"The patch's leaking," said Gettler.

"Shut up and get busy." Jeb lowered himself into the warm water, waded across to the muddy ground ahead of the plane. "I'll find something to wedge the patch tighter."

He glanced up at Monti, nodded toward Gettler.

She raised the muzzle of the rifle to where Jeb could see it.

Monti watched Jeb explore the island for bits of driftwood. She heard David moving on the cabin top, Gettler working at the floats.

The still, steamy air above the river felt unbreathable, and made her lungs gasp in deep unsatisfactory gulps of vapor. The day grew hotter as the men worked.

It can't possibly get any hotter, she thought.

But it grew hotter.

Jeb came around the left side, lifted the cowling, began working on the motor. Presently, he appeared at the cabin door, leaned in toward Monti.

"Anything in your suitcase I can use to wipe away moisture in the motor?"

"I'll see."

She climbed into the rear seat, groped behind it, came up with a translucent red nightgown. It smelled of mildew and there was a green streak of rot across it. She handed it to Jeb.

"Here. Use this."

And she thought: *Now there's a macabre twist! That little bit of red fluff was supposed to save my marriage. Now ... maybe it'll save my life!*

She shook her head, slid across the seat, peered out at Jeb.

"How's it going?"

"I think the ignition shorted out. Everything's soaked. It's getting plenty of gas."

She glanced up at the sky.

"Why aren't there planes out looking for us now that the weather's clear?"

Jeb continued to work, spoke without looking at her.

"The clear weather may be local. We don't know what it's like downstream.

"But couldn't they just fly up the river?"

"Maybe ... maybe not."

"They must've missed us by now!"

"Don't count on it."

Her voice sank to just above a whisper: "I'm famous, dammit. They won't just leave me and forget me." She raised her voice. "We heard that one plane! There'll be more."

Jeb stopped, looked at her.

"That was over a week ago, Monti."

"They'd search at the rancho first," she said. "That's natural."

"If they've missed us, they may suspect that we found a chunk of mountain in a cloud ... or crashed into the jungle." He stared out across the flooded river. "The jungle can swallow a plane in a week—grow over it so that it'd never be found." Again he looked at her. "Why should anyone expect us to be on a river that curves all over hell's half acre?"

She put a hand to her eyes, shook her head.

Jeb leaned against the cowling as a trembling of weakness passed over him. He felt that he had passed beyond hunger.

"The floats are as dry as I can get them," said Gettler.

Jeb straightened, looked down at Gettler standing in the water ahead of the plane. A look of feral cunning veiled the man's eyes. Unconsciously, Jeb put his hand to the revolver in his belt.

"You're going to have to crank her," said Jeb.

"How?"

"Beach the canoe between the floats, and stand in it." Jeb looked at the prop. "Ever do this before?"

"No."

"You grab the prop with both hands up here, stand well back; you haul it down and step clear all in one motion."

"When do I do this?"

"Get the canoe in position. I'll tell you when. We'll prime it first. You have to be careful when I yell contact." He looked down at the canoe. "Fall back into the canoe if you have to.

Let's get moving."

Jeb climbed into his seat, checked the controls, nodded to Gettler.

The motor coughed on the second try, then settled into its familiar banging, spitting roar. Jeb adjusted the carburetor, leaned out his door, shouted: "Tie the canoe to the float and shove us off!"

Presently, the nose of the plane swung out into the river. Gettler appeared standing on the right hand float.

"Why're you using the motor?" asked Monti.

"To dry it out."

"Is David all right up on top?"

"Yes. He was lying down flat when I got in."

"If we just had enough gas," said Monti.

"It'd save some blisters all right," said Jeb. He glanced up at the wing tank gauge on his left, looked down to the temperature needle. "That should do it." He turned off the ignition.

Gettler rapped on the door window beside Monti.

"We going to have to crank her every time?"

Jeb shrugged.

David slid down to the cowling, dropped to the left float, climbed into the rear seat.

"Boy, it's hot up there!"

A wavering diagonal current took the plane around a thin neck of tree-garlanded land. Again they heard the sound of falling water. The river below them stretched more than half a mile wide with a straight line slanting across it. Vapor whorls hung above the line.

"A shallow falls," said Jeb. "Maybe three feet." He looked left to right. "Clear across!"

"What'll we do?" asked Monti.

"Gettler!" called Jeb. "Crank her!"

Gettler moved forward along the float.

The motor caught on the first turn.

Jeb swung toward the left shore in a wide, curving arc.

Oil smoke fumed back into the cabin.

Monti coughed.

"What're you going to do?" she asked.

"Look at those trees," said Jeb. "See the water beyond them? Means it's open. No place for an ambush."

She nodded.

Jeb cut the motor, slipped down to the float. The plane coasted in among drooping vines. He caught one, tied it to the strut.

"Plantain," said Gettler.

Jeb looked at him. "Huh?"

"Bananas." Gettler pointed into the narrow peninsula.

Jeb followed the direction pointed, saw a tree of thick fronds with red-skinned fruit showing through the green.

Gettler already was off the float, forcing his way through the undergrowth. He returned with three thick stems of the fruit, passed two to Jeb.

"Are those bananas?" asked David. "They're red."

Jeb handed Monti one of the stems of fruit.

"They ought to be cooked if you want to take the time," he said. But he already was peeling and eating one.

The food felt leaden in his stomach, and he suffered a sudden cramping pang of nausea. It passed, and he ate a second one.

Gettler squatted on the muddy shore, staring at the nose of the dugout beneath the plane. If he closed his eyes, he knew that he would see rapids around him, feel the canoe fighting the savage water beneath him, the cane pole vibrating in his hands.

Curious, he thought. *I wasn't afraid.*

And he realized that he had never once doubted his ability to shoot the white water safely. The feeling had come over him as he crouched in the dugout to escape the dart attack, and watched the plane drift away. But all the same ... something had happened back there: a new kind of awareness tingling in his nerves.

He saw David come out of the cabin and onto the float beside Jeb.

"May I go pick some more of that fruit?" he asked.

Gettler absently pinched off a tick on his leg.

Jeb studied the peninsula to the left where it curved off into higher ground, looked across the flood waters on the other side at the feathery green hills, a great softness of hills bending down to the river. There was a desolate, sweltering emptiness to the landscape, all motion crushed by the pressure of heat.

And Jeb knew that the emptiness was a false image.

"I'll be careful," said David.

"Let him pick some of the fruit," said Monti. "It's open in there. Nothing could be hidden."

A black and scarlet dragonfly buzzed across the cowling of the plane, hummed in among the trees.

Jeb shrugged. "Be careful."

"Yes, sir."

"And keep your finger out of the water."

David leaped to the mud beside Gettler, skidded, caught himself on a vine. He made his way toward the fruit still showing through the green.

Jeb turned to bail out the floats.

"How're you planning to go over those falls?" asked Gettler.

"Skim over them under power," said Jeb.

Gettler sniffed.

"And what about the canoe?"

"We'll let it go over by itself and recover it below." Jeb glanced at the canoe. "Untie it and beach it for now."

Gettler straightened stiffly, moved to obey.

Monti leaned out the door. "Where's David?"

Jeb glanced at the shore. No sign of the boy.

Monti pulled back, looked into the rear seat, on the floor, under the front seats.

"Jeb, he's got the other gun: the twenty-two," she said.

There was an edge of panic to her voice.

"It's all right," said Jeb. He moved to the front edge of the float, called: "David!"

No answer.

And again, louder: "David!"

Monti dropped down beside him, shouted: "David!"

No answer.

Gettler beached the canoe, climbed up the muddy shore.

"David!" he called.

A hummingbird darted past him with a musical whirring of wings. No other sound except the roaring of the falls.

"He can't have gone far," said Jeb.

Gettler returned to the canoe for the machete, went back into the underbrush.

Monti put a hand to her cheek.

"Something's happened to David!" Her voice bordered on hysteria.

"Stay here!" said Jeb.

He leaped to the shore, scrambled up toward the fronds that trembled to Gettler's movements.

Gettler emerged from the bushes, machete dangling in his right hand. "His tracks lead off toward the mainland."

"What's he thinking of?" Jeb cupped his hands around his mouth, shouted: "David!"

"He can't hear you above the sound of the falls," said Gettler. "He's following the tracks of a river pig."

"Following the ..."

"He thinks he's going to get us some meat," said Gettler. "I heard her say he took the gun."

"What's wrong?" called Monti.

Jeb returned to the bow of the canoe, explained.

Monti's glance darted fearfully along the line of the peninsula.

"Logan," said Gettler.

Jeb turned.

"I'm going after him," said Gettler. "Let me have your gun."

Jeb shook his head. "You're staying here ... without a gun." He lifted the revolver from his belt, hefted it. "I'll find him."

"Stay where you are!" ordered Gettler. He lifted the machete.

Jeb brought up the gun muzzle.

And Gettler laughed, a brutal, chopping sound. "You're not the killer type, Logan. And that's why I'm going after the boy."

Gettler whirled, crashed into the underbrush, through it.

Jeb started after him.

"Wait!" called Monti.

He hesitated.

"Don't leave me," she said.

"Sonofabitch!" muttered Jeb.

Gettler was already out of sight.

Jeb felt a sudden chill, thought: *He could wait for me in there, chop me down with the machete.*

Slowly, he made his way back to the plane, jumped out to the float.

Then he thought about the twenty-two, glared at Monti.

"Christ!" he whispered. "If he gets that gun away from David, he could pick us off here like sitting ducks!"

"What'll we do?" gasped Monti.

Jeb rammed the gun under his belt, scrambled after the canoe, held it by tossing the grapnel into it. He slashed the vines tying the plane, pushed off, brought the grapnel. The canoe drifted free.

"Get inside!" ordered Jeb.

"What're you doing?"

"Get in there!"

She climbed into the cabin, gazed at the shore.

Jeb joined her, primed the motor.

"Pray there's enough juice in the battery."

He pulled the starter.

The motor kicked over, coughed, belched a cloud of black

smoke, settled into its uneven, banging.

Jeb let out a long breath.

"You're stranding them!" shouted Monti. "What're you doing?"

Jeb pointed the nose of the plane upstream, cracked the throttle a notch. They drew away from the falls.

"We'll recover the canoe and anchor below the falls in that big pool there."

"But they ..."

"The peninsula comes right down to the edge of the falls. We can pick them up there. Gettler can't shoot us. It'd strand him without transportation."

He swung the plane around in a wide arc, pointed it downstream. Oil smoke pouring from the cowling screened off the view ahead momentarily, and Jeb saw that the motor already was beginning to overheat. He threw off caution, pushed the throttle all the way ahead. The plane burst through its smoke screen, and the line of falls loomed up ahead like a pencil mark drawn across the river.

"Pray!" gritted Jeb.

The controls felt sluggish, soft, and the drag of the patched float forced him to use heavy left rudder. But some of the purpose built into this metal and fabric still lived. The plane wavered up onto the step as the falls came underneath. There was a bouncing sensation, a tortured roaring from the motor. They shot outward, dropped with a sodden splash that sent spray rattling against the fuselage and up under the wings.

Jeb eased off the throttle, kicked right rudder.

"There's the canoe!" shouted Monti.

It floated upside down beneath the falls, held there by the back surge of current.

Jeb killed the motor at the last minute, coasted up to the canoe, into the warm spray and rising mist. He slipped down to the float, caught the canoe, righted it, tied it alongside with a length of fish line.

The plane drifted slowly back from the falls into the wide pool.

He tossed out the grapnel, felt it bite into the river bottom.

The line tightened, and they swung around to face upstream.

Jeb bailed out the canoe, straightened.

Monti stared toward the peninsula above the falls. A dove-grey mist boiled up from the disturbed water to veil the shoreline. There was a dream quality to the forest wall.

"Monti," said Jeb.

She chewed at her lower lip, continued to stare shoreward.

"I know this can't mean much now," he said. "But I'm sorry I let him go."

"You didn't let him go," she said. "We all let him go. Even Gettler."

A deep sense of weariness dragged at Jeb. He tipped up the visor of his cap, rubbed his forehead. The insects they had evaded in moving the plane, found the new location, settled around the two humans, buzzing and biting. It was like being struck with thousands of pins. Jeb ignored them out of a deep feeling of fatigue. Monti forced her mind away from the horror of them until she felt that she was actually outside herself, an interested onlooker.

And she thought about Gettler with a new clarity.

If David's alive, Gettler will find him.

She held onto this thought like a thin flame of sanity.

A gentle flowing of wind pushed across the plane, turned it slightly. The wind brought a false coolness that made the after sensation of heat more unbearable. Again the wind surged across them—stronger this time. They could hear it in the struts, across the wings: a thin metallic vibration.

Jeb looked up into the wind.

A thick billowing of dark clouds filled the eastern horizon. There was a feeling of depth and weight and blackness to them. Lightning flickered soundlessly from beneath the rolling front. A long interval passed before the thunder came: a low, sodden hammer stroke.

A feeling of soundless suspense came over the river and the jungle. Even the pulsing of the falls became muted.

The current crawled beneath the plane like a writhing serpent, a muddy grey velvet oozing motion that harried the plane. Wind and current fought for domination over the creaking metal.

Again, lightning flickered over the jungle, and the growl of thunder came faster, sharper. The sound set off a band of howler monkeys on the eastern shore, and their cries echoed across the river.

Luminous grey darkness flowed across the plane, flattened all shadows. A line of rain surged over the water, whipped up violent bursts of wind. The storm broke over the plane as night fell. It was a blackness filled with the rattling of rain and shuddering wind.

A fork of lightning speared the darkness.

Jeb's eyes carried an afterglow image of the distant forest wall and veiling rain: everything frozen in a stark blue-white glare. He climbed into the cabin.

Monti leaned against him with a quick, seeking motion.

"Oh, God, I'm scared," she whispered. "Oh, God, I'm scared. Oh, God, I'm scared."

He had no words to comfort her. Their world and everything it demanded of them had gone beyond words into an elemental flow of feeling and emotion.

Monti shuddered, clutched at him. Abruptly, she pushed away, dragged in a sobbing breath.

A gust of wind and rain shook the plane.

She stared out into the blackness. It was impenetrable oblivion: a foretaste of death. She jerked her mind away from this thought, fumbled in her pocket for the cigarette lighter. The wheel rasped against the flint in the darkness. A thin spray of sparks shot across the wick, ignited it. The flame was a warm spot of yellow that sent wavering shadows into every corner of the cabin.

Jeb looked at it.

"What's that for?" he asked.

She reached out, balanced the lighter atop the instrument panel, stared at the tiny flame.

"Call it a candle in the window," she whispered. "Could they see it?"

"You couldn't see that light a hundred feet away through this rain."

"Jeb, what if they come back to the shore and find us gone?"

"They'll wait for morning."

"But the storm ..."

"It's rough, sure. What else can we do, though?"

She buried her face in her hands. "If I could just stop my mind! Stop thinking!"

Abruptly, she dropped her hands, whirled against him. Their lips touched, then bruised together.

An uncaring recklessness came over Monti. There was nothing more important in the world than the need to drive away thoughts, to win a blank passage of forgetfulness. She pulled her lips away from Jeb, whispered: "The body knows how to forget."

Jeb reached up, clicked the cap down on the lighter, extinguished it.

His mind took one fleeting glance into the jungle before he surrendered himself to his own need to forget. He saw the rain beating into the eternal mud, and two human figures crouching there. He felt that they were together.

Their lips met.

Cold blue gleams of lightning flared across the night: prongs of fire in an ebony sky. Thunder rolled and muttered and clapped. There came the crashing of uprooted trees in the jungle.

The lightning glare penetrated the forest ceiling only as a faint wash of blueness. But the thunder burst like an irregular cannonade through the avenues of tree trunks. Rain water ran off every leaf in curving torrents.

David crouched between two upsloping roots of a thick tree. He held the little twenty-two revolver straight out in front of him with a rigid fearfulness. Each shock of thunder sent an involuntary trembling through his muscles. He wanted to give himself up to sobbing terror, but part of his mind said: *"That would be stupid thing to do."*

Far off through the trees there came the tearing, crashing sound of a tree falling.

He bit at his lower lip, willing himself to feel only this pain, but the thought of pain brought a dull throbbing to the stump of his finger.

Gettler heard the tree fall as though it were directly on top of him. The sodden earth shook at the impact, and mud spattered him.

Close! Christ, I should've brought the flashlight!

Before darkness sealed off the jungle, he had seen David's footprints move toward higher ground. There had been an aimless wavering to the boy's tracks: a sure sign that he was lost.

The brief blue wash of lightning flitted across the jungle floor, revealed the fallen tree on his left. An immediate clap of thunder and smell of ozone told of the nearness of the bolt.

Gettler stumbled forward through the muddy darkness, slipping, falling. He knew it was useless to move when he could see nothing, but there was in him a need to *do*.

Again, lightning *fixed* the forest floor.

And David saw a crouching shape off through the trees where there had been no shape in the previous flash. In a paroxysm of terror, he squeezed the trigger of the twenty-two. The shot cracked loudly, and a yellow-orange flame gouted from the muzzle.

David's ears rang. He trembled.

Gettler heard the shot, saw the spurt of flame about a hundred feet to his left. The bullet spatted into a tree beyond him. He picked himself up from the mud, shouted: "David! It's Gettler ... I'm here! Where are you?"

David heard the voice in the night, and his careful hoarding of calmness broke. He began to sob, and called out: "I'm here! Over here! I'm here! Oh, please hurry!"

Gettler blundered through the slippery mud, stumbled into the tree where David crouched, brushed against the boy, gathered him into an enfolding hug.

"I got lost," sobbed David. "I was scared." He buried his face against Gettler's rough jacket, and cried.

"It's all right," whispered Gettler.

He felt the gun in David's hand, took it, set the safety, pushed it into a pocket.

"It got dark," said David. "And I was afraid you'd go on without me."

"No!" growled Gettler. "We'd never do that!"

He pulled the boy down between the roots, sheltered him under part of the jacket.

Now, all the fear and rage and protest that had driven Gettler settled into a small throbbing within his temples. Lightning flashed, and thunder shook the air. Rain drenched him. And he felt that he was withdrawing from his body:

acutely aware of David and every sound in the darkness. It was as though the essential core of himself existed in a curious vacuum: one step removed from his senses, experiencing everything as through the body of a stranger. The world of the night, its danger and terror, did not seem to apply to himself except in a mathematical way—like the function of a complex formula.

Gettler closed his eyes, and experienced a vision in brilliant clarity. It came with the flare of lightning against his closed lids, set off by the shock of thunder. He saw an endless network of interlinked rooms, and sensed himself in each room with nothing hidden. An open door drew him, and he followed the vision with rapt concentration. In the room his father whipped the child Franz, and followed the whipping with a lecture on morality.

The words dripped from the father's mouth, red and splashing.

And Gettler remembered.

He floated through a series of rooms, above each door a glittering sign: *"Thou Shalt Not!"*

In each room the puppets acted, every action and detail perfect.

And Gettler remembered.

Quite suddenly, Gerda stood beside him in the middle chapel of their parish church. Father Braun, the kindly old one, intoned the marriage litany. And it was no longer a matter of puppets: Gettler re-experienced the scene with a draining sense of sweetness.

And when the scene was an empty husk, he moved on to a new experience out of his past. There came over him the slow realization that each memory thus seen became a room, and the rooms collapsed behind him like dusty shells destroyed by his passage. He saw the good times and the bad times in a swift kaleidoscope of images.

A moment came when he felt that he could thus examine the day of infinite horror, drain it dry in the same way. The puppets moved: his own figure came up the stone walk past the rose arbor—under his arm the paper-wrapped telescope: the gift for Peter. And now he realized that an emotional veil—the wonderful anticipatory lift of homecoming—had hidden from him the unnatural stillness of the house.

There came the remembered pause, the curious swaying sense of something wrong, an emptiness. Gettler abandoned the jungle night, flowed into the puppet figure of his memory, opened his front door, walked down the silent hall and into the demolished universe of his own living room.

It was a tableau: the gouts of blood, the twisted naked figures of Gerda and Peter, and over them the vacancy of death. The grinning S.S. officers, stripped to the waist, watched him with eager eyes. And for the first time Gettler saw the sadistic torturers as sufferers.

They looked for an answer to themselves in my pain! By their power over me they tried to force me to betray the secret of life. They wanted words to free them from their prison of words! Power? That dies in its instant of use. And cowardice never lives.

Again he felt the rage that grief-shock had suppressed. Now he permitted it, felt it spill out of him. After that, the rooms were easier to enter: even the one where he killed Bannon. He came to know that the horror of that homecoming had shattered him, strewing lost pieces everywhere. But now he saw where all the threads went, and he gathered them in.

Gradually, the world of the night re-established itself. He felt David against his side, realized that the boy slept in the exhausted reaction to terror. Like the remembered glare of lightning, Gettler saw the lost dreams he had projected onto this boy, saw the destruction that madness had worked.

David must live! No matter what, David must live!

The boy stirred in the throes of a dream.

Gettler's arm tightened with convulsive protectiveness around David's shoulder. A clarity of mind like the aftermath of fever filled Gettler. But he knew it for a tenuous thing with hungry chaos waiting all around.

David slept in the shelter of Gettler's arm.

The nervous voice of the forest sank to a waiting hush, and daylight crept through the rain pall.

Gettler awoke the boy, headed downhill toward the river. Rain had obliterated their tracks, but he had an instinct for the jungle.

The first rainy light of morning found the plane sawing gently at the end of its anchor line. The metal had dulled to a grey that blended into the dove-grey mist of falling water. There was only a place where the river surface wasn't cratered by raindrops.

Jeb slipped out his door and down to the pontoon. Both pontoons floated low, sloshing out hollow echoes with their burden of water.

Monti looked out at him.

"What's wrong?"

"We took a lot of water during the night."

He found the dipper Gettler had made, bent to bailing out the pontoons, and he scanned the shore while he worked. It was a pastel shore, mysterious behind the downpour—all colors pearl-washed by the rain.

Monti clambered down to the right hand float, stood beneath the wing behind him.

"Jeb, what if we miss them?"

"They'll signal. We can't miss them."

"If it'd only stop raining! We can't see anything!"

"We'll hear them."

"What if it was a trick, Jeb? What if he isn't looking for David? What if he's gone on without us?"

Jeb shook his head.

"I'd bet everything I own—including my life—that he'd look for David until he found him."

"But what if the Indians get to them first?"

"Let's fight our battles one at a time, Monti."

She buried her head in her hands. "I feel like I'm being punished."

He capped the float, stood up, put a hand on her shoulder. "Monti, if you're ..."

She shook off his hand. "Don't touch me! I have to think with my head ... like a man."

Again he reached out for her to comfort her.

"No!" she said. "When you touch me I think with my body. That's why I'm being punished."

"That's nonsense, Monti!"

"No it isn't!"

Jeb started to reply, stopped as a strange sound wavered across the river.

"Hallooooooo!"

Monti and Jeb whirled, stared toward the peninsula.

"It's Gettler!" said Monti. "There! I see him! In front of that tree!"

"Yes!"

"Where's David? I don't see David!"

Jeb untied the canoe, grabbed up the cane pole.

"Let me go with you!" cried Monti.

"No! Stay with the plane! Be ready with the rifle."

He pushed off, headed for shore.

"Hallooooooo!" called Gettler.

Jeb's cane pole bit into river bottom, sent the canoe surging toward shore. Abruptly, he saw movement in the tree high above Gettler: an arm waving something bright—the machete!

David!

The canoe slipped through a line of reeds, grounded, and Jeb saw the handle of the twenty-two jutting from Gettler's pocket. But Gettler was intent on helping David scramble out of the tree.

Jeb pulled the magnum revolver from his belt, waited.

Gettler turned, held David in front of him.

"Logan!" he called.

Jeb cursed under his breath. Gettler was shielded by the boy.

"I'm going to give you the revolver in my pocket," said Gettler. "This is to show you that I don't have to!"

He let go of David.

It's a trick! thought Jeb.

He waited tensely for David to move aside, and almost pulled the trigger when the rifle roared from the plane behind him.

His first thought was that Monti saw the impasse on shore and was shooting at Gettler. But a spear suddenly sailed over the brush from the flooded backwater to their right, buried itself in the mud beside David.

"Canoe!" screamed Monti.

And again the rifle roared.

Gettler charged forward, swept up David, dumped him into the dugout, shoved off and leaped into the other end—all in one blinding motion.

"Shoot, you jackass!" he roared. And he grabbed the cane pole, sent them skimming toward the plane.

Jeb snapped out of his shock, fired at the bushes.

Again the rifle roared.

They cleared the end of the peninsula, saw a canoe drawn up above the falls on the other side.

Jeb shot into the undergrowth ahead of it.

Another spear sailed out of the greenery, fell short of the fleeing dugout.

David crouched low, still clutching the machete.

Something flicked into the water beside him.

Gettler grunted, shot the canoe under the right wing of the plane, caught the float.

"Out!" he roared.

Jeb helped David onto the float.

"Inside with you!"

He saw Monti on the opposite side. She raised the rifle, fired at the shore.

Jeb clambered onto the float, brought in the grapnel line. But the grapnel refused to come free of the bottom. He ducked back along the float, took the machete from David in the cabin, returned and slashed the grapnel line.

Immediately, the current turned the plane to the right, swept it away from the falls.

Jeb returned the machete to the cabin floor, looked down at Gettler, who still sat in the canoe, holding the float. Gettler was bent forward. As Jeb watched, his hand started to slip from the float. Jeb crouched, grabbed the canoe.

"Gettler!"

No response.

Then Jeb saw the tuft of kapok on Gettler's right sleeve, the dark spot within the kapok.

Dart!

He threw a loop of the fish line around the canoe, cinched it, dragged Gettler half onto the float.

"Monti! Help me!" he called.

She came through the front of the cabin, took one of Gettler's arms.

"What's wrong?"

"Curare dart!"

David grabbed Gettler's other arm.

Between them, they hoisted him into the cabin and across the seat back.

"What can we do?" whispered Monti.

"David! Give me the first aid kit!" barked Jeb. "Monti, keep an eye out for another attack."

David brought the green metal box from the rear compartment, thrust it into Jeb's hand.

"Take your pocket knife and cut away the jacket there," said Jeb. He nodded toward the fluff of kapok.

David wet his lips with his tongue, stared wide-eyed at the protruding tip of the dart.

"Hurry up!" barked Jeb. He snapped open the first aid kit, fumbled in it for the hypodermic.

David swallowed, brought out his pocket knife, clenched his lips together, began cutting away the jacket.

Suddenly, Gettler whispered: "I'm all right."

Jeb hesitated, looked at Gettler.

The man's eyes were open.

"The race ... from shore ... wore me out," husked Gettler. "Weak."

Jeb turned back to the hypodermic, brought an ampoule from the first aid kit.

"What can we do?" asked Monti. "It's poison." She stared at Gettler's bare arm.

Part of the dart bent downward.

"It's broken off," said David.

"That's the way the bastards make 'em," whispered Gettler. "Poison part breaks off inside." He lifted his arm, stared at it.

Jeb lifted the hypodermic.

"What's that?" asked Gettler.

"Prostygmine," said Jeb. "No time for niceties like sterilized needles." He swabbed a dab of alcohol on Gettler's arm above the dart, sank in the hypodermic needle, depressed the plunger, removed the needle.

"Give me the knife, David," said Jeb.

David handed it to him.

Jeb poured alcohol on the blade, turned back to Gettler's arm, slashed once across the embedded tip of the dart.

Gettler winced, bit his lip. Blood poured down his arm.

Jeb flipped the dart tip with the point of the knife, pressed his mouth against the wound, sucking out the poison. He spat over the side, repeated the operation. And again.

Gettler's head lolled.

"Salt tablets in the kit there," said Jeb. "For the heat. They're marked. Dump out all but a couple of cups of water from the water bag, drop in a dozen of those tablets.

David grabbed up the kit, obeyed.

"What's prostyg ... whatever you said?" asked Monti.

"Specific for curare," said Jeb. He took the water bag

from David, turned Gettler's head, dribbled water between his lips.

Gettler gagged, coughed.

"This's why you have prostygmine in your jungle kit," said Jeb.

He dribbled more water between Gettler's lips.

"Swallow it!" he ordered.

Gettler gulped, swallowed. Slowly, he drained the water bag.

"Why the salt water?" asked Monti.

"That's how the Indians treat themselves for curare poison," said Jeb. "It works.

"What's it do ... the poison?" asked David.

"It makes the muscles relax," said Jeb. "You suffocate ... or your heart stops."

Gettler suddenly turned, arched his back, sagged in the seat. His breathing became labored, uneven. His head sagged forward.

"What if he stops breathing?" whispered Monti.

"Artificial respiration," said Jeb. "David, mix some more salt water."

David dipped a water bag over the side, began pouring salt tablets and purifier into it.

"Any sign of the Jivaro?" asked Jeb.

Monti jerked upright, glanced around. "No."

"Mr. Logan!" hissed David. "I almost forgot!"

"What?"

"When I was in the tree back there. I saw a big black cliff downstream. It had a hole in it. I thought maybe it was another canyon, but the rain got worse. I couldn't tell for sure."

Jeb turned, looked downstream, back at David, down to Gettler.

The man's breathing had become slower, shallower, each time he exhaled seemed more like a final collapse.

"Here's the salt water," said David. He passed the bag forward.

Jeb tipped Gettler's head back, dribbled water between his lips. Once, Gettler's eyes flickered open, closed. He swallowed with a convulsive gulp.

Gettler heard the conversation around him as though it happened behind a thick curtain of unimportance. His mind drifted through a series of velvet explosions. He shuddered, opened his eyes, closed them. Fire coursed through his veins, then ice. Again he opened his eyes, moved his lips.

Jeb bent closer.

"Oscar Wilde was wrong," whispered Gettler.

"Don't try to talk," said Jeb.

"Thousand lives," husked Gettler, "worth thousand deaths!" He smiled, closed his eyes.

Jeb forced more salt water down his throat.

Gettler turned his head aside. "Gotta tell y' something," he whispered. "Memory catches everything ... like a fisher–man's net."

"Drink this water!" ordered Jeb.

Gettler shook his head.

"'Simportant! 'Sbeautiful! Everything's got to change." He forced his head off the seat back. "Can't stop changing! And anything's possible! Anything!" His mouth opened, closed. "It's holy!" He let his head drop back against the seat.

"Sure," said Jeb. "Now stop trying to talk. Take some more water."

Again he forced salt water between Gettler's lips. And again Gettler turned away.

"Gotta 'splain," he whispered. "Something's holding us on the river. 'S time! River's time. Words holding us!"

"Can't you make him stop raving?" asked Monti.

"Circle," whispered Gettler. "All creation. Mustn't stop circle. "Sdeath! Motion's holy." His voice dropped. "Creation ... fire ... circle."

"What's he saying?" asked Monti.

"He's delirious," said Jeb.

"It's my fault," said David. "If I hadn't tried to be smart ...

but I was so hungry, and I saw those tracks. Then the storm came, and I was afraid ..." He began to cry "... the Indians ..."

"Did you see Indians?" demanded Monti.

"Not until the river."

"Storm saved him," said Jeb. "Indians take cover in a storm."

Again he dribbled water between Gettler's lips.

"He seems to be breathing easier," said Monti.

"I think so," said Jeb.

He turned to bandaging Gettler's arm, thought: *Why didn't I let him die? Sonofabitch!*

"How's your hand, David?" asked Monti.

"Oh, it's all right."

"That bandage looks muddy."

"I fell."

"Let me change the bandage, David," said Jeb.

David put the bandaged hand behind him. "It's all right."

"Let's see it!" snapped Jeb.

Slowly, David brought his hand around.

Jeb took it, gently cut away the dressing.

David looked away.

"Christ!" said Jeb.

"What is it?" whispered Monti.

"It's infected."

"Badly?"

"Any infection's bad out here!"

Jeb dug in the medical kit, brought out the terramycin. "Take these. I'll pack it with this sulfa ointment."

Monti watched Jeb work—short, angry movements.

And Jeb thought: *I didn't let Gettler die because he saved David ... and probably saved me ... and ... No. I did what I had to do for him.*

It came to Jeb abruptly that this simple idea explained Gettler: *He did what he had to do.*

Jeb tied off David's bandage.

"There's what I saw," said David. He looked out the right

hand window.

Jeb and Monti turned.

The rain mist had thinned. Through it they saw a great black face of lava rock about a mile away. It towered above the jungle growth like the side of a monster ship. To the left it appeared split, and the air showed a thicker hazing of mist there.

"It looks farther away," said David.

"River's curving all over the landscape through here," said Jeb. "Monti, open your door."

She obeyed.

A faint roaring came to their ears.

"More rapids?" asked Monti.

"Could be the wind," said Jeb.

A gust of wind pushed a black line up the river toward them, pulled a rain veil across the lava cliff. The downpour whipped around the plane, thudded against the cabin top. As quickly as it had come, the wind passed and the smooth current slipped them onward through a somnolent hiss of falling rain.

Gettler stirred, groaned, opened his eyes.

Monti looked across him at Jeb, who was sitting half out of the cabin to make room for Gettler.

"How do you feel, Gettler?" asked Jeb.

"Thankful," whispered Gettler.

"Thankful?"

"For your jungle kit. German in your ancestry. Has to be. Too thorough."

"Do you feel up to crawling into the back?" asked Jeb.

Gettler nodded.

They helped him over the seat. He slumped back beside David, glanced at David's bandage.

"Invalids in the rear, eh, son?"

"I'm sorry I caused so much trouble," said David.

"Not you," said Gettler. "The jungle." He looked out his window. "Indians live in the jungle, and the jungle lives in them—passed through them. Nothing resists. Take a white man, though: it's like our skin wouldn't let the jungle in. One of us has to break. Drain that swamp! Kill those bugs! Clear away that forest!"

"Give it back to the Indians," said Monti. "Every man to his own jungle."

She tipped her head against the seat back. "It's so hot ... so damp. If it wasn't so goddamn damp! I smell mildew all over me."

Jeb slipped down to the float, kicked away a floating island of sedge that had lodged there, ignored the cloud of insects that arose at the disturbance. He saw that the rain was slackening. It shimmered away to a glistening mist, and even that faded.

The river took on a flat and oily look: a stretch of shimmering glass dotted with tufts of sedge like a tabletop display laid out on a mirror with a label: "South American jungle river—Amazon headwaters." It became an enchanted river: slow, hypnotic. The plane was a toy plane shrunken by jungle sorcery—lost in a magic immensity of flooding current.

"White men weren't meant to live in this country," muttered Jeb.

He felt that they drifted in a moist pocket of air that had been drained of all vitality. The smell of the jungle pressed in upon him: a dank piling up of life and death on the forest floor, rotting and festering. The odor hung across their track—a physical substance of smell that they encountered in waves.

A soft breeze puffed across the plane from the right hand shore, brought a new odor. Jeb sniffed at it.

Gettler stirred upright in the rear seat, hissed: "Cassava root! I smell fresh cassava root!"

"What is it?" asked Monti.

Jeb stared across the plane's cowling.

"Village," he said.

"Where?"

"Back in the jungle across there."

"I don't see anything," said Monti.

A stagnant silence settled over the plane.

Presently, Monti said: "The air's so hot. I feel like it was pulling all the oxygen out of my lungs."

Jeb looked downstream at a line of shock-headed palms along the far shore. As he looked, a flock of golden-beaked toucans lifted out of the trees in a frenzied cloud, filled the air with their dog-pack yelping.

"Something disturbed them!" hissed Gettler.

"What?" asked Monti.

"Maybe an animal," said Jeb. He glanced in at Monti. Her cheeks were indrawn, pale hollows. He rubbed at his beard, felt the sharp line of cheekbone beneath.

"Possession isn't nine points of the law here," said Gettler. "It's all the law there is."

Jeb closed his eyes, felt the weariness draining him, sleep like a narcotic mist waiting at the edge of awareness. He experienced a nightmare sense of dreaming through their entire journey to this point. His eyes snapped open. He put a hand against the warm metal of the cowling, wiped at a smudge of oil smoke stain.

"It's so hot," said Monti. She pulled the back of her hand across her forehead.

The river downstream suddenly glistened with uncounted sparklings.

Jeb looked up: great cracks of blue were spreading through the clouds. The sun came out. It hit the plane with a sense of physical pressure, reflected off the water into every corner beneath the wings. Jeb turned away, saw the silver wheel of a spider web stretched between fuselage and float. It brought to his mind the vivid remembrance of the spider on the ceiling of his bedroom in Milagro (*How long ago?* he asked himself) and this recalled his nightmare premonition.

Death and a river ... a river and death.

A feeling of helplessness came over him, a giving up to the belief that he was caught like a fly in a web, held by a force too strong to resist.

And he recalled with a dull uncaring that he had neglected to take the twenty-two revolver from Gettler's pocket.

It doesn't matter, he thought. *Nothing matters.*

"Mr. Logan," said David.

Jeb shook his head slowly.

"Mr. Logan!"

It took a conscious act of determination for Jeb to turn his head toward David in the cabin. The boy was leaning forward, unbandaged hand pressed against Monti's forehead. Monti was curled in her corner, eyes closed, head thrown back against the seat.

"She feels awfully warm," said David. "She's been moaning."

The idea refused to register in Jeb's mind, but he nodded as though he understood. Realization swam upward through his consciousness like a fish rising from the depths.

"Fever?"

"I think so, sir."

"See if she'll take ... one of the pills we gave you."

"Yes, sir."

Downstream, a curving ripple of current swept away from the left shore. Jeb saw it, looked beyond it, became aware that the river curved, too. It swept to the right in a wide arc.

The plane glided into the ripple track, bobbed and danced, turned. Dull sloshing sounds came from the floats. A faint roaring came to Jeb's ears—like the echo in a seashell.

Jeb started to turn in the direction of the sound, but David suddenly leaned out the door, pointed upstream.

"Mr. Logan! Look!"

Jeb looked.

A line of canoes stretched across the upstream reaches of

the river, coppery bodies giving off an oil sheen in the hot sunlight.

"They're chasing us!" said David.

The roaring sound grew louder.

Both Jeb and David turned, looked downstream.

"That's what I saw!" cried David.

About a mile downstream, sheer black walls of lava rock squeezed the river into a rumbling agony of white water. Waves cresting over unseen rocks sent up a crazy splendor of violence that climbed in a milk-and-amber mist above the chasm.

And Jeb thought quite calmly: *Yes. That's probably what he saw.* The river track curved away from it, then back.

He became aware of movement along both shores between the plane and the raging water. The movement aroused a feeling of curiosity.

More canoes, by God!

"They've got something stretched across the river!" shouted David.

Gettler sat upright beside the boy. "Whh ..."

And Jeb saw what David had seen.

"It's a rope or a net," he said.

He felt a detached admiration for the Indians. "They're persistent devils," he said.

"Do something!" cried David.

A screaming shout arose from the canoes downstream, was answered by the Indians following.

The dreamlike detachment suddenly snapped off of Jeb like a sheet whipped from a statue.

"What am I doing?" he asked.

He whirled around, shot a glance upstream.

The pursuing canoes had closed the gap between them and the plane.

"It's a trap!" screamed Gettler.

Jeb leaped into the cabin, primed the motor.

Beside him, Monti opened her eyes, shook her head.

"Strangest dream," she whispered.

A booming roar came from the right bank. Something slammed into the tail of the plane.

Jeb pulled the starter.

A slow grinding sound arose from the motor.

"Battery's dead!" shouted Jeb. He whirled. "David, see this knob? Pull it the minute the motor catches. I'm going out to crank it."

Jeb clambered across Monti, who stared blankly around. He dropped down to the float, saw the dugout tied beneath the fuselage, grabbed the machete off the cabin floor, cut the fish line fastenings. The machete clattered against metal as he tossed it back into the cabin.

A many-throated scream filled the air behind them. He ignored it, worked his way forward, leaned out, grasped the propeller, jerked it down.

No response.

Again.

The motor roared to life, and Jeb almost fell off the float getting out of the way of the propeller. A pall of black smoke floated upstream as the plane gathered way. A screeching sound of friction had been added to the other rackets from the motor.

Jeb scrambled back into the cabin, kicked the right rudder. They swept around toward the canoes upstream. The canoes parted, and he saw that they too carried a net across the river. He allowed the plane to sweep around toward the savage torrent in the canyon.

A raging defiance filled Jeb.

The dugout that he had cut loose loomed ahead. He swerved to dodge it, roared toward the downstream trap rope and the chasm.

This is the only direction to go! he thought.

The battered plane skidded across a cross-eddy, skimmed toward the rope. Now, the river spread out in a glossy black pool. And beyond the rope, the water creased into steeper and steeper furrows before flashing outward and down into the gorge.

Slowly, the rope ahead lifted from the river like a dripping snake to reveal the dark pattern of net squares below. Eager hands on each shore pulled the net higher.

And the plane swept into the net, rocked forward. A thunderous grinding and whipping sound lifted above the plane as the propeller slashed through the net ropes.

The motor stopped short.

But the net had been cut.

A savage scream arose from the Indians, rising above the devil drums of roaring water. The current swept the plane to the right, crunched it against the first obsidian buttress above the torrent. A scraping and wrenching of metal competed with the mounting roar of the chasm.

Gettler shouted something that was lost in the avalanche sound of the water. The plane bounced outward, whirled, pounded across two infolding steps of explosive current. A vast pulsing roar like the crashing of ocean waves onto rocks deafened them. The spiral cone of a whirlpool sucked at them, shot them into a new, more savage turbulence.

They heard the rasping, crunching, grating of rocks grinding in the maelstrom. A glistening ledge of black rock, its face scarred by the current, loomed directly ahead. The plane smashed against it, recoiled.

The people in the plane were shaken about like pebbles in a box. *Wham!* The left door slammed open and wedged against the strut. The right wing crumpled against the chasm wall, and the plane whipped around to the left.

Jeb watched the motion jolt the rifle off the cabin floor into the river. He was powerless to prevent the loss. A heavy rumbling sound from the shattered right wing added to the din. The plane's nose lifted on a boiling, spume-hurling upsurge of water, and they slammed down into a black maelstrom beyond.

Monti held fast to the safety straps on both sides, caught

in a fascination of terror by the view over the cowling. She felt herself plummeting with the plane: *down! down! down!* whipped around, and back through undiluted violence that crashed around her like a crazy carnival ride.

A frothing spiral of current shot them around broadside to the channel, then back until they faced downstream. Again they lifted over a millrace chute, slammed down into another roaring cavity of water.

David hugged both arms around the seat back directly ahead of him, head turned sideways. He could see out the side window: a cresting of amber spray, the flopping right wing, a pocket of damp green shade along the water-scarred cliff. Solid white water washed over the window, and the wing was gone.

Gettler lay wedged on the floor between front and back seats, his head just below the level of the left side window. From this viewless position, sound dominated his world: a deafening cymbal dissonance gone wild; magnification beyond human endurance of the highest savagery in noise. He felt the sound as a physical thing that grated through him in an unchecked rhythm like a giant's fingernails scraping across a cosmic blackboard.

A washboard of white water dropped off beneath the plane, shot it through a staccato of jarring *slap-slap-slaps* that sent solid spray geysering over the cowl.

Jeb tried to see through the spray, glimpsed only a rippling blur of motion. He had seen the right wing go, felt it like something torn from his own body. His hands were numb from clutching the control wheel, and his shoulder ached. The wheel moved freely forward and back, but he could not remove his fingers from their grip on it to gain a hold on something more solid.

Can she take more of this? he asked himself.

He expected momentarily that the plane would disintegrate, dumping them into the chasm: motes in an immensity of violence.

A great brown turtle back of smooth current rolled over directly in front of them, and the spray washed down the windows to give Jeb and Monti a clear view of the prospect.

Monti closed her eyes.

The plane surged up onto the smoothness with a sliding and gentle deceptiveness. There, it hesitated, then dove down the lower side. The nose with its twisted propeller smashed squarely into a black wall of water. There came a wrenching, screeching of metal. Then the tail slammed down, lifting up a torn and gaping hole where the motor had been.

A whirlpool caught them, twisted them around until they faced upstream. The river hurled them tail foremost over another boiling mound of water. A wrenching and grating came from the tail as it ripped against the rocks. The plane whipped around with the tail as a pivot.

And Jeb watched the dark torpedo shape of an overturned canoe shoot past them ... and another.

The Indians tried to follow us into here! Or they chased us too close to the chasm and were trapped!

The left wing raked the black lava wall, and the plane twisted momentarily sideways, shot with blinding abruptness into the glare of sunlight. They floated across the false calm of a broad pool that absorbed the turbulence of the rapids, and revealed this turbulence only in bubbles, thin and swift runnel lines converging and spreading.

The plane emitted a metallic gurgling, tipped to the right. The damaged left wing flopped upward.

Jeb looked out to the left, saw the pontoon floating almost a foot beneath the river. Water began to creep across the cabin floor as the plane tipped farther to the right. He swept one frantic glance around: four overturned canoes floated in the pool, but all were too far away.

"We're tipping over!" cried Monti.

"Everybody to the left," said Jeb.

He slipped out the left side, stood with one foot on the

strut. It grated loosely. The door flopped farther open, leaned forward. He pushed it, and it tipped on the lower hinge, splashed into the river. It was like a piece of death to Jeb. He watched the glinting metal of the door sunfish back and forth into the depths until muddy water hid the reflection.

Water touched his ankle, and he saw that the left side had slipped farther down. He glanced back toward the roar of the rapids: no sign of the Jivaro. His attention went to the plane's tail assembly: it had been torn loose, and now dangled in the water. He looked downstream. A barren point of land jutted into the river about a quarter of a mile away at the lower end of the pool. It reached out from a high wall of jungle on the left.

"Gettler," said Jeb. "I'm going to climb on top. Pass me the survival kit, the machete, and anything else lying around. Everybody come up there after me. She's sinking slowly, and we may be able to make it to that point on the left down there." He pointed.

"Get moving," said Gettler.

Jeb clawed his way onto what remained of the cowling, braced himself there, accepted the articles passed to him, helped the others onto the cabin top, and joined them. They all looked downstream at the point: rain-flattened reeds steaming in the sun above a thin mud bank. Their attention went to the tangled green forest wall about a hundred yards back from the tip of the point.

Gettler found the machete, lay across the fuselage, began paddling with the broad blade. He could see the point past the torn stump of the right wing.

"Behind us!" hissed David.

They turned.

A line of Indians emerged onto a rocky shingle below the rapids, three canoes on their shoulders. They squatted in unison, slipped the canoes into the river.

"Give David the twenty-two," said Jeb.

Gettler turned on his side, slipped the gun from his

pocket, handed it to David.

"One shot to make them keep their distance," said Jeb.

David sighted, squeezed the trigger. The bullet spattered water beside the lead canoe. The Indians back-paddled.

Another six inches of the left strut sank beneath the river. The cabin now was half filled with water.

Jeb took another look at the point. The plane was angling across into the back eddy that swept toward the jungle along the upper end of the barren tongue of land.

There's where we die! he thought.

Death and a river.

A quick sensation of near panic tightened his throat muscles. His body fell into a terror reaction, shivering with primitive and abysmal emotion: a rapture of fear that locked onto his mind, and released it with only one clear thought: *Living is a luxury.*

The pulse of life had never tasted so sweet.

Something caught the right float, stopped it some fifteen feet from shore a third of the way down the point.

"We're on the mud," said Jeb.

Gettler stopped paddling.

Slowly, the left float, which was higher in the water, drifted around. The tip of the left wing slipped into the muddy shore, stopped the motion.

Jeb grabbed up the black bag of the survival kit, ran along the wing, jumped into the low reeds. He drew the magnum revolver from his belt, eyed the forest wall.

David and Monti followed.

Gettler came last, the machete dangling from his right hand.

"This is the place," he said.

"Out to the tip of the point," said Jeb. "A spear or dart could reach us here." He motioned the others ahead, brought up the rear.

The canoes upstream inched closer.

"Give them another warning," said Jeb.

"I could hit them easy," said David.

Jeb hesitated, and an instinct warned him.

"No." He shook his head. "Just tell them we're ready."

David squeezed off a shot that smacked the paddle from the hand of one of the Indians. An angry shout lifted from the canoes, but they paddled back to the edge of the shingle.

"You do that on purpose?" asked Jeb.

"Yes, sir."

"Okay. Save the rest of your shots for real. Fill that clip again and get the spare ready."

"Yes, sir."

"Look out!" screamed Monti.

They whirled.

A spear arced from the jungle, splatted into reeds and mud opposite the plane. The handle of the spear jutted upward, a tassel of monkey fur and kapok dangling from its tip.

"There's your answer," said Gettler. "The spear of vengeance." He smiled, a skull grimace of teeth in the matting of his beard.

A smoking arrow followed the spear, hissed into the river beside the half-sunken plane.

"Fire arrow!" snapped Jeb.

They crouched.

Another arrow followed the first. It hit metal, skidded into the river. A third arrow arced into the gaping front where the motor had been. Instantly, a sheet of flame leaped upward, enveloped the entire front of the plane. An acrid smoke of gasoline and oil drifted across the point.

"Duck!" shouted Jeb. "It'll blow what's left in the wing tank!"

A sharply booming roar erupted from the plane, and a section of wing sailed across the point spewing a trail of fire. Gobs of flaming gasoline spattered into the reeds.

"Why'd they do that?" whispered Monti.

"To destroy our magic," said Gettler.

"What'll they do now?" asked David.

"I don't know," said Gettler. He sat back in the mud, the machete held across his knees, looked from the jungle at the base of the point to the downstream reaches of the river. A bend cut off the view about a mile downstream. Terraces of massive trees stepped away from the bank there, blended into a mossy curving of hills. The water was a glaring reflector that magnified the hammering of sunlight. The point felt smaller and smaller, as though it were drawing back from the forest skyline.

Jeb glanced at Gettler. The man's personality had undergone a transformation: the shedding of a false cloak that opened up deep strength. His eyes when he looked back at Jeb revealed anguish that had gone beyond all turmoil to a pervading calmness.

"Helluva place to die, eh, Logan?"

Monti began sobbing.

What's the difference? thought Jeb. But he reached out, patted her shoulder.

"The uncertainty's what's bad," murmured Gettler. "Enough uncertainty, and you welcome anything."

Jeb looked at where the plane had been. A torn strip of fuselage lay stretched along the mud: nothing more.

My little piece of civilization didn't make it, he thought. *I won't outlast it for long.*

His attention went to the green wall, glistening leaves, silence.

An arrow lifted out of the green, slanted into the mud ten yards in front of them.

"Can they reach us?" whispered Monti.

Gettler nodded. "Probably."

"What's keeping them?" she screamed.

Gettler grunted, shifted his weight forward, got to his feet.

"They've seen David," he said. "Listen."

A low chanting sound drifted from the jungle. "They're

making counter magic."

"What about David?" asked Jeb.

Gettler laughed with a chopping abruptness, a wild sound. He bent forward, jerked the revolver from Jeb's hand before Jeb could react.

Jeb started to rise.

"Stay put," said Gettler. He stepped toward the jungle, lifted his voice in Quechua, roared: *"Hear me, people!"*

The chanting in the jungle stopped.

"What's he saying?" whispered Monti.

"He's asking them to listen," said Jeb.

"I am the one you want!" shouted Gettler. *"I am the only one. The others are blameless!"*

Jeb translated in a low voice.

Again Gettler shouted.

Jeb spoke to Monti and David out of the side of his mouth.

"He says that David is the son of their brother, their brother Bannon ... that you are their brother's woman ... that I was a mere ... hired canoeist. That's the only comparison in their tongue."

Gettler fell silent, waited.

No sound came from the green wall.

Gettler spoke to the three behind him without turning.

"I've done what I can. See if you can make them parley." He shrugged. "Well, thanks for everything."

"Wait!" hissed Jeb.

But Getter already was striding toward the jungle with a stiff-legged, rocking gait. He held the revolver close to his side.

"They'll kill him!" shouted David. He started to rise, dash after Gettler.

Jeb pulled the boy down.

Gettler broke into a staggering run toward the ominous green silence. Everything was held suspended in soundless waiting. Then Gettler raised the gun, began firing as he advanced: a shot ... a step ... a shot ... a step—into the jungle—a shot ... a shot.

Sudden babbling of Indian voices.

Silence.

A shadow passed across the point, and it began to rain with the on-switch tropic abruptness: driving bursts of water that drenched across the three people at the tip of the land.

Monti stared at the mossy green wilderness of scrambled vines, leaves and limbs periodically blurred behind the waves of rain.

"Don't let them take me," she whispered.

Jeb reached down to David's hand, removed the twenty-two from the boy's limp fingers, handed him the machete that Gettler had dropped.

"The extra clip," said Jeb.

David passed it to him without looking from the jungle.

Monti put a hand to her throat, rubbed it.

"Why do they do that ... to the head?" she asked.

"Religion," said Jeb.

He had a momentary mental image of a Jivaro witch doctor working over the small fire: the hot sand, the careful needlework across dead lips. Five heads dangling from the ridgepole of a *jambai* house. Big *jambai*. Big medicine.

Unconsciously, his left hand repeated Monti's gesture, rubbing his throat. Horror remained distant, held back by a great curiosity. He felt suddenly utterly sensitive to himself—a state of relaxed alertness where everything around him happened only with his express permission. And he thought that he could turn off his world by the simplest decision. But still the power of curiosity overwhelmed him like the flow of a river, like the flow of time. And he was lost in a swimming duality unable to make the decision that would stop existence.

The rain stopped. Sunlight returned. Steam spiraled and fumed above the point, thickened to a vapor, dispersed in a light breeze.

A black centipede crawled across a length of reed in front of Jeb. He stared at it, experienced an abrupt rapport with the tide of jungle life, a quickening of soul: the busy silence of it filled him. He lifted his attention to the forest wall, attracted by a flicker of motion.

An Indian appeared in front of the jungle, flung there by a sorcery that produced his image out of a natural camouflage in one movement. Ebony eyes glinted from beneath a straight line of bangs. Red whorls of achiote streaked his face. Scarlet macaw feathers protruded from a red string that bound the upper muscle of his left arm. He carried a spear held vertically in his right hand. A monkey skin bag dangled heavily from his left hand.

"What's he doing?" whispered David.

"Showing us that he has the *tzantza*," gritted Jeb.

David stepped in front of his mother, hefted the machete.

"Better the devil you know than the devil you don't," said Monti. She spoke in an almost conversational tone.

A whole line of Indians appeared in front of the jungle by the same magic that had revealed the first. Every face carried the red achiote streaks that spelled out their mission: a war of vengeance. They carried spears, clubs, bows, blow guns ... and here and there an ancient muzzle-loader. Two of the Indians stepped ahead, converged, advanced together a cautious ten paces. The entire line moved up behind them. More Jivaro appeared from the jungle.

They pressed forward.

"No sudden movements," whispered Jeb.

The line of Indians stopped some twenty feet away, the two leaders only about ten feet from the waiting trio.

Jeb passed his gaze along the glowering line, realized that none of the Indians were looking at him. All of the dark eyes focused on David.

The image of the father, thought Jeb.

And he suddenly understood Gettler's words: *"They've seen David."*

One of the Indians stepped closer to David, spoke in jungle Quechua: *"Boy child, how do you have the face and hair of my brother?"*

"The child does not speak with your voice," said Jeb.

Eyes turned toward Jeb.

"This is the son of your brother," said Jeb.

"And woman is this child's mother?"

Jeb swallowed in a dry throat, nodded.

Dark eyes probed at Jeb.

"The demons of the rapids did not slay you, even when we made our strongest medicine," said the Indian.

"What are they saying?" hissed Monti.

"Quiet!" snapped Jeb. Then: *"The demons do not slay those of pure heart."*

"Ari ... yes." The Indian nodded. *"But how came you to shelter the maná-wakani, the demon creature with an animal soul in a human body?"*

"He told us that you slew his partner, Roger Bannon," said Jeb. *"You were many. We were afraid. We fled."*

"Ari."

Indian heads nodded all along the line.

"Yes. You ran. You were afraid."

"Gett ... ler was pitalala, *the poison snake,"* said the Indian. *"His tongue spoke in two directions. He slew our brother, then fled our vengeance. That is the truth of it. You will tell the soldiers?"*

"Soldiers?"

"They come in many canoes," said the Indian. He held up his left hand, two fingers. *"Two days."* Three fingers. *"Three days. No more."*

"He says soldiers are coming in canoes," said Jeb.

"Three days at the most."

Monti buried her face in her hands.

"Tell the boy that his father's soul will rest quietly," said the Indian. *"We have seen to this. He was our brother."*

"What's he saying?" demanded David.

"He says that their quarrel was with Gettler. That it's settled."

"Gettler killed my dad, didn't he?" asked David.

"Yes."

"Then why don't I hate him?"

Tears began streaming down David's face. He shivered.

The Indian turned to his followers, barked an order, returned his attention to Jeb. *"A storm comes. We will build you a shelter here where you cannot miss the soldiers."*

Indians began filing back across the point into the jungle.

David turned his back on them, walked around his mother to the river's edge.

"Are we really safe?" asked Monti.

"Yes."

"One moment they were deadly, threatening ... Now ..."

"It's their religion ... their code," said Jeb. "They see the evidence in David's face."

"He's the image of Roger."

"Yes."

A lean-to shelter of brush and bark was erected on the point facing the jungle, a fire built in front of it. Indians appeared with a pig, spitted it above the flames. The air above the point vibrated with heat devils. The last of the day's sunlight stabbed out along the silver furrow of the river like a thrown lance.

Darkness clapped down upon the scene.

Little fires appeared at the Indian's shelters along the forest wall. Stars glittered overhead like holes punctured in a velvet bowl. An orange moon lifted over the trees, flung its track along the river.

Jeb squatted inside the lean-to, facing the fire. The meat weighed heavily in his stomach. He could see the faint outline of David seated beside him, and Monti beyond in a dark corner.

Insects fogged the air of the shelter, keening thinly, pushing, crawling, biting. Bats laced the air overhead. There came a splashing, whiffling sound from downstream on the far bank. The chime call of river frogs lifted from the muddy shoreline, and distantly, he could hear the rapids.

Wind shook the lean-to, stirring the rain-rinsed air. Clouds blotted out the stars and moon. A dull splattering rhythm began to beat on the bark roof above them. The air took on a swift feeling of freshness. A crashing roar of almost simultaneous lightning and thunder shook the ground: a thermal flare that left them blinking in the after-darkness. The sharp bite of ozone came to their nostrils.

"That was close," whispered Monti.

"Off in the jungle downstream," said Jeb.

Another snake-tongue of light forked the sky downstream. Thunder rumbled behind it. In the brief glare they saw Indians standing beside their fires at the jungle's edge: caught in frozen motion between darkness and darkness. More lightning flickered across the forest: three swift strokes, one after another, spearing the darkness. In each brief flash the river stood out like a dark sheet of rippled blue steel.

Now the rain sheeted down in savage spasms torn by bursts of wind. The tongue of land seemed to rock and twist in the gusts with the remembered motions of the plane. A steady hissing of rain on water could be heard behind the louder beat of it against the bark above their heads.

And Jeb thought about the future.

I've been running away, he told himself. *I don't fit down here. I'm not the expatriate type. I belong on a nice safe milk run with regular hours and regular pay. A wife at home ... and kids.*

He didn't picture Monti in this role.

There came over him a great need to sink into the flowing movement of his own kind of people, into their security and protective coloration.

I'm not really a rebel, he thought.

Monti, too, thought about the future. She suddenly saw

herself as a kind of latter day religious courtesan in her own temple of love, and the idea amused her.

The studio'll make a great thing out of this, she thought. *Probably do a picture about love in the jungle.* Silent laughter shook her. And she considered Jeb as briefly as he had considered her.

Another passing affair.

She knew that she would miss him no more than she had missed a half a hundred others.

Suddenly, her throat tightened with unshed tears, and she pushed away an image of Roger.

I don't need you anymore! she thought desperately. *I'll never need anyone but myself ever again!*

But somewhere inside herself she knew that she lied.

Another lightning flash glimmered dimly through the rain. Distant thunder rumbled.

And with it came ghost memories of Franz Gettler.

He murmured to Jeb: *"Go home."*

He murmured to Monti: *"Go home."*

And he whispered in the close stillness of David's mind: *"You live in an endless circle ... and you have no home."*

Made in the USA
Lexington, KY
02 December 2014